Also by Tarquin Hall

From the Files of Vish Puri, India's Most Private
Investigator

The Case of the Missing Servant

The Case of the Man Who Died Laughing

The Case of the Deadly Butter Chicken

Nonfiction

*Mercenaries, Missionaries and Misfits:
Adventures of an Under-age Journalist*

*To the Elephant Graveyard: A True Story of the Hunt
for a Man-Killing Elephant*

Salaam Brick Lane: A Year in the New East End

The Case of the Love Commandos

From the Files of
Vish Puri, India's Most Private Investigator

TARQUIN HALL

Simon & Schuster
New York   London   Toronto   Sydney   New Delhi

Simon & Schuster
1230 Avenue of the Americas
New York, NY 10020

First Simon & Schuster hardcover edition October 2013

SIMON & SCHUSTER and colophon are registered trademarks of Simon & Schuster, Inc.

For information about special discounts for bulk purchases, please contact Simon & Schuster Special Sales at 1-866-506-1949 or business@simonandschuster.com.

The Simon & Schuster Speakers Bureau can bring authors to your live event. For more information or to book an event contact the Simon & Schuster Speakers Bureau at 1-866-248-3049 or visit our website at www.simonspeakers.com.

Manufactured in the United States of America

10 9 8 7 6 5 4 3 2 1

Library of Congress Cataloging-in-Publication Data
Hall, Tarquin.
   The case of the love commandos : from the files of Vish Puri, India's most private investigator / Tarquin Hall.—First Simon & Schuster hardcover edition.
      pages   cm
   1. Private investigators—India—Fiction. 2. Murder—Investigation—Fiction. 3. India—Fiction. I. Title.
   PR6108.A495C35   2013
   823'.92—dc23   2013009100

ISBN 978-1-4516-1326-1
ISBN 978-1-4516-1329-2 (ebook)

For Ta

The Case of the
Love Commandos

Prologue

The Love Commando watched the black Range Rover pull in through the gates of the University of Agra. Laxmi—the Commando's code name—could make out the portly profile of the driver, the one who was so fond of chicken tikka, desi sharab and the accommodating ladies of the local bazaar.

Next to him sat the goon with the gorilla nose and droopy eyes. He looked like he'd have had trouble spelling his own name. But it would be a mistake to underestimate him, Laxmi noted. Naga, as he was known at his local gym, was a power-lifting champion with fists the size of sledgehammers.

"They're pulling up now," she said into her mobile phone, the line open to her fellow Love Commando volunteer Shruti, who was waiting inside the gymnasium building where the examinations were about to begin.

It was ten minutes to four.

The driver had kept his end of the bargain. Now Laxmi would have to live up to hers. Last night's surveillance video of his dalliance with that bar girl would not find its way into the hands of his wife after all.

From behind the Licensed Refrigerated Water "Trolly"

1

positioned across the road, she watched the driver alight. He looked up and down the busy street. Satisfied that the coast was clear, he opened the Range Rover's back door.

The revulsion Laxmi felt for the driver paled in comparison to the contempt in which she held his boss, who emerged. Vishnu Mishra personified everything the Love Commandos were attempting to change about India. In north Indian parlance, he was known as a Thakur, literally "lord"—a hereditary landowner with no qualms about exploiting the caste system that still doomed tens of millions of low-caste Indians to subjugation and poverty. His immaculate appearance despite Agra city's heat and dust owed everything to this gross imbalance. An army of servants attended to his every whim: cooks, cleaners, sweepers, even a personal barber–cum–shampoo wallah who kept his nails immaculate, buffed his skin and, rumor had it, dressed him in the morning. Managers oversaw the day-to-day running of his numerous commercial activities. His eldest son managed his political ambitions. And a mistress called "Smoothy" ensured that during many an afternoon in apartment 301D of Avalon Apartments, his carnal needs were sated.

Mishra even had a ready vote bank of thirty thousand subjugated tenant farmers whom he maintained in a perpetual state of poverty and hunger.

Still, there was one task he was evidently prepared to take care of himself: Vishnu Mishra was prepared to kill.

As he climbed down from his Range Rover, Laxmi caught a flash of the semiautomatic inside his jacket.

He stood for a few seconds, surveying the street and waiting for Naga to alight from the other side of the vehicle. Then he beckoned for his daughter to step out.

This was the first time Laxmi had laid eyes on Tulsi. She'd been under lock and key for the past three months in the family's Agra villa, barred from having contact with even her closest female friends. Indeed, the only visitors she'd seen in all that time were prospective grooms and their families, all of them vetted and introduced by an "upscale" marriage broker.

"Beautiful, homely, fair and proper height" was how Cupids Matrimonial Agency had described her. Laxmi could see that this was no exaggeration. Tulsi had mother-of-pearl skin and dark brown eyes set amidst a flurry of long black lashes. She looked to be in good health, with plenty of color in her cheeks. If she bore her father any ill will, it certainly didn't show in her doting smile.

Had she buckled under the relentless pressure of parents and family? Laxmi wondered.

She'd known it to happen before. Tulsi's boyfriend, Ram, might have been a handsome boy with liquid brown eyes, but he was still an "untouchable," or Dalit—a caste so low and noxious to the highborn Hindu that, until recent times, the slightest physical contact with a member had been considered personally polluting.

Vishnu Mishra would stop at nothing to prevent his daughter from seeing Ram again. He'd blocked all communication between them and left the young man in no doubt about what would happen if he attempted to contact Tulsi again.

"I'll kill you at the earliest opportunity, Dalit dog," he'd promised over the phone.

But Ram hadn't been scared off. He'd appealed to the Love Commandos for help. The charity helped Indian couples from disparate castes and religions to marry and settle down, often under aliases. The founders and volunteers believed that the arranged-marriage system was holding back society and that if young people were able to choose their own partners—to marry across caste lines and therefore break down the ordained divisions once and for all—then India would become a more progressive place.

Laxmi, who'd met with Ram a fortnight ago, had taken a shine to the young Dalit and his commitment to Tulsi.

"She has hair that smells like raat ki raani," he'd told her.

Did Ram understand how hard it was for "love marriage" couples to make their way in Indian society without parental support? Did he comprehend how especially hard it would be for them given that Tulsi was from a Thakur family and he a Dalit one? Possibly not. "Without blossoms there is no spring in life," he said, quoting from the poet Ghalib. Ram sounded naïve, but Laxmi was willing to risk her life for the lanky love-struck student nonetheless.

And what better place for the Love Commandos to strike again but Agra, home of the Taj Mahal, the world's greatest monument to love?

Now the whole plan hung on whether Tulsi would be true to her feelings—and whether she was brave enough.

If she wanted to avoid an arranged marriage at the Harmony Farms wedding venue a week from today, then she would have to be. This was her only chance of escape, her finals being the one commitment Vishnu Mishra would ensure that she didn't miss.

"She's heading in now," Laxmi reported to Shruti. "Be ready."

Vishnu Mishra led Tulsi inside the examination hall past clutches of students. Naga followed a few steps behind. His steroid-enhanced muscles ensured that he moved like a gunslinger in an American Western, with legs splayed and arms hanging stiffly by his sides.

The driver, meanwhile, stepped over to the Licensed Refrigerated Water Trolly and demanded a glass of nimboo pani. He gulped it down, some of the liquid trickling onto his stubbly chin, and eyed Laxmi, who was posing as the vendor.

"Want to be Radha to my Krishna, baby?" he said with a lecherous grin.

She ignored him and he tossed a couple of coins onto the top of the cart before returning to the Range Rover.

A few seconds later, her phone vibrated with an SMS. "Dad's here!" it read.

Laxmi cursed under her breath. Vishnu Mishra had gone *inside* the examination hall. He must have come to an arrangement with the adjudicator—no doubt a financial one.

"Stick to plan," she messaged back before donning her helmet, jumping on her scootie and kick-starting the engine.

Crossing over the road and mounting the pavement, she headed down the alleyway that ran alongside the gymnasium building. It was littered with chunks of loose concrete and dog turds. She pulled up beneath the window to the ladies' toilets.

A few minutes later, she received another SMS confirming that Tulsi had been slipped Ram's note asking her to run away with him.

All Laxmi could do now was wait—and pray.

Forty-five minutes passed. Laxmi was beginning to give up hope when a set of painted fingernails appeared over the window ledge.

A pair of anxious dark brown eyes followed. It was Tulsi.

"Are you with Ram?" she whispered.

"Yes, I'll take you to him!" answered Laxmi.

The Love Commandos had placed a bamboo ladder in the alley earlier that morning. She picked it up and leaned it against the wall.

"I'm not sure I can do it!" said Tulsi as she looked down.

"We've only got a few minutes before you're missed. Hurry!"

It took the young woman a couple of attempts to get one elbow up onto the windowsill. The other followed. Then a foot.

"That's it, you're almost there!"

Just then, there was a thud inside the toilets—a door slamming against the wall. A man's voice shouted, "What the hell? Get down!"

He grabbed Tulsi by the leg and tried to pull her back inside, but she kicked. "No, Papa! Stop! Let me go!"

Laxmi heard another thud—Vishnu Mishra falling backwards into a toilet cubicle—and suddenly Tulsi was free and scrambling out the window.

Within seconds, she'd reached the bottom and Laxmi sent the ladder clattering to the ground. Mishra's curses rained down on the two women as they clambered onto the scootie and sped away down the alley, slaloming through the debris.

They reached the front of the gymnasium to find the pavement occupied by a crowd of students demonstrating against poverty, chanting and holding up placards that read: IF I GIVE CHARITY YOU CALL ME A SAINT, IF I TALK ABOUT POVERTY YOU CALL ME A COMMUNIST!

Honking her horn and motioning the students out of the way, Laxmi wove between them.

Out of the corner of one eye, she spotted Naga bursting out of the gymnasium doors. He pushed through the crowd and knocked over three or four students. "Stop!"

He would have caught her had it not been for Laxmi's colleague Sanjoy, a third Love Commando volunteer, who'd been mingling with the students.

Stepping forward, a can of pepper spray at the ready, he nailed the goon right in the face.

Naga reared up, roaring like a wounded animal, clasping his hands to his face, and staggered away. Sanjoy then climbed onto the back of the scootie and he, Tulsi and Laxmi sped off toward the main gate.

Behind them Vishnu Mishra ran into the middle of the street. He was wielding his revolver and gesticulating wildly to his driver to start the engine. But the man was fast asleep at the wheel of the Range Rover. The knockout pill Laxmi had slipped into his nimboo pani had done the trick.

The trio passed beneath the red sandstone ramparts of Agra Fort and crossed the sluggish, polluted waters of the Yamuna River. Between the iron supports of the bridge, they glimpsed the gleaming white marble of the Taj Mahal before plunging headfirst into a maze of filthy alleys and lanes as cramped and teeming as an ant colony. The shop fronts of ironmongers, jewelers, dried-fruit sellers and cigarette-paan vendors interspersed with light industry units housing ironworks, printers and cardboard recyclers all appeared in rapid succession like the frames of a cartoon viewed through a Victorian zoetrope. Motorbikes and three-wheelers bullied their way through a multitude of pedestrians, cows and goats. Children spun metal bicycle wheels along the ground with sticks. At a water pump, men wearing chuddies lathered themselves in suds.

Tulsi bore the stench of raw sewage and diesel fumes and potholes without complaint. Only after they'd emerged into a landscape of houses dotted amongst virgin paddy fields on the edge of the city did she call out, "Where are we going? Where's Ram?"

The answer was a nondescript building of red brick that served as the Love Commandos safe house.

"I can't believe we got away!" gushed Tulsi as she dismounted from the scootie, shaking with fear and excitement. "Oh my God, I don't know how to thank you!"

Laxmi didn't respond. Her attention was focused on the front door of the building. It was hanging, broken, from its hinges.

"Is Ram inside? Can I see him?" asked Tulsi.

"Keep her here," Laxmi instructed Sanjoy as she stepped forward to investigate.

Pushing the door aside, she discovered a flower pot lying shattered in the corridor beyond. In the room where Ram had been staying, there were signs of a struggle. His new pair of black shoes, purchased for his impending wedding, had been thrown at the assailants who'd broken in. There were a few spots of blood on the concrete floor as well.

Laxmi searched the rest of the house, fearful of finding a body, but it was empty.

Somehow—God only knew how—Vishnu Mishra's people had finally tracked Ram down. They'd waited until he was alone and then grabbed him. That, surely, was the only explanation.

Laxmi went outside to break the bad news to Tulsi.

Her face fell and turned pale. "Pa will kill him!" she cried. "Oh my God! I've got to talk to him!"

Laxmi handed the young woman her phone.

Tulsi's hands shook, but she managed to dial the number. "Please pick up, Pa. Please, please, please," she kept saying.

Laxmi put her head close to the phone so she could eavesdrop on the conversation.

The call was answered by a gruff male voice. "Who is this?"

Tulsi's answer caught in her throat. "Paaaa . . . I'm . . . soooo . . . saaarreee," she wept.

"Where are you, beta?"

"Please don't hurt him, Pa. I'm begging you."

"Hurt who?"

Tulsi let out a couple of long, hard sobs. "Raaaaam!" she wailed. "I love him sooo much!"

"Listen, I don't know what you're talking about. Now I'm going to come and get you. Tell me where you are. I'm not angry. Your mother and I want you home—that is all."

Tulsi wiped her wet cheeks and managed to compose herself. "Let me speak with Ram first," she said. "I want to know he's all right. Let him go and I'll come home. Papa, I'll never forgive you if anything happens to him."

"Listen to me very carefully, beta. I don't know where he is. And I don't care. My only concern is your future. Tell me your exact location immediately."

"You're lying, Pa. He's not here."

"Where is *here*? Tell me! I'm your father!"

Laxmi grabbed the phone and disconnected the call.

She and Tulsi stared at each other, confusion and disbelief writ across their faces.

"What did he say?" asked Sanjoy, who looked equally baffled.

"He says he doesn't have Ram," said Laxmi.

"You believe him?"

"He sounded genuine," said Tulsi.

One of the neighbors, whose house stood a couple of hundred yards away, pedaled past on his bicycle. Had he seen anything? Laxmi asked.

"A black SUV with tinted windows was parked here earlier."

"Did you see who was inside?"

"Two men got out."

"What did they look like?"

"I was too far away."

"Did you see anyone leave with them?"

"A young man, I think. They dragged him out of the house."

Laxmi thanked the neighbor and hurried back into the safe house to grab her bag. She emerged again to find Tulsi in a flood of tears.

"I should just go home. That way no one will get hurt," she said, gripped by grief.

"I don't think that's the answer," said Laxmi as she tried to comfort her. "Now, listen: I promise we'll get to the bottom of this. For all we know Ram was taken by someone hoping to get a reward from your father. I've a friend who can help—a private detective. In the meantime I need to get you somewhere safe. You're going to have to trust me. Will you do that?"

Tulsi thought for a moment and then gave a nod. They remounted the scootie.

"We should split up," Laxmi told Sanjoy. "Rendezvous at the bus station in three hours. Make sure you're not followed—and change your mobile chip."

She disposed of her own down a drain and then headed back through Agra's burgeoning suburbs.

Once Tulsi was out of harm's reach, she'd call Vish Puri using another number.

The fact that he was supposed to be going on a pilgrimage with the rest of his family wouldn't prove an issue. The man hated taking time off.

Still, it was going to prove awkward having to explain what she, Laxmi—or rather, Facecream, the sobriquet Puri always used for her—had been doing in Agra when she was supposed to be enjoying her offs sunning in Goa.

One

It had been a quiet month—as quiet as it ever got in a nation of 1.2 billion people.

The start of June had brought a desperate call from the Khannas. The couple had arrived to take possession of their new apartment in Ecotech Park Phase 7, greater NOIDA, on a day deemed auspicious by their astrologer, only to find another family simultaneously trying to move in. Vish Puri's task had been to track down the double-crossing real estate broker, whom he'd located in the bowels of northeast Delhi.

Next, celebrity chef Inder Kapoor had commissioned Most Private Investigators Ltd. to find out who hacked his computer and stole his mother's famous recipe for chilli mint marinade. Puri's reward for identifying the culprit had been several helpings of homemade papri chaat drizzled with yogurt and tamarind chutney spiked with pomegranate, black salt and just the right amount of fiery coriander-chilli sauce.

"Should you have need of my services, I am at your disposal night or day," Puri had told Kapoor after finishing every last morsel.

Then last week he'd played bagman for Mr. and Mrs. Pathak and got back their precious Roger from his kidnappers. How they could have brought themselves to pay the five lakh rupees was beyond him. It was a staggering amount—more than the average worker made in ten years. But what was even more shocking—"absolutely mind-blowing" in Puri's words—was madam's claim that she would have paid ten times that amount after receiving the "traumatizing" ransom video that showed her pooch being "tortured"—lying on a dirty concrete floor rather than a silk cushion.

The detective almost wished he hadn't bothered delivering the cash. He would rather have enjoyed the prospect of the kidnap gang carrying out their threat to eat Roger. And they would have done it too, given that they hailed from Nagaland, where pug kebab was considered something of a delicacy. But being "a man of his word and integrity, also," Puri—along with his faithful team of undercover operatives—had caught the goondas by using a miniature pinscher as bait.

June had also brought in a few standard matrimonial investigations—although with the monsoon almost upon them, India's wedding industry had taken a honeymoon.

And then there was the Jain Jewelry Heist.

Puri had caught the thieves. Within seven hours of receiving the call from his client, First National Hindustan Insurance Corporation Inc.

"These Charlies left so many of clues when they decamped with the loot, it is like following crumbs to the cookie jar," Puri declared at the time, certain that he'd broken some kind of record.

But then he'd hit something of a brick wall.

Of the 2.5 crore of jewelry taken from the Jains' multimillion-dollar luxury Delhi villa, Puri had recovered just two pairs of earrings, four bangles and a couple of hundred thousand rupees in cash.

Delhi's chief of police gloated, telling the baying press corps that "amateurs" were not up to the task. And yet the chief fared no better, soon coming to the stunning conclusion that the gang had stashed the loot at some secret location between the Jains' palatial residence and their hideout.

Desperate, the chief had then reverted to a "narco analysis test." Although a violation of an individual's rights under the Indian constitution—not to mention a form of torture according to international law—this involved injecting the accused with a truth serum and monitoring their brain patterns.

The results were comic at best. Under the influence, the gang members, who all giggled as they "deposed," told their interrogators that they might care to find the jewelry in a variety of different locations. These included the top of Mount Everest and up the chief's rear passage. Yet, when sober, they strenuously denied having taken anything more than the earrings, bangles and cash.

"That was all there was in the safe!" their leader insisted.

In the three weeks since, Puri had questioned everyone who'd had access to the house. He'd also put every known fence or dealer of stolen gemstones in north India "under the scanner" in case one of them had been passed the consignment. But to no avail.

"Only one case has slipped through my fingers in my long and illustrious career and that through no fault of my own," Puri reminded his executive secretary, Elizabeth Rani, as he sat in his office at Khan Market that Saturday morning.

The Jain Jewelry Heist file lay on the desk in front of him. The words STATUS: CASE SUCCESSFULLY CONCLUDED AND CLOSED, which he'd hoped to stamp in bold definitive letters across the front some days ago, were conspicuous by their absence.

"Even the most rare of diamonds has flaws," he added. "Yet when it comes to Vish Puri's performance, 'til date you will not find a single one."

Elizabeth Rani had brought him a fresh cup of masala chai only to find the last one still lying untouched on his desk along with his favorite coconut biscuits. This was unprecedented. Usually the refreshments lasted only minutes. Things must be bad, she reflected.

"I'm sure it will only be a question of time before you locate the jewels," she said, as supportive as ever. "It has only been a few weeks after all. No one evades sir forever."

"Most true, Madam Rani, most true. Even Jagga, one of the most notorious dacoits to terrorize India 'til date, did not escape the net."

Puri's eyes wandered listlessly around his office, lingering on the portrait of his late father, Om Chander Puri, who'd served with the Delhi police. Next to him hung a likeness of the patron saint of private investigators, a man synonymous with guile and cunning—the political genius Chanakya.

The sounds of flapping feathers and cooing came from outside the office window as a pigeon landed on top of the air conditioner unit. The detective's attention was drawn to the darkening sky beyond. A squall was brewing. It perfectly reflected his mood.

"Madam Rani, there is no point ignoring the elephant in the room: the case has gone for a toss," he said. "I am clueless in every way and Mr. Rajesh of First National Hindustan Insurance Corporation Incorporated is getting worried—and justifiably so. What all I should tell him, I don't know."

"You visited the house again this morning, sir?"

"I have come directly from there, only. I was doing follow-up interviews of the employees. As you are very much aware, there has not been one shred of doubt in my mind from the start that an inside man or inside female was there. Some individual guided them—that much is certain."

"Perhaps one of the Jain family, sir?"

Puri gave an exasperated sigh. "Naturally, Madam Rani, I considered that as a possibility some days back. But I am satisfied none of them were party to the crime."

"Yes, sir."

She eyed the clock. It was almost six. Sir was due to leave for the railway station in fifteen minutes. She was growing concerned that he was stalling.

"Should I call the driver?" she asked.

Puri didn't seem to register her question. His eyes remained fixed on the Jain Jewelry Heist file.

"Who all provided the gang with the insider information? That is the question," he said, half to himself.

"Sir, your car?" prompted Elizabeth Rani.

Puri looked up, puzzled.

"Ma'am must have reached the station by now," she said.

By "ma'am," she meant his wife, Rumpi.

The detective responded with a half shrug like a child who didn't want to take his medicine. "Really I don't see how I can go out of station. What with this case pending and all, it is really impossible. Should Mr. Rajesh of First National Hindustan Insurance Corporation Incorporated come to know, my reputation would lie in tatters," he said.

Elizabeth Rani had feared as much. Given his workaholic nature, Puri was always loath to take offs. In the twenty-odd years she'd worked for Most Private Investigators Ltd., he and Rumpi had enjoyed only a few holidays away—and invariably these had combined work with pleasure.

Take that Bangalore trip four months ago, for example. It had coincided with an international conference on digital forensics and cyber crime. Since then, he hadn't spent a single day at home.

A short break would do him a world of good. And the exercise—the family was due to make the pilgrimage to the

15

top of the Trikuta Mountain to visit the popular Vaishno Devi shrine—would be no bad thing, either.

Besides, Elizabeth Rani had made plans of her own. Tomorrow being Sunday, she'd be at home with her father. But she'd been promised Monday and Tuesday off as well and arranged to take her nephews to see a movie at Select Citywalk mall. She was also looking forward to doing some shopping in Lajpat Nagar, getting her eyebrows threaded and having tea with her childhood friend, Chintu.

How best to handle him?

It wasn't in her nature to bully. And arguing would get her nowhere. Any attempt to appeal to his need for time off would simply be met with a weary riposte like "Man was not made to sit idle, Madam Rani."

What was needed was a subtler approach. Sir, like most men, suffered from an acute fear of failure. If she could convince him that all would be well with the unsolved case, then she was in with a chance. A little massaging of his ego wouldn't go amiss, either.

"Sir, you owe it to yourself to take some offs," said Elizabeth Rani.

"And why is that exactly?"

"Such sacrifices you make of yourself every day, assisting people from all walks of life. No doubt everyone will understand if you are absent for a short while."

"And what if some Tom, Dick or Harry has need of my services for some emergency or other? What then? Lives could be at stake."

"That of course is possible, sir," she conceded. "Such incidents can occur at any time without warning."

"Crime knows no boundaries, nor distinguishes between night and day, Madam Rani."

"But it is not only here in Delhi that people require your

valuable assistance. Who knows what might occur during the pilgrimage? What if it is your karma to be there on the pilgrimage?"

Puri despised astrology and all forms of stargazing, often describing it as a social evil that afflicted his fellow countrymen and women. Yet he was not altogether immune to superstitious thinking. Nor from perceiving himself as the sun around which the solar system orbited.

"Most true, Madam Rani, most true," he intoned. "Who is to say what the God has in store for us, no?"

He went thoughtfully silent for a moment, then added, "Naturally, duty to family is there also. They will be looking for me to lead them on the pilgrimage."

Elizabeth Rani reminded him that his senior operative, Tubelight, was also hard at work on the Jain Jewelry Heist case. He and his boys were trawling the underworld for any clues as to the whereabouts of the missing loot. "So it is hardly as if the case is lying idle," she added.

Puri's countenance began to brighten. "I suppose a few days cannot hurt," he said. "It is a pilgrimage after all. Some blessings will be there. Perhaps the goddess will offer me some sort of guidance with regard to the case."

"Some time away will help you see things in a fresh light, sir, I'm sure."

"My thoughts precisely, Madam Rani."

He picked up the file, put it inside the drawer of his desk and gulped down the second, still warm cup of chai. "To be perfectly honest and frank, I had already made up my mind to go," he said in a confiding tone. "Just I was playing devil's advocate, actually."

He spent the next five minutes frantically packing his things and calling out reminders to his secretary to do this and that while he was away.

"Be sure to get Door Stop to polish the sign on the door each and every day." "Ensure he doesn't waste milk." "Dusting of my personals is required, also."

Elizabeth Rani noticed him slip his pistol into his bag along with a box of ammunition. This was unusual—Puri rarely carried—but then sir had received a tip-off recently that con man Bagga Singh, who'd sworn to "finish" Puri, was back in Delhi.

"I can be contacted night and day, round the clock, come rain or shine," he said as he paused at the door. "Should any development be forthcoming regarding the robbery, I would want to know without delay."

Elizabeth Rani watched Puri make his way down the stairs and disappear into Khan Market's Middle Lane.

She closed the door, returned to her desk and relaxed back in her chair, relishing the silence. Although she was keen to get away as soon as possible and buy some Safeda mangoes in the market (it was nearly the end of the season and these would be the last she'd taste for the next ten months), she knew better. Sir would call en route to the station to remind her to attend to some of the tasks he'd already mentioned, and if the phone went unanswered he would have fresh doubts about leaving Delhi.

No doubt he would also need another pep talk to assure him that Armageddon wouldn't happen in his absence.

The phone rang five minutes later.

Elizabeth Rani was surprised to hear Facecream's voice on the line. "How is Goa?" she asked her.

At the mention of the word "emergency," her heart sank. "He's on his way to the station. You'll reach him on his portable," she said before hanging up.

So much for the nice quiet break.

Two

Clouds the shade of smudged charcoal rolled over Delhi like some biblical portent. A torrid wind spitting sand began to buffet the trees and stirred a maelstrom of loose leaves, twigs and plastic bags. The light took on an ethereal quality, the greens of the city's flora rendered psychedelic in their intensity. In Connaught Place, that paradigm of whitewashed British imperial architecture, tourists and locals alike ran for cover. Even the ubiquitous touts selling carved wooden cobras and Rajasthani puppets abandoned their pitches and took shelter between the colonnades.

The traffic thinned and bicyclists, motorcyclists and auto rickshaw drivers joined the beggars and migrant workers beneath one of the city's numerous overbridges. Dozens of black kites, giant wings stretched wide, wheeled and cried overhead. And then the first drops of rain fell—big, angry dollops that banged down on the roofs of cars and left long streaks on red sandstone facades.

Puri had always relished these summer squalls. As a child, when they'd rolled in from Rajasthan (as they generally did in the weeks preceding the arrival of the monsoon), he would run up onto the flat roof of his father's house in Punjabi Bagh. Despite the threat of lightning and strong, unpredictable gusts, he'd put his face up to the sky, relishing the sensation of cool droplets splashing down upon his flushed skin. Not even Mummy's chiding would persuade him to come down until the storm had passed and the air was thick with the strangely intoxicating smell of steaming concrete.

This evening, however, he had no wish to get wet. He was wearing his favorite black Sandown cap and a new safari suit, a gray one made by his tailor, Grover of Khan Market. Besides, it was unseemly for gentlemen of his maturity and reputation to run around in storms. Such behavior was allowed only on Holi and when participating in a wedding baarat. Furthermore, the Jammu Express would be pulling out of the station in less than twenty minutes, and with the electricity knocked out by the storm and the traffic lights on the blink, the gridlock on the approach to the station was threatening to delay him still further.

Not even satellite imaging could have made sense of how the jam had formed. A vehicular stew, it bubbled with angry drivers honking and gesticulating at one another, the two-finger twist synchronized with a jerk of the head by far the tamest expression of their frustration. Puri watched, helpless, as the rain came down in earnest and gusts drove litter across the street. Everything was dripping wet now: the backpacker hotels and crowded eateries with their forlorn facades and cockeyed signs; the fruit-and-vegetable wallah's barrows on the half-dug-up pavements; the omnipresent crows perched on the sagging overhead wires. Only the beggar children seemed to be enjoying the downpour, broad grins of brilliant white teeth beaming from tawny faces as they danced in the puddles.

Handbrake, Puri's driver, inched the Ambassador forward and, with only ten minutes to go, finally turned into New

Delhi Railway Station. Passengers were hurrying from their vehicles and dashing zigzag between waterlogged potholes toward the terminal building. Parking touts were gesticulating wildly like gauchos herding cows. Coolies in red tunics and soggy turbans peered through steamed-up car windows touting for work.

"Which train, saab?" "How many pieces?"

An elderly coolie, whose bare, sinewy legs showed between the folds of his dhoti, hoisted Puri's bag onto his head and set off for the terminal. The detective struggled to keep up with him—umbrella held at forty-five degrees against the wind, eyes fixed on the backs of the man's callused heels, which squelched rhythmically in his rubber chappals.

They'd covered about a third of the distance when disaster struck: a gust plucked away the umbrella as easily as a balloon from a child and sent it rolling across the car park. Puri had the presence of mind to clasp one hand to the top of his head, thereby saving his cap, but in so doing, he forgot to watch where he was treading. Looking down, he found his right leg knee-deep in muddy water.

With a curse, he hurried to the station building and took cover. His mishap had engendered a collective whoop from the crowd sheltering beneath the overhang. Many of them were still smiling as he brushed away the muck from his trouser leg. Puri could barely mask his displeasure at being considered a figure of fun. After being reunited with his umbrella, which was brought to him by a helpful parking attendant, he strode purposefully into the ticketing hall, water seeping from the sides of his shoe.

The security check beyond proved as haphazard as ever. The metal detector beeped constantly as departing passengers coursed through it unchallenged. The jawan manning the X-ray machine yawned. When the image of the detective's bag appeared on his screen, the impression of his .302 IOF pistol went unnoticed.

Puri, who had a license to carry the firearm, felt tempted to give the idiot a piece of his mind. Sloppy security had helped facilitate the success of the 2008 Mumbai terrorist attack, after all. But he hurried on, deciding instead to report the incident upon his return to Delhi.

Finding the station's only escalator broken—BY ORDER OF THE STATION MANAGER according to an official notice—gave him something further to grumble about. But once he'd climbed the steep steps up to the iron bridge that spanned the platforms, spied the roofs of the trains below and heard the lowing of the horns, his pulse began to quicken. Puri was still caught up with the romance of train travel. No other means of transport came close. With a car you simply got inside, told the driver where to go and sat back, a passive observer. Buses were even worse. But with trains there was ritual and expectation: pick up a couple of magazines from the A. H. Wheeler's bookstand; find your carriage; claim your berth; watch the stragglers hurrying to get on board; listen to the final whistle as the bogie shuddered forward.

There was no substitute for the tamasha of being amongst the jostling crowds of passengers in the stations, either. In New Delhi they were drawn from every corner of the country. While crossing the bridge, he found himself amongst Sikhs, Rajasthanis, Maharashtrians, Tamils and Tibetan monks. He passed a family of Gujarati villagers, who'd evidently disembarked from the Varanasi train and were carrying plastic containers of holy Ganga water. Behind them appeared a group of Baul minstrels, easily identifiable in their patched cloaks, their instrument cases tucked under their arms. All the while over the PA system came announcements about the departures of trains bound for some of the furthest destinations in the country—Jaisalmer in the Thar Desert; Darjeeling in the foothills of the Himalayas; Thiruvananthapuram, a three-thousand-kilometer journey to India's southern tip.

If there was anything that provided Indians with a sense of living in one nation, it was the railways, he reflected. The Britishers had at least bequeathed that.

"Carriage number, sir-ji?" asked the coolie.

He'd been waiting at the bottom of the stairs on Platform 11 for his customer to catch up with him. Despite the heavy bag balanced on his head, he wasn't the one sweating profusely.

"S3 number," panted the detective. "Second-class AC."

The Jammu Express was preparing to depart. Along the platform, relatives stood waving off their loved ones. The coolie wove his way between heaps of cargo and the odd fortune-telling–cum–weighing machine, and reached the carriage with a few minutes to spare.

Inside, passengers were settling down for the journey. Bags were being stored under bunks, the sore feet of elderly aunties were being attended to by dutiful daughters-in-law, packs of cards were being shuffled in preparation for games of teen patti, and sections of stainless steel tiffins containing home-cooked food were being separated and laid out on newspaper like mini buffets.

The detective brazenly pushed his way down the aisle between the bunks until he found his family members, who numbered six in total.

"Chubby, so wet you are, na!" exclaimed his mother. "What all you've been playing at?"

Rumpi, too, reacted with little sympathy. "What have you done to your new suit?" she asked. "Such a state!"

He looked down at the offending trouser leg. A small pool of water had started to form around his shoe.

"It is raining, my dear," he stated.

"Well, main thing is you made it just in time," said Rumpi. "Come. The train's leaving any moment. Your berth is that one."

She pointed to the one across from hers. It was occupied by his nephew Chetan, who was fifteen, grossly overweight and an irritating busybody.

"Hi, Uncle!" He grinned, his mouth full of chocolate.

Puri greeted him warily, never altogether comfortable with the young man's overly familiar tone, and felt suddenly thankful that he wasn't going with them.

"Actually, my dear, something most urgent has come up," he said.

"Don't tell me you're not coming, Chubby!" replied Rumpi, who struggled to make herself heard over a babble of disappointment from the others.

The detective put up his hands in a defensive posture. "Believe me when I say it is not by choice. My heart was set on coming, actually."

Rumpi stared at him in disbelief.

"My dear, allow me to assure you, I'm the one who is disappointed. But one matter of life and death is there," he said.

"Something serious?" piped up Mummy.

Sometimes Puri forgot that his mother wore a hearing aid that seemed to give her almost superhuman auditory perception.

"Not at all, Mummy-ji," he answered.

"But you said 'life and death,' na."

"Must be you heard the words 'wife' and 'theft' and got them mixed up. I was referring to a minor robbery, only."

Mummy shot him a skeptical look. "Then why it can't wait a few days?" she asked.

"Most likely I would be able to join you tomorrow or next day," he answered, his words addressed to the entire family. "Meantime, sincerest apologies all round and safe travels."

He took Rumpi to one side. "Believe me, it is not my fault—quite the reverse in fact," he said. "The situation is a grave one. A young man's life hangs in the balance."

She could tell that he was speaking the truth. Chubby might have lied consistently about his calorie consumption, but he never exaggerated about the nature of his work.

"Such a pity," she said. "I can't remember the last time we got away. I was hoping we'd perform the darshan together. At least promise me you'll take a few days once it is all over."

The train gave a jolt.

"Absolutely, my dear," he called back to her as he started back down the aisle. "I've been invited to lecture at Pune, actually."

"No, Chubby! None of your conferences! I want to go to Singapore or some such place."

"Yes, my dear!"

Puri soon found his way blocked by a man coming in the opposite direction. The stranger was his girth twin. Neither of them could pass without the other backing up.

"I would be alighting the train," explained the detective, who could feel it moving.

But the man didn't give ground; instead, he turned side-on and the detective was left with no choice but to do the same.

The two men's stomachs pressed together like a couple of beach balls. For a moment, Puri felt like he was going to get stuck.

"Seems we're both expecting!" joked the stranger, whose breath reeked of garlic.

Puri responded with an awkward, perfunctory smile and then let out a loud yelp as his toes were crushed underfoot.

"Was that your foot? Clumsy of me! So sorry!" apologized the stranger.

Struggling free, the detective limped to the door and managed to step down onto the platform without causing himself further injury.

"Bloody fool needs to go on a diet," he muttered to himself as he watched the Jammu Express pull away.

Rajnath, otherwise known by Puri as "Magician Ticket Wallah," was waiting for the detective on Platform 3. Once again he'd achieved the miraculous at short notice and secured Puri a berth in a first-class, air-conditioned compartment on the next train to Lucknow.

Puri didn't ask how he'd done it and preferred not to know. He simply took the ticket, thrust it into his pocket and, having thanked Rajnath, sent him on his way. With some twenty minutes to spare before his train departed, the detective then headed to the platform dhaba and, as the coolie waited with his bag, ordered a couple of samosas and a cup of chai. What with the storm and the rush to see Rumpi off, this was the first opportunity he'd found to reflect on Facecream's phone call.

His Nepali operative had always been an enigma. Details about her past remained few and far between, even after years of unremitting service. But the revelation that she'd become involved with the so-called Love Commandos had come as a shock. Puri had read about the organization in the papers and considered it to be something of a joke. He also disapproved of its work. Love was all well and good, but when it came to marriage, the approval of elders was sacrosanct in his book. It was not just about a girl marrying a boy; on the day of her shaadi, a bride became a part of her husband's family. If she hailed from another community or a totally different caste with a conflicting set of values and habits, what then?

His own marriage had been arranged and it had worked because he and Rumpi shared similar backgrounds and their families had got along from the start.

"Our mutual affection and devotion for one another grew over time rather than with so much groping in the back of a cinema hall," he'd written recently in a letter on the subject of "premarital relations" to the honorable editor of the *Times of India*. "So much of hormones going unchecked are like genies out of the bottle."

Still, Facecream had never asked for his help before and he wasn't about to turn her down. The details were these: A young male Dalit student called Ram had been abducted from the Love Commando safe house. His girlfriend's father, a notorious Thakur by the name of Vishnu Mishra, had vowed to kill him, yet claimed to have no knowledge of the boy's whereabouts.

"There's something else going on here—something I'm missing," Facecream had said over the phone, before going on to explain that Ram and Tulsi had met at the University of Agra, but both hailed from rural Uttar Pradesh, India's most populous state. Ram's village was to the west of the state capital, Lucknow, and it was there that Puri suggested they try to pick up his trail. He had a hunch (which he'd kept to himself) that the young man had decided to go back on his commitment to the girl. No doubt the father, Vishnu Mishra, a wealthy man, had bought Ram off. Thus the boy had staged an abduction and run away.

Puri's Lucknow-bound train pulled onto the platform.

In the first-class carriage, he found two young men already occupying two of the four berths. They greeted him with respectful nods, eyes lingering on his dirty trouser leg. The coolie placed Puri's bag on the floor and the detective reached inside his safari suit to take out his wallet.

It wasn't there.

"By God," he mumbled, struck by an uncommon panic.

He began to pat himself up and down as if there were insects crawling on his skin. But his pockets were empty. The wallet was gone.

"There's some problem, Uncle?" asked one of his fellow passengers.

"Yes, I, well . . . my wallet." Puri sounded uncharacteristically unsure of himself. "Seems to be gone, actually."

He thought back to where he might have lost it. He'd definitely had it with him when he'd left the office . . . the only time he'd needed any money was to pay the dhaba owner and for that he'd used loose change.

And then it came to him.

"Maaderchod!" he cursed to the shocked bemusement of his fellow travelers.

Out on the platform, the station manager was blowing his whistle.

The coolie, who wore a "Likely story, saab" expression, held out his hand. Puri fished out the last hundred rupees from his trouser pocket and handed it to him. The old man touched the note to his lips, then his forehead, and hurried toward the door.

Three

Puri wasn't one to jump the gun. His father had drummed it into him from an early age never to assume anything. Gather the facts and weigh up the possibilities before drawing conclusions, he'd always said—advice that had proven both invaluable and wise.

In this case, however, Puri was in no doubt as to the identity of the individual who'd stolen his wallet: that fat bloody bastard who'd blocked the aisle on the Jammu train.

He'd used classic distraction tactics—the old stepping on the toes and garlic-pickle-breath ploy—while slipping his hand inside the detective's safari suit.

"Must be he is a master pickpocket," Puri explained to his fellow passengers once the train was under way. "He had the advantage, actually. What with the train getting started and all, I was in a hurry to alight."

"Not to worry, Uncle, it could happen to anyone," said one of the young men. They were sitting on the lower bunk opposite the detective. "There are pickpockets everywhere these days."

"But my wits are always about me," insisted Puri. "Nothing escapes my notice. My radar is working twenty-four hours a day, three hundred sixty-five days a year, only."

"You've got extrasensory perception is it, Uncle?" asked the second young man with a playful smile.

The fact that he was being teased didn't escape Puri's attention. His tone became officious. "There is nothing *extra* about it," he said, his chin jutting out from the folds of his throat. "It is my job to notice what all is going on around me. I am a private investigator after all."

"You're a jasoos?" asked the first, who sounded surprised.

"Perhaps you have heard of me? Vish Puri is my name. Most Private Investigators Ltd. My offices are in Khan Market above Bahri Sons."

They both shrugged.

"I'm winner of six national awards and one international, also," he added. "The Federation of World Detectives saw fit to name me super sleuth some years back. My picture was on the cover of *India Today*. Probably you must have seen it."

"Sorry, Uncle, I think I missed that edition."

The young men turned to their BlackBerries, their indifference compounding Puri's sense of indignation at having been robbed.

Fighting his inclination to try to impress them further—another thing Papa had often tried to teach him was never to show off—he considered the best course of action to retrieve his wallet.

Inspector Malhotra, the Jammu deputy chief of police, was a good fellow, both reliable and honest. He was also discreet. Puri could ask him to meet the train and have the pickpocket searched on some pretense or other. But first he needed him located and identified.

He tried to think of someone in any of the towns en route who might be able to help on short notice. Only fellow private investigators came to mind and he ruled them out. Puri would rather have dropped the whole affair and never seen his wallet again than let it be known in professional circles that he'd been hoodwinked.

There was only one option: he'd have to call Rumpi and ask her to locate the pickpocket's berth number. By checking the chart—a list of passengers with confirmed berths was always pasted on the outside of each carriage—she should be able to ascertain his name.

Under no circumstances, however, was Mummy to get involved. Not because she wouldn't be able to help. On the contrary: she had an uncanny knack of getting to the bottom of things. But then he'd never hear the end of it.

As it was, she brought up the Case of the Deadly Butter Chicken every time they met, never failing to remind him of her involvement and how, in her words, she had "solved the case." And although Rumpi implored him not to rise to the bait, he didn't always keep his cool.

"Yes—eventually!" Puri would thunder. After keeping vital information about the case to herself and thus jeopardizing its outcome, Mummy had identified the killer. And yes, she had been in a unique position, given her involvement with certain events in 1947, to assist with *his* investigation. But had it not been for his own bold and daring crossing into Pakistan—at a good deal of risk to his own life—the case would not have been successfully resolved.

Furthermore, Mummy was quite wrong in asserting that he'd promised to work with her. He had only given his word to look into the odd matter that she had brought to his attention—and this for the sole purpose of keeping a closer eye on her. She was always going off on her own, sticking her nose in other people's business, after all. One of these days she was going to land herself in a hot soup.

How many times did he have to reiterate that he was the only detective in the family? Mummy-ji, as he'd put it to

Rumpi recently, should "stick to what she is best at: making gulab jamuns and all."

Puri stepped into the corridor of his carriage and dialed his wife's number.

"Chubby, that you? Hello? You're on another train, is it?" asked a familiar voice.

"Mummy-ji, why are you answering Rumpi's phone?"

"Just she's currently indisposed. Something is the matter? Some tension is there?"

"No tension," Puri lied, feeling his stress levels steadily rising. "Just I—"

"One moment hold. She's reverted."

He heard Mummy say, "It's Chubby. Something urgent sounds like."

Hands fumbled with the phone before Rumpi's voice came on the line.

"Anything the matter?"

"I would require a private word if at all possible."

"You'll have to speak up. I can hardly hear you."

The reception was indeed terrible. It didn't help that Puri's train was still trundling through Delhi's moribund outskirts and the driver was blowing his horn to clear the people walking along the tracks ahead.

"I would need a private word, my dear!" repeated the detective, his voice raised and distinctly edgy.

Rumpi made her way to the section of the train between her carriage and the next.

"All that is required is for you to locate the said individual and make a note of where exactly he's seated," said Puri after explaining what had happened.

"Yes, I suppose I can do that," said Rumpi, although she couldn't have sounded less confident or enthusiastic.

"Tip-top. Once you reach Jammu, Inspector Malhotra

will do the needful. Your help could be required in pointing out the guilty party, that is all."

"What if he's dangerous, Chubby?"

"Not to worry, my dear—a common chain snatcher, only."

She thought it over for a moment and then sighed. "I just don't understand why you can't ask Mummy."

The question provoked a predictable diatribe about how mummies aren't detectives. She held the phone away from her ear for a moment or two and then said, "OK, Chubby, have it your way. I'll do my best. What was in your wallet, by the way?"

Puri ran through the contents in his head: a couple of bank cards, a few thousand rupees in cash, various counterfeit IDs, multiple fake business cards and two SIM cards for untraceable mobile numbers.

"This and that," he answered.

Even if Rumpi had wanted to—and she didn't—it would have been impossible to keep the theft of Chubby's wallet from coming to her mother-in-law's notice. Mummy-ji had radar like a bat and their berths were all of three feet apart.

Besides, Rumpi didn't like all this cloak-and-dagger sneaking around. She was a housewife, content to attend to her home and family, volunteer two days a week with a charity helping street children, and make her mango achaar, which was generally regarded as being in a class of its own.

If Puri wanted his wallet back, he'd just have to put up with Mummy getting involved. She was the most capable person by far. Only recently, she'd managed to entrap a con man posing as an electrical meter reader by letting him into her Punjabi Bagh home, showing him the cupboard under the stairs and then locking him inside.

The said con man had robbed numerous elderly citizens prior to meeting his match in the form of this diminutive, gray-haired lady and Mummy had been heralded as a local hero. There was even talk of an award.

Why Chubby would never acknowledge her obvious talents and allow her to put them to use in an open and free manner was beyond Rumpi. He loved and respected his mother, of that there was no doubt, but when it came to work, he was intensely possessive. Or was it competitive? Either way, he behaved totally irrationally whenever he got wind of his mother "playing" detective and Rumpi could never make him see sense.

"Just I knew something was going on!" exclaimed Mummy five minutes later as they stood conferring in the section of the train between the carriages. "Chubby said earlier, na, some life-and-death situation is there."

"I hate to disappoint you, but it's not all that serious," said Rumpi, who went on to explain about the wallet and the fat pickpocket.

Mummy responded with a dismissive tut. "Probably left it at home," she said. "So forgetful men are."

"Chubby's usually careful with his things. If he says it was taken, then it probably was."

"He's certain it was this concerned individual?"

"That's what he said. And he's not one to point fingers, either."

"That is true also."

Encouraged, Rumpi repeated Chubby's description of the pickpocket.

"Achcha," said Mummy once she had taken it all in. "This thing is obvious. After identification we'll alert the train inspector. He can do personal searching of his possessions."

"No, no, that's not what Chubby asked me—sorry, I mean *us*—to do." Rumpi made a face, immediately regretting her faux pas, which she could see had not been lost on her mother-in-law.

Mummy crossed her arms in front of her chest and made a face of her own. "Let me guess. Chubby said to keep me in the dark—Mummies are not detectives and all," she said.

"You know what he's like."

"Exactly. So why I should do assistance, you tell me?"

"Because *I* need your help. I'm useless at this kind of thing."

Mummy sulked for a moment or two longer before saying, "Fine. But the proper and right way is to alert the inspector. Robbery was done on the train, na?"

"But Chubby said he's going to have the police waiting in Jammu."

The doors to the adjacent carriage to theirs opened and a shifty-looking male passenger with a large stomach emerged. He eyed the two women with what appeared to be suspicion and stepped into the toilet.

Mummy gave Rumpi a knowing look. "Could be that one."

"Except Chubby said he was wearing a suit."

Mummy went thoughtfully quiet for a moment and then suggested a plan. "Here's what to do: just I'll take one photo to send to Chubby via my portable."

"Your portable?"

"Naturally. It is having eight megapixels."

"But then Chubby will know you're involved, Mummy, and I'll be the one who has to put up with all his cribbing."

"Fine. I'll take photos and do Bluetooth to your phone. Then you can do forwarding."

"How are you going to take a picture without him noticing?" Rumpi asked.

"Never forget I am old," she said.

"What does that mean, Mummy-ji?"

"Didn't you know? Old is gold, na."

• • •

Puri had hung his trousers to dry, changed into his pajamas, called his bank to cancel his debit and credit cards, and was now lying on his bunk (still wearing his cap, which he never took off in public), staring up at the ceiling and feeling in something of a funk.

All did not seem right with the universe. First, he'd failed to solve the Jain Jewelry Heist case. And now he—Vish Puri, best detective in all India—had been pickpocketed.

He glanced over at his fellow passenger on the opposite bunk. He could tell that the young man was Bengali (his "Z"s came out as "J"s), he worked for a call center or a BPO (his headset had left a distinctive red mark on his temple) and it was highly likely that he was allergic to dairy (the white spots on his fingernails indicated severe calcium deficiency). So why couldn't he figure out what the gang had done with the loot? And how could he have been so easily duped by a common pickpocket?

There was surely only one answer: "nazar lag gayi"—the evil eye was upon him. No doubt this had come about because of his success, which had fostered envy. The evil eye was known to fix itself on those who enjoyed well-being and happiness yet failed to disguise their good fortune. Bad luck would now plague him unless he could shake the gaze free. To do this, he would need to make an offering to Shiva, the destroyer of evil.

Crucially, Puri would also need to play down his accomplishments from now on. He'd start by telling Elizabeth Rani to put away his framed *India Today* cover and all his awards. Just as a mother blemishes an infant's features with kohl to disguise its beauty, he would have to strive to appear flawed, no matter how hard this might prove.

Just then his phone vibrated—an SMS from Rumpi with a photo attached.

Part of the image was obscured by a curtain. The rest showed a fat man in an undershirt lying on a bunk asleep.

It wasn't the pickpocket: his moustache was Hitler-like.

Puri sent back an appreciative message saying that this wasn't the man.

He got a reply from Rumpi assuring him that she had another candidate in her sights.

In her carriage alone, Mummy found a number of men with large bellies. Two matched Puri's description, and she managed to snap pictures of them both. The first was asleep, which made the task easy; the second she caught unawares while he was brushing his teeth and clearing his nasal passages at the communal faucet outside the toilet.

Neither of them was the pickpocket, however, and so Mummy moved on to the next carriage. It was identical to the one in which she was traveling: six berths per section, each separated by flimsy curtains. In those sections where the lights were still on, Mummy was able to get a good look at all the occupants without having to intrude upon their privacy. But where necessary, she didn't shy from intruding. And although she provoked some cold or inquisitive stares, no one raised any objection, privacy being something of a tenuous concept in anything other than first class.

Methodically and with a certain natural discretion, she passed through five more carriages, doubling back where necessary, and loitering here and there to make sure that every passenger was accounted for. She came across four more males with ample bellies, many of them already snoring loudly, but only one with a moustache.

Finally Mummy came to the first-class carriage, which boasted six self-contained compartments with sliding doors. Lights burned inside four of them and she began to knock on each door in turn. To whomsoever answered, she explained, somewhat absentmindedly, that she was looking for her berth and then apologized when told that she was in the wrong carriage altogether.

A knock on the fourth compartment, however, engendered a hostile response. "What do you want?" a woman's voice screeched.

"Apologies, I'm looking for my berth," called out Mummy, to which the response was "Are you blind *and* stupid? Check your ticket!"

Mummy couldn't believe her ears. "That is not the proper way, na!" she said.

But the woman upbraided her again, bawling, "Oh, just get lost, you pain!"

Deciding that she must be some kind of demon, and remembering the old axiom that the only answer to a fool is silence, Mummy moved on to the fifth compartment. Through a gap in the curtains hanging in the window, she could see the interior. Two men were sitting opposite each other studying what appeared to be a diagram. One of them was short and thin with a pinched, weasel face. The other, who had his back to Mummy, was a man of large proportions. He was wearing a suit. Mummy also spied the curl of a moustache.

Fat Man was doing the talking and kept pointing at the diagram and running his finger along a portion of it. At one point, he made a movement with one hand as if he was giving something a hard push. Then he folded up the map and pulled out a thick envelope from the inside pocket of his suit jacket. This he handed to Weasel Face, who promptly opened it, running his fingertips over a thick wad of thousand-rupee notes. The two then stood up and shook hands.

Mummy retreated into the shadows halfway down the corridor, where she stopped and turned, mobile phone at the ready.

When Fat Man emerged from the compartment, she got two quick snaps of him without being noticed. She then watched as he knocked three times on the compartment occupied by the demon woman.

"Where've you been?" she demanded as the door slid open.

"Taking care of business," he answered.

"I'm hungry. Where the hell's my dinner?"

"Patience, patience, my rose. I'll serve you momentarily."

Fat Man was about to step inside the compartment when a voice called out, "Mummy-ji! There you are. What are you doing up here? We've been worried."

It was Chetan.

Mummy motioned for him to keep quiet.

"Why? What's going on? Why are you taking pictures?"

Chetan had got Fat Man's attention. He started down the corridor toward them, his forehead crumpled into a quizzical frown.

"Go! Phat-a-phat!" she told her nephew, and gave him a push.

They hurried back through the train, only stopping once they'd reached their berths.

Mummy turned off all the lights and told Chetan to get under his sheet and keep quiet.

After fifteen minutes, when she was sure they hadn't been followed, she checked her phone. The pictures weren't the best quality but good enough.

Within a couple of minutes they'd been forwarded to Rumpi's phone and then on to Chubby.

His reply read, "Bingo!"

Four

Puri arrived at Lucknow's magnificent Charbagh railway station at five thirty in the morning, groggy after half a night's sleep in the air-conditioning. He'd been tormented by a recurring nightmare in which his humiliation at the hands of the pickpocket had been exposed on national TV. While facing the glare of the cameras, he'd looked down to find that he was naked apart from a nappy. Mummy had then appeared, telling the press that her son needed his daily dose of iron tonic. "Bed rest is required for tension purposes," she'd informed the hacks as the detective had started howling like a toddler.

He was still trying to shake off the sensation that the dream didn't belong entirely in the realm of the subconscious when he found Facecream in the station car park. Their mutual choice of greeting was a formal handshake rather than a namaste or the side-on hug commonly observed between Indian men and women. It denoted a certain professionalism and mutual respect.

"You've heard anything from the boy?" asked Puri as they both squeezed into the back of the hatchback she'd hired.

"No word, sir. No trace."

Facecream had traveled from Agra through the night and slept no more than a couple of hours. Her complexion, which was usually aglow, had lost its luster. The worry showed in the creases around her eyes and the way in which she ground her molars together. And yet her natural dynamism hadn't waned.

"One thing you should know, sir: Vishnu Mishra left Agra on the highway headed this way at midnight," she said.

"He will go directly to Ram's village," reasoned Puri. "His daughter has absconded—and if, as you say, he is not in possession of the boy, he will take someone hostage."

"Ram's parents?"

"Definitely."

Facecream looked skeptical. "But if anything happens to them, he'll be the prime accused. Ram registered a complaint against Mishra after he threatened to kill him. Also, Tulsi called him again and told him not to touch Ram's family, not if he ever wants to see her again," she said.

"Think a Thakur type will worry about such details? Believe me, he will stop at nothing to get his daughter back. It takes a father to know."

They passed along dark empty streets where stray dogs roamed and litter lay awaiting the reed brooms of sweepers. It had been three or four years since Puri had last been in Lucknow, once celebrated as the Constantinople of the East. In the dim, expiring light, he could see that the crush of contemporary India was slowly taking its architectural toll on the city. Malls and office blocks, about as imaginatively designed as cardboard boxes, now cluttered the place. Building sites appeared around every corner, with concrete superstructures cloaked in bamboo scaffolding.

Vestiges of this once-great center of culture and learning remained, however, in the domes and towers of palaces and mosques etched against the somber sky. The British influence remained conspicuous, too. They passed a church with a spire that wouldn't have looked out of place in a Cotswolds village, and the old Residency building—scene of some of the bloodiest fighting during the 1857 First War of Independence ("the Mutiny" to the Britishers)—its brickwork still pockmarked by cannon fire.

The driver turned on his radio. When the newsreader spoke of the burning of Korans in Afghanistan and subsequent rioting in Kabul, Puri noted similarities between that conflict and the one of 1857. The ramifications of colonialism always proved disastrous. Indeed, Uttar Pradesh, one of India's most lawless states, was yet to recover from the legacy of the Britishers in the detective's opinion. The British Empire had destroyed the fabric of the indigenous economy as well as the old nawab culture, which, for all its faults, had produced an educated intelligentsia. Since independence, the vacuum had been filled by something far less sophisticated. Uttar Pradesh's modern rulers possessed none of the intellectual acumen of the likes of Mahatma Gandhi, Jawaharlal Nehru or Dr. B. R. Ambedkar, the Dalit leader responsible for writing the Indian constitution. Today's politicians were crude men and women guilty of everything from smuggling to rape and murder. Their route to power was not competence or judiciousness but exploiting caste vote banks.

The latest leader to ascend to the state's highest elected office was the son of a hereditary laundry man. Thanks to the affirmative-action "reservation" system for so-called backward classes, the new chief minister had been the first in his family to receive an education. Popularly known as Baba Dhobi, this former bureaucrat had tapped into the resentment of the long-oppressed untouchable castes to win power.

"We will thrash the Brahmins with our chappals!" had been his main slogan.

Since becoming chief minister four years ago, Baba Dhobi had sought to consolidate his cult standing by using state funds to build lavish monuments and statues to the leaders of the Dalit movement, himself included. Bronze effigies of this stocky, thick-nosed character—unmistakable in his simple dhoti with the unshorn tufts of hair growing from his ears—now stood at major intersections across the state. With new elections looming in a couple of months, his smiling image also stared out from myriad billboards and posters across Lucknow.

But from what Puri had read in the newspapers, Baba Dhobi was languishing in the polls. The crucial Muslim vote looked set to abandon him, and there were even grumblings amongst his Dalit base, who claimed that their lives had improved only marginally during his tenure. It was the detective's understanding also that crime was still on the rise. Often referred to as India's badlands, Uttar Pradesh was deeply feudal, with a caste landscape that was bewilderingly complex. Mafia-like networks controlled every aspect of the economy, and dacoits indulged in kidnapping, smuggling and carjacking.

Puri was glad to have his pistol with him. But before heading into deepest, darkest rural Uttar Pradesh, he needed to perform a puja to help ward off the evil eye. He explained to the driver his requirement and soon the ornate shikhara of a temple, its shrine strung with colored lights, came into view.

"Fifteen minutes is required, only," Puri told Facecream as the car stopped.

He got out and then remembered that he didn't have a paisa on him. Unable to tell even Facecream about his embarrassing secret, he made some excuse about his ATM card not working and asked to borrow three thousand rupees. With a small portion of this money, he bought from a stand in front of the temple some ghee, a coconut, and a garland of marigolds. He found a dozen other worshippers crowded before an effigy of Shiva, intoning "Om Nimah Shivayah." Puri explained his evil eye issue to the priest, who suggested an appropriate puja. He then chanted some shlokas from the Hindu holy texts and made an offering of ghee to the deity. The marigolds were draped around the idol's neck and the coconut duly blessed.

The detective stood with his eyes closed and his hands pressed together, entreating Shiva for protection from negative forces conspiring against him. The priest then smeared his forehead with a daub of vermillion paste, gave him a string of rudraksha beads, and pressed blessed halva and a few sultana raisins into his upturned hands.

With the god duly on his side, Puri returned to the car and shared the prasad with Facecream and the driver.

To the west of Lucknow, past rains had carved deep gorges into the earth's crust. They spread like fractures in a pane of glass across the umber-colored landscape—perfect hideouts and smuggling routes for the likes of the infamous Bandit Queen, who'd once been the scourge of the area.

Despite the evidence of bygone deluges, this year's monsoon was late here too, and the earth was wracked with thirst. Even at this early hour, it was evident that today would bring no reprieve. There was not a wisp of cloud in the sky: just the reds and pinks of dawn and the promise of a harsh, punishing sun.

The legions of truck drivers, who spent the best parts of their lives in cramped cabs hauling goods over thousands of miles, knew this better than most. Their battle-scarred carriages jostled for position along the highway, charging at one another like angry bison in a race against the fiery globe inching over the horizon. The tiny hatchback found itself boxed in amongst monster wheels and lopsided loads that threatened to topple over at any second. Engines roared and air horns blared, drowning out any attempt at conversation. Puri and Facecream were forced to pass most of the journey in silence. Indeed, it wasn't until they'd covered nearly a hundred miles and the traffic had begun to thin that the detective outlined how he intended to proceed.

"Better if I travel to Ram's village alone," he said, reasoning that it would be a mistake for them to be seen together. "We will find a dhaba or some such place on the highway where you can wait."

Facecream could sense a certain distance in Puri's manner. This was born, no doubt, from her admission to moonlighting with the Love Commandos. He was somewhat possessive, after all, and probably looked down on the organization's activities to boot. Puri could be stubbornly old-fashioned about certain things, and the institution of arranged marriages was one of his pet issues. She'd heard him voice opinions on the subject before. Although he was no caste apologist, he'd sounded pompous and out of touch.

She soon realized that despite dropping everything and rushing to her assistance, he also harbored serious misgivings about the case and even suggested that the whole thing might be a ruse.

"Sir, there's no doubt Ram was abducted," Facecream insisted. "There was every sign of a struggle and all his possessions were left behind."

"You're certain, is it? No chance whatsoever he decided not to go the marriage way?"

"No, sir. I've no doubt he loves Tulsi very much."

Puri's expression suggested he considered this a flimsy

argument. "There are other considerations in life, also," he said.

"Sir, I agreed to help Ram because I believe in him," said Facecream. "In this day and age, why shouldn't he be able to choose his life partner freely and she hers?"

Puri frowned and Facecream decided not to push the point further. She was deeply grateful to him for coming all this way. In spite of his quirks, he was the one person she could rely on to help.

"All I can tell you is that Ram planned to marry her," she reiterated. "We were planning to take them to the temple right away."

"And these other volunteers, your Love Commando types, they're all to be trusted?"

"No question."

"What if one of them betrayed Ram?"

"If you met them, sir, you'd see they're all loyal and dedicated."

Puri's nod indicated that Facecream's judgment on this matter at least was good enough for him.

"What else you can tell me about the boy?" he asked.

"I'd call him brave. He's not backed down despite everything. He's resourceful as well. As a child he didn't go to school. His family are traditionally swine herders. But he saved enough to buy books and taught himself. Eventually, with his mother's help, he got a place in a high school in Lucknow and moved into the city. When it came to getting accepted into university, he had to fight hard to get a place. Despite the reserved seats for his subcaste, he faced a lot of discrimination. He's been beaten up more than once."

"When did you see him for the last time?"

"Yesterday, before we set off for Agra University to fetch Tulsi."

"How you would describe his mental state exactly?" asked Puri.

"He was nervous—no doubt about that. Very jittery and preoccupied, in fact. But then you would be too, if a man like Vishnu Mishra had sworn to kill you."

"You know where all he'd been staying these past weeks?"

"He'd managed to rent a room somewhere in Agra. I got the impression that he'd visited his village in the past few days, though. He mentioned seeing his mother after a long time. They are very close."

Facecream paused. She felt a sudden inclination to explain to him why she'd volunteered for the Love Commandos, why she was so passionate about the cause. Perhaps if she told him about her past, he'd understand. But then his phone rang and as he answered it, the moment passed.

The approach to Govind, Ram's village, looked timelessly idyllic in the pearly morning sun. A sandy lane led through fields of ripening wheat, and beyond, humpback zebu cows pulled wooden plows through the dark alluvium. Water being pumped from bore wells formed little streams that glistened in the sun like some magical elixir. Even the fumes from petrol generators hanging above the landscape like morning mist looked enchanting.

They passed a single-story building that stood on its own in the middle of a fenced-off plot. A red cross painted on its side indicated that it was a clinic. The rusty padlock on the door and the weeds growing in the cracks of the porch suggested it was government funded.

Govind's only school was next—a collection of simple buildings with bars in the windows arranged in a semicircle around a banyan tree. There was a marked lack of activity here, too. It was now half past seven and the front gates were closed. An empty chair stood sentinel.

Twenty yards beyond, farmsteads with cow dung patties drying on their walls marked the outskirts of Govind proper. Chickens pecked about in patches of chaff where wheat had been threshed by hand. An old man with languid eyes sitting on a charpai stared at the hatchback as if it was the first car he'd ever seen. His wife crouched on the doorstep of their house sweeping away the dust with a reed broom while holding the pallu of her brightly colored sari across one side of her face.

Gradually, the buildings grew denser, the lane narrowed and the car entered an open space in the center of the village. To one side stood a small shop offering everyday products like hair oil, soft drinks, cigarettes and strips of foil pouches containing gutka and paan masala.

Puri wound down his window and asked the shopkeeper for directions to Ram's home. The man seemed to anticipate the question and made an impatient gesture with his hand. The "salla bhangi," as he referred to the Dalit, lived on the other side of the village. "Take the lane to the left and follow the smell."

The detective's face showed marked disgust as he told his driver to carry on. Delhi society might have been acutely hierarchical, but nowadays, amongst the middle classes at least, money generally counted more than caste. A Dalit with the means could buy his way into any neighborhood; similarly, Brahmins no longer found themselves at the top of the pecking order by right of birth. But this wasn't Delhi. And although untouchability had been outlawed as long ago as 1947, and it was no longer unheard of for Dalits living in rural India to be invited to upper-caste weddings (and occasionally even eat off the same plates), Puri could see that Govind remained strictly segregated. Away from the large houses and cars, the sacred bathing pool and the richly adorned temple complete with a well-fed and especially smug-looking pandit, the Dalit ghetto was grim. Perched on a rocky slope that led down to a trench filled with garbage, a collection of mud and thatch houses stood alongside a filthy stockade holding a few cows and water buffalo.

There weren't many people about—some men tanning hides, a few women milking the cows, three or four kids playing cricket with a tennis ball. One by one, they all stopped what they were doing and hurried indoors. By the time the hatchback came to a stop and Puri got out, there wasn't a single person in sight.

The detective considered knocking on one of the doors and explaining the purpose of his visit, but decided instead to go and sit in the shade of the only tree and wait for someone to come to him.

Gandhi, he reflected, had seen village life as essential to the survival of Indian society. "If the village perishes, India will perish too," he wrote. His romantic notions of the rural ideal were shared by many an Indian even today. As a younger man, Puri had shared them as well. But experience had changed this perception. The former Dalit leader Dr. B. R. Ambedkar's assertion that the village was "a sink of localism, a den of ignorance, narrow-mindedness and communalism" had proven closer to the truth in the sixty or so years since independence. Sitting there, Puri thanked his lucky stars that he had born and brought up in a city, even if he often bemoaned the negative sides of urban living and the creeping Westernization of the nation's youth.

Ten minutes passed. And then a man approached. Like the other Dalits, his clothes were old and dirty and he was clearly malnourished. His face and body bore signs of an additional indignity: he'd been badly beaten within the past few days and his cheeks and forehead were bruised. Had Puri not known better, he might have attributed the stranger's cautious, subservient demeanor to the violence he'd endured and not a natural timidity born of a lifetime of repression.

"Saab, I am the government-appointed village chowkidar and it is my duty to ask you your business here," he explained in Hindi, hands pressed together in a namaste.

Puri improvised. "I've come to make a full report about the incident," he said without elaborating.

"You're with the police, saab?" asked the chowkidar.

"From Delhi." He was certain that mention of the far-off capital would be enough to establish his authority. Taking out his notepad and pen, he added, "Tell me what happened to you."

The chowkidar eyed the items with apprehension. "Which incident, saab?"

"You've been beaten."

A coy smile spread across the man's face. "It's nothing, saab," he said with a shake of his hand. "A misunderstanding."

"With whom?"

A schoolboy giggle spilled out of him. "What's done is done. No complaint."

"Were the men who did this to you looking for Ram Sunder?"

The chowkidar pressed his hands together again, this time in supplication. "Please, saab. I'm a humble man. I don't want trouble."

"Then tell me this: when was the last time you saw Ram?"

"Just three or four days back, saab. Since then we've not seen him. Believe me! If he were here, I would tell you willingly. Why should we suffer for him?"

Puri gave a nod. "How long did he stay?"

"A few hours. He came late at night. By morning he'd gone."

"Has anyone else come today looking for him?"

"No, saab."

"Last night?"

"No one."

Puri checked his watch. It was almost eight. If Vishnu Mishra was coming, he would be here soon.

"Show me Ram's house," he said.

"It's the one over there. The brick one."

Shielding his eyes from the sun, Puri looked to where the chowkidar was pointing. The house stood at the bottom of the slope and was indeed built of brick, the only one of its kind in the Dalit section. There was another thing: the construction was new.

"Saab, it was made last month."

"What does the father do?"

"Nothing. He sits around. She's a midwife."

Midwives were traditionally considered polluted and were invariably all Dalits. They earned a pittance.

"Then where did the money come from?" asked Puri.

"Ram sent it. He's the only child."

The detective noticed a satellite dish on the roof—an incongruous sight given the inherent impoverishment of this part of the village.

"They have a TV?" he asked.

"His father bought it."

"With money sent by Ram?"

"Yes, saab."

"When?"

"A few weeks back."

"There's electricity?"

"It comes and goes."

Puri started toward the house. They passed a water pump, the only one in the Dalit section. It appeared to be broken. A well-trodden path ran down through the fields beyond the village to a river about a mile away. It explained why the chowkidar smelled of river water.

"Are Ram's parents at home?" the detective asked as they approached the house.

"His father is there."

"And the mother?"

The chowkidar didn't answer.

"Where is she?" Puri demanded.

"She left, saab."

"Left the village?"

"Yes."

"When?"

"Last night. After dark."

"And she hasn't come back?"

The chowkidar shook his head, eyes cast down.

There was a sudden urgency to Puri's step as he strode up to the front door of the house. This might well be a serious business after all. The boy's life, the mother's too, perhaps, was at stake. He found the door open and hanging off its hinges, a boot tread clearly visible across the grain.

Puri pushed his way inside. The room beyond was sparsely furnished, the floor bare concrete. A man sat snoring in a lone chair, his head resting on his chest. The TV in front of him had a cracked screen and a dent in its side, yet it still worked and was tuned to the Filmy channel. Bollywood's Govinda was gyrating his hips in front of a Swiss Alpine landscape.

"Is this the father?" Puri asked the chowkidar, who'd entered the house behind him.

"That's him, saab."

There were a couple of empty plastic bottles lying discarded on the floor. Puri didn't need to pick up and examine them to tell what they had contained. The whole place reeked of tharra.

His attention was drawn to the far wall of the room, which was plastered with posters, flyers and cutouts from newspapers all depicting Uttar Pradesh's Chief Minister Baba Dhobi.

"For Ram's parents, he is God," explained the chowkidar, as he stood behind the detective. "When the party sends buses, she goes to his political rallies. Any opportunity to see him."

"And you? You voted for him?"

"Of course. We all did. He gives us hope."

Puri took a closer look at the collection on the wall. There was a photo mixed in. It showed a handsome young man in a T-shirt and jeans standing next to a village woman. They were posing in front of a statue of Baba Dhobi.

"That's Ram and his mother, Kamlesh," said the chowkidar. "They traveled to Lucknow last year."

Puri took the photograph off the wall, slipped it inside his safari suit and went to rouse the father.

"Hey, you, wake up!" he bellowed, and gave the man a rough shake. "I want to talk to you!"

The man snorted a couple of times and opened his bloodshot eyes.

"Kya?" he said with a grimace.

"He's with the police," bawled the chowkidar in a belligerent tone that could not have been more different from the one in which he addressed Puri. "You'd better answer his questions!"

The detective could see now that the father had also been badly beaten in the past few days.

"Do you know where your son is?" he demanded.

His question was drowned out by the sound of "dishooms!"—the exaggerated fight-scene sound effects coming from the TV. Puri turned off the set and repeated his question.

"He was here but he left," replied the father.

"Where did he go?"

"How should I know?"

"How does he make his money?"

"I don't know anything."

"Who beat you?"

"Some men. They were looking for Ram."

"Who were they?"

"I don't know."

"What did you tell them?"

"What I told you."

Puri rolled his eyes and gave an exasperated sigh. This was a waste of time. What brain cells this simpleton had ever possessed had been destroyed by seventy-proof moonshine and Govinda movies. He went to look around the rest of the house and found two bedrooms, a basic kitchen equipped with a sigri and a few pots and pans, and a bathroom devoid of plumbing.

There were, however, a couple of items of interest: a newly opened mobile phone box and, plugged into an electrical socket, a charger with a cord that had recently been uncoiled.

Pushing open the back door in the kitchen, he found himself in a small, walled enclosure. To one side there was a hole in the ground about a foot deep. Next to it lay a pile of freshly dug earth.

Retracing his steps into the kitchen, Puri found what appeared to have been retrieved from the hole: a stainless steel box with traces of dirt inside.

He carried the box into the main room. What had it contained? he demanded from the father.

"Kya?"

"Who dug the hole in the ground?"

"Kya?"

The detective finally lost his temper and shouted, "Does your wife have a phone?"

It was the chowkidar who answered. "Yes, saab, she has one. Ram gave it to her," he said.

"About a month back, no doubt?"

"Yes, saab."

"Do you know the number?"

The man giggled again, as if this was the silliest thing he'd ever been asked. "No, saab."

Puri left the house and walked back to the car. It would take a less direct approach to find out what had happened here—and for that he would use Facecream.

"Which way did the mother go—when she left last night?" Puri asked, pausing by the open door of the hatchback.

"Through the village to the main road, saab," the chowkidar answered.

"Was she carrying anything?"

"Just a plastic bag."

"Did anyone pass her on the way?"

"Saab, it is possible," he said, his hands pressed together again. "But it was dark and the night belongs to the owl and the jackal."

Five

Puri was making his way back to the highway from the village when he spotted a plume of dust rising above the narrow lane ahead. A black Range Rover soon came into focus, traveling at high speed. In little more time than it took him to mumble to himself, "I don't like the look of this, actually," the vehicle closed the distance between them and came to a grinding halt.

With the way effectively blocked, Puri's driver had no choice but to stop as well, although he did so in rather less dramatic fashion. He then made his displeasure known by pressing down on his horn, which emitted a sound like a duck quack, and gesturing through the windscreen as one might to a lowly rickshaw wallah.

His railing ceased abruptly, however, when through the haze of fine sand stirred up by the Range Rover's tires, a large goon wielding a shotgun stepped out of the vehicle.

The driver's exact words were: "Mar gaye!" ("We're dead!")

Puri, too, was taken aback by the size of the man and the sheer thickness of his jaw. But he wound down his window nonetheless and was perfectly friendly.

"Beautiful morning, no?" he said.

The goon's skin was red and blistered around his eyes and nose. This was Naga, the thug Facecream had described.

"Come," he grunted, the shotgun held across his chest.

Puri smiled up at him. "Direct and to the point, haan? Well, how I can refuse when you put it in such a gracious manner?"

He exited the car and Naga motioned him toward the Range Rover. A back window slid down, revealing an unshaven man in a white collarless shirt and a silk half-sleeve jacket.

Vishnu Mishra wasn't someone who would have possessed a great sense of humor at the best of times, Puri observed, and right now he looked like he was ready to take on the whole world.

"Who are you? What are you doing here?" he asked, his voice dispassionate.

"Sir, with due respect and all, my mummy-ji told me not to speak with strangers," said Puri, conscious that Naga was now standing directly behind him.

"That was bad advice," said Mishra. "Some strangers won't take no for an answer."

"I'm not in the habit of providing information of a professional nature to any and all persons," answered the detective.

Mishra said nothing to this. He simply gestured to Naga, who promptly grabbed Puri by the shoulder, twisted him round and drove the butt of his rifle into his stomach.

The detective's ample padding absorbed a good deal of the blow, but he felt the wind go out of him and bent double.

The goon gave him a moment and then straightened him up by the arms. "Aaan-saar!" he bawled.

It took a moment for Puri to catch his breath. "I'm Inspector Lal Krishna, Delhi Crime Branch," he wheezed.

Mishra looked him up and down. "What's a Delhi cop

doing out here?" he said, doubtful. "And why are you being driven in a hire car with Agra plates?"

"Chasing a con man. His name is Ram Sunder."

"A con man? What are you talking about?"

"He plays on girls' sympathies, gets them to agree to marry him, then absconds with all their valuables and such. We've been tracking him for some months."

Mishra studied Puri's expression as intently as a portrait painter, weighing up his story, then said, simply, "Search him."

The goon promptly pushed Puri up against the Range Rover, patted him down and went through his pockets. He found a few clear plastic bags, one of which contained some pasty residue from a samosa, a mobile phone, and a forgotten, oily receipt from Dosa Heaven.

"ID?" demanded the goon.

"It's in the dickie," said Puri with impatience.

Naga gave him a shove and the detective staggered back toward the hatchback. His heart was beating furiously. Had his wallet not been stolen, he'd have used his Inspector Lal Krishna, Delhi Crime Branch, fake ID. His only option now was to get ahold of his pistol. Otherwise he had no doubt that Mishra would order his goon to beat the truth out of him.

With shaking hands, he opened the trunk and unzipped his bag.

"My wallet's in here somewhere," he said as he felt amongst his clothes for the metal of the pistol.

He found it near the bottom and gently wrapped his finger around the trigger.

"Jaldi!" bawled Naga.

"Moment, yaar," insisted the detective. "It is in here somewhere."

Slowly, he took his pistol out of the bag and pushed the toe of his right shoe down into the sandy surface of the lane. His plan was to kick some dirt into the goon's face and then draw on him. If he had to shoot, he'd aim for the legs.

Puri took a deep breath to calm his nerves. On the count of three. One, two . . .

On three, as if by a miracle, Puri heard sirens in the distance. He looked over the roof of his car and, to his relief, spotted a police jeep racing toward them.

"The cavalry," he said with a smile.

Naga cursed, ordered Puri to stay put and hurried back to the Range Rover. The police jeep pulled up moments later and disgorged an inspector and four jawans.

Mishra couldn't have looked less concerned. He greeted the officer with an irritated "What is it, bhai?"

The police wallah, whose nametag read GUJAR, was nervous. "Sir, I've been ordered to place you under arrest," he half-apologized.

"For what?"

"Murder, sir. Ram Sunder's mother was found in the canal close to your ancestral village two hours back. At the hospital she was declared 'brought dead.'"

Mishra made a face like a customer in a restaurant who's discovered his food is cold. "Who gave the order for my arrest?" he asked.

"Sir, I've been told to bring you to the station, where you'll be charged under section 302," said Gujar.

Mishra waved his hand as if to brush away a fly.

"Go have your khana," he said. "Tell them I wasn't at home."

For a moment, the Inspector looked as if he might indeed back off. His expression betrayed the agony of indecision. But he stood firm and unclipped his service revolver.

The jawans, too, readied their rifles and trained them on Naga.

"Sir, I respectfully request that you alight from your vehicle," said Gujar.

"Sure you know what you're doing, Superman?"

"Sir, I've my orders."

Mishra opened the door to his Range Rover and stepped out. He maintained a commanding presence even as he was cuffed.

"Careful what you start, bhai," he said as he squared up to the inspector. "Once you have dirtied your hands, only death will remove the stain."

He shook off the jawans' grip on his arms and walked, slowly, to the waiting jeep. Naga and Mishra's driver were taken into custody as well, and they were all driven back along the lane toward the highway.

Puri, whom Gujar had noticed but ignored, followed behind.

One thousand kilometers to the northwest, another police wallah was preparing to question a suspect. Inspector Malhotra, the Jammu deputy chief of police, stood on the platform as the Delhi overnight train pulled into its final destination three hours late. He was soon approached by Mummy, who was the first passenger to disembark.

"Pranap Dughal is the suspect's name," she informed him. "It is written there on the chart."

"Very good, madam," said Malhotra. "But understand, at most I can check his identity. If there are any irregularities, then only I will be able to take action."

"Irregularities" could be construed as almost anything in the state of Jammu and Kashmir, where the security forces had special powers to fight the ongoing insurgency. Mummy therefore took succor from his statement and waited at the back of the platform to watch what happened.

The Dughals were slow to disembark and the reason for the holdup soon became obvious. Mrs. Dughal was so large that she required two porters to carry her down onto the platform. She then had to be hefted into a wheelchair, her lower frame wobbling like blancmange.

"That is she—the one who was doing shouting," Mummy told her daughter-in-law, who'd joined her on the platform.

"She doesn't look like a very happy person, does she?" observed Rumpi.

They watched as Inspector Malhotra interviewed Pranap Dughal, who listened and smiled, and made an amiable gesture that suggested he had nothing to hide. He then reached into his back pocket for his wallet. As he took it out, half the contents spilled onto the platform. Cards, bank notes and receipts scattered in all directions.

"Such a pagal!" scolded Mrs. Dughal. "Why don't you watch what you're doing! I'm always telling you not to keep your wallet there!"

Her husband looked embarrassed and flustered as the porters scrambled around after his personal effects and returned them to him.

Once he'd found his ID, he handed it to the inspector the wrong way up.

"He doesn't look like he'd make a very competent pickpocket to me," said Rumpi. "Think maybe we've got the wrong man?"

"Definitely not," replied her mother-in-law. "Just he's doing acting."

It was at this point that Chetan came running down the platform. "Aunty-ji, Mummy-ji! Look! I found it!" he shouted.

Rumpi and Mummy shot him an irritated look and told him to "chup!"

"No, no, you don't understand. Here, here, see!" Chetan was in a state of breathless excitement. "It . . . it . . . was on the floor . . . under the table. Between the . . . the berths."

He handed Puri's wallet to Rumpi.

The outburst caught Inspector Malhotra's attention and he approached. "Is this Puri sahib's?" he asked with a frown.

Rumpi checked the contents and confirmed that it was indeed her husband's property.

"Looks like we owe you an apology, Inspector," she said. "I'm so sorry to have wasted your time."

But Mummy wasn't convinced.

"No, no, something is not right, na," she interjected. "Definitely the wallet was not there! Just it has been planted by this fellow in the wee hours. Inspector, I tell you this Dughal is guilty as charged."

"Now, Mummy, that's enough," said Rumpi. "We've got Chubby's wallet back, buss."

Inspector Malhotra cleared his throat. "If there's nothing more, madam, I've my duty to attend to," he told Rumpi in a polite but firm tone. "With your permission I'll take my leaves."

He went and handed Pranap Dughal back his ID and wasted not a second in making for the station exit.

Rumpi placed a hand on her mother-in-law's arm and gripped it tenderly. "Come, Mummy-ji, we should get a move on," she said. "Jagdish Uncle's come to pick us up."

But her mother-in-law didn't budge. "He's a cunning one," she said. "Must be he came to know he looted the wallet belonging to a certain jasoos. No doubt, he was already regretting his mistake, na. Then thanks to Chetan my face becomes known to him. Thus he does two and two and checks the chart. There he finds my good name—that is Puri, also. What to do? Return the wallet, that is what. Thus he slips it under the curtain in dead of night."

"But, Mummy-ji, you told me you were up all night—keeping 'vigil,' as you put it."

"Correct. In case he fled the train."

"So don't you think you would have noticed a man that size coming through our carriage?"

"He's got a compliss."

"An *accomplice*? Now, Mummy, I've heard enough. I'm going to call Chubby, tell him the good news, then let's just forget the whole thing. Come. Everyone's waiting."

Mummy had been watching the Dughals over Rumpi's shoulder. The porters had struggled to get their bags—they looked uncommonly heavy—up onto their heads and were now heading for the exit. Pranap Dughal was pushing his wife's wheelchair and she in turn was berating him.

"How could you let that police wallah harass you without a protest? You should have given him a piece of your mind! Who is *he* to ask to see your ID? What are you, a man or a mouse?"

Mummy looked for Weasel Face, but there was no sign of him. He must have left the train from a door on the other side, unseen, she decided, and reluctantly she went with Rumpi to join the rest of the family in the station car park.

Her mood was not improved by their teasing—"Better bring your magnifying glass next time, Mummy-ji," joked Chetan. And when Rumpi gave her a gentle reproach—"You have to admit, you got a bit carried away"—she bristled.

"Not at all, Chubby was looted for sure," said Mummy with crossed arms. "He himself told you, na."

Indeed, Puri, although delighted to hear that his wallet had been retrieved, was adamant that he'd been pickpocketed.

"There is no way I dropped it," he insisted when Rumpi called him while the bags were being loaded onto the roof of Jagdish Uncle's car. "Definitely it was taken by that bloody bastard."

"Well, I don't know what to say," said Rumpi. "I've got your wallet. Just tell me what you want me to do with it . . . Wait, your mother's trying to say something."

She handed the handset to Mummy.

"Hello? Chubby? Listen," she said. "Definitely this concerned person, name of Pranap Dughal, got hold of your wallet. What is that?"

Mummy held the handset away from her ear for a moment. She rejoined the conversation with "Yes, I came to know. I was the one to get that snap on my portable. Do checking of police files. He's a charge-sheeter, no doubt."

She listened to him for a few seconds and then let out a loud tut. "Just I'm trying to be of assistance, Chubby. Making so much of effort on your behalf. Thanks to me your wallet got returned. But fine. Have it your way."

She disconnected the line and handed the phone back to Rumpi.

They both sat in silence, brooding, until they reached Jagdish Uncle's haveli.

After Puri's run-in with Vishnu Mishra, Facecream spent a couple of hours in a small town five kilometers from Ram's village where there was a hole-in-the-wall establishment that offered long-distance calling, prepaid mobile charging and photocopying. Internet access was also available, subject to electricity, with seven partitioned booths equipped with PCs. All but one was occupied by young men surfing social media sites and ogling busty snaps of Bollywood starlets.

Facecream's searches were mundane by comparison. On

the official website of the state government of Uttar Pradesh, she found details about the Govind village school. The current teacher, who was charged with the education of some fifty-two children between the ages of four and eleven, was a certain Mr. P. Joshi. After accessing the Most Private Investigators online database of Indian logos, she then forged all the official paperwork she required. With half a potato, her trusty switchblade, a red ink pad and a laminating machine, she also fashioned herself an ID.

An hour later, after buying some dour cotton suits, a pair of bookish glasses, and a few notebooks and pens, she arrived at the school in the guise of Miss Padma Jaiteley, an assistant teacher from Lucknow.

An elderly Muslim caretaker wearing a prayer cap sat in a metal chair behind the gates. There was not a gram of fat on him, his sun-baked skin stretched taut over his bones and joints.

"I'm looking for Mr. Joshi," Facecream explained, brandishing a letter for him from the Uttar Pradesh state Education Ministry, which appointed her as his deputy. But the caretaker, whose name was Atif, said he wasn't there.

"He went for a family wedding."

"When?" asked Facecream.

"Oooh, long time. A month at least."

She spotted some children playing hopscotch in the shade of a banyan tree. There were roughly twenty in all.

"Where are the rest of the students?" she asked.

"Working in the fields, mostly. Some go to a new private school. It's a few miles up the road."

Atif took her bag and led the way across the compound. The children greeted her enthusiastically and followed her as she inspected the school buildings.

The only classroom was dusty and littered with insect carcasses. It contained a few old desks, some metal chairs that were all bent out of shape, a couple of rusting almirahs and a pile of textbooks missing half their pages. A dog was asleep in one corner.

The "kitchen" was a room with an open hearth and a metal bucket for washing dishes. There, the cook, a miserable-looking local woman, was preparing a heap of spotty potatoes. Watery daal containing a minimum of onion and garlic was boiling in a large aluminum pot.

"The pradhan provides us with the worst-quality rations," complained Atif, referring to the village headman. "It's barely enough for each child."

"What does he do with the rest? Sell it?" asked Facecream.

"In the local market."

She stepped outside into the sunlight and stood for a while watching the children who'd returned to their play. She'd been wondering why they still came to school despite the absence of their teacher. Now she understood: they hailed from the poorest families and their parents didn't want them to miss out on the pitiful, adulterated gruel cooking in the kitchen.

A sense of hopelessness, of defeat in the face of insurmountable corruption, swept over her. The village headman skimming the children's only meal was but one of thousands doing the same across the country. The whole system was as rotten as that heap of potatoes. Little wonder that the Mao-inspired Naxalite movement was gaining ground across huge swaths of the country. But violence wasn't the answer. She'd learned her lesson the hard way as a young idealistic teenager when she'd joined the Maoists in Nepal in their fight against the state. Change could only come from the grassroots, from people producing their own legitimate leaders and then holding them accountable. For that to happen, there needed to be universal education. The words of Rabindranath Tagore came to mind. Even for those at the extremes of poverty, he'd once written, "there can be no question of blind revolution." By far preferable was a "steady and purposeful education."

The thought reassured her, and she walked over to the banyan tree to address the children. Class would begin tomorrow, she announced, and asked that they spread the word through the village.

Between then and now, she would stock up on chalk and slate tablets. That was all that was needed in terms of equipment, Facecream reflected, remembering the example of biochemist Hargobind Khorana, who had received his early schooling from village teachers under a tree and went on to win a Nobel Prize.

She also resolved to do something about the food situation. A visit to the pradhan was on the cards.

But there was no forgetting why she had come to Govind in the first place, of course.

Ram's mother had been found dead in a canal a mile from Vishnu Mishra's ancestral home, Puri had informed her. Facecream's priority was to find out what had possessed Mrs. Sunder to leave the village on foot last night and to retrace the unfortunate woman's final earthly steps.

Six

The body lay on a table in a crude surgical theater that doubled as an autopsy examination room. A Lucknow Government Hospital bedsheet was draped over it. Where the crisp cotton had come into contact with the skin, damp stains had formed.

That the deceased was a woman was immediately obvious to Puri. A shock of long hair, leaves and bits of twig caught in its gray tresses, hung over one end of the table. A petite hand, wan after hours lying in muddy canal water, and a set of pigeon toes, deformed by a lifetime of walking barefoot, also protruded from beneath the sheet.

"To be honest, I'm not a forensics man," said Dr. Naqvi, who had a big booming voice and was strangely jovial given the morbid surroundings. "Whenever a body turns up and they suspect foul play, a Jallad first cuts open the body and removes the organs and then the cops ask me to take a look. Lucknow doesn't have a coroner. In fact I don't believe there's one in the whole of Uttar Pradesh. No one would want the job. Imagine training for all those years to be a doctor just to spend your time in some stinking place like this."

He went on: "I've done quite a bit of reading, of course—

Dr. Ludwig's handbook has come in very handy. And I've learned a lot from watching American crime shows as well. *House* is wonderful, but I think *Quincy* remains my firm favorite. Sometimes I feel a bit like him—Quincy that is. You know—trying to figure out how someone like this poor lady ended up in such terrible circumstances."

Puri, who'd persuaded Dr. Naqvi to allow him to take a look at the body, dearly wished he would shut up. His conversation would have been tedious at the best of times and Puri didn't have much time. He'd passed Inspector Gujar in the corridor outside the "morgue," and if he was discovered illegally examining the body, the police wallah could make his life difficult. Besides, if there was one thing the detective was averse to (apart from flying, working with Mummy and having to deal with Mrs. Col. P. V. S. Gill, Retd., at the Gymkhana Club), it was spending time around dead bodies. There were four more lying uncovered on the floor, and the stink of formaldehyde and the sight of all the surgical instruments, which looked like they belonged in a Spanish inquisitor's torture kit, was making him light-headed.

Puri remained scrupulously punctilious in his manner, however. Naqvi was under no obligation to help him. And as a doctor he commanded respect.

"You're certain it was foul play, sir?" asked the detective, who was holding his handkerchief over his mouth.

"I didn't get you," said Dr. Naqvi.

Puri lowered the handkerchief slightly and repeated the question.

"Oh, without doubt," came the reply. "Any first-year medical student could tell you that. This unfortunate lady met with a frightful end. She was shot through the head. Would you like to see?"

"W-well . . . I suppose," stuttered Puri.

Taking this as a yes, the doctor promptly pulled back the sheet to reveal her face. Puri grimaced to see the ashen skin, the color drained from it as assuredly as life had left the body. The eyes, glassy and vacuous, were fixed on a point far beyond the confines of the hospital theater. Yet somehow her mouth remained contorted in a silent, terrified scream, and her brow was fixed in a questioning frown that spoke less of terror than bewilderment.

"The bullet entered here, through her left temple," said Dr. Naqvi, pointing to the wound. "I found what seems to be powder residue, so the weapon must have been held very close."

"This was an execution," said Puri, his mouth filling with an acidic taste brought on by nerves. He swallowed it back, wishing he'd brought a bottle of water, and asked the doctor if he could take a guess at what kind of weapon had been used.

"As I indicated, I'm not trained in these matters. All I can tell you is the bullet exited down toward the back of the skull." Dr. Naqvi pointed again. "See here."

It wasn't so much a wound as a gaping hole, the hair around it caked with congealed blood.

"By God, that poor woman," mumbled Puri. He walked over to the window to take in some fresh air. "Thank you, Doctor, I think I've seen enough," he said.

Dr. Naqvi pulled the sheet back over Kamlesh's face. He said, "She died instantly and not by drowning as the police assumed."

"That much is certain," said Puri as he turned back into the room. "We can assume the killer was taller than she, also. Up to one and a half feet, in fact."

"That would make him around six foot."

"Six one by my calculation. And a lefty."

"Left-handed?" Dr. Naqvi considered Puri's assertion for a moment and then concluded, "You're right! He faced her, held the weapon up like so, and fired into her right temple. You see, it is like being Quincy!"

Puri groaned silently. Who was this person the doctor kept mentioning? And why had he been named after a fruit?

"You make an estimate time of death at all?" he asked.

"Hard to say given that she's been in the water. At a guess twelve hours, but don't quote me on that."

"You came across anything else, sir?"

"Such as?"

"Physical abuse of any kind?"

"None."

"You had a . . . well, thorough, um, look, is it?"

"At the vaginal area?"

"Yes . . . right . . . that."

"I saw no sign of bruising if that's what you mean."

Puri took out his notebook and jotted down a couple of lines on a fresh page.

"Any personal possessions and all?" he asked.

"Some bangles, toe rings."

"No mobile phone was discovered on her person?"

"Not that I'm aware."

"And she was totally, um, without clothes and all when she came to you, is it?"

"She was wearing a sari. It's over there." Dr. Naqvi indicated the material draped over a chair.

"Mind if I take a look?"

"Help yourself."

The doctor went to wash his hands in a washbasin in the far corner of the theater and, while rigorously lathering his hands, sang to himself. "*What to do with the drunken sailor?*"

Puri tried his best to ignore him while giving the sari his full attention. Despite having been in the water, it looked relatively new. There was another thing: the cotton was of a high quality—far better than a Dalit village woman would wear while going around her everyday chores or traveling to, say, the local market.

What had prompted Kamlesh to don her best before heading out of the village just before dusk?

He stepped back to the table and took a close look at her hands. The left offered nothing of interest. However, on the top of the right, he discovered a symbol—a smiley face. It had been stamped onto the skin with indelible ink—the kind of stamp punched onto the hands of customers at, say, a fairground or water ride as proof of payment.

Puri took out his mobile phone, managed to locate the camera icon and clicked a picture of the symbol. Dr. Naqvi didn't notice.

Inspector Gujar was standing on the front steps of the hospital briefing a rabble of reporters on his arrest of Vishnu Mishra. Puri stopped to listen to the police wallah outlining his case. Kamlesh Sunder's body had been found less than a mile from Mishra's ancestral village, the police wallah explained. Vishnu Mishra's daughter, Tulsi, had eloped yesterday with Kamlesh Sunder's son, Ram, in Agra. Therefore Vishnu Mishra's motive was clear. He had abducted the woman from her home, killed her and dumped the body in the canal.

"The evidence is undeniable," he added as the reporters let rip with a barrage of questions.

Where are the couple—Ram and Tulsi—asked one.

"Both of these individuals are missing," said Inspector

Gujar. "We appeal to anyone with information about their whereabouts to come forward."

Could sir confirm that Tulsi Mishra was sprung from Agra University?

"It's my understanding that an FIR was filed subsequently by her father yesterday evening," the inspector answered.

Puri tarried a little longer and then went in search of his car. He was getting hunger pains and considered stopping en route to the canal to get something to eat, but decided against it. The sooner he reached the spot where the body had been discovered, the better. Already, the scene would be "getting stale."

The emptiness of his stomach was not the only discomfort Puri felt during the hour-long drive. There were a number of points about the case niggling at him—"brain itches," he called them.

Number one, how was it that young Inspector Gujar had acted so quickly? It was not like the Uttar Pradesh police, or any Indian force for that matter, to be so efficient. Kamlesh's body had been discovered at dawn this morning and within a few hours there'd been an arrest. What's more, the suspect was a powerful man—not the kind of individual a lowly inspector simply picked up on a whim. Obviously, someone high up had given the order.

Second, Inspector Gujar had stated outside the hospital that he believed Vishnu Mishra had abducted Kamlesh from her village. But according to the village chowkidar, she'd left at dusk, when Mishra was still in Agra. Also, if he had indeed killed her, why return to the village this morning?

The questions kept coming. What had been buried behind the house? Where had Kamlesh got that smiley stamp on her hand? Where had Ram, supposedly an impoverished student, found the money to pay for the construction of a brick house, a TV and a mobile phone?

Puri listed all these points in his notebook, a process that helped declutter his mind and put everything into a certain order. Then he sat back, looking out the window.

The image of the mother's face kept appearing in his mind's eye. There was something in that terrible, contorted expression—something that held the key to understanding who it was who'd murdered her.

The exact spot where the body was discovered hadn't been marked, let alone cordoned off by the police. Puri had to stop to ask directions from a group of local boys diving off a lock into the muddy waters of the canal. Dripping wet and as dark as dates, they crowded around the car, each more eager than the last to answer his questions.

"Yes, yes, we can show you!" they all chorused. "We're the ones who found her!"

They all set off at a trot north along the grassy verge, motioning for the driver to follow. After roughly a mile, they stopped. "Here! Here!"

A branch lay in the water. The body had caught against it, they explained.

"*Here?*" Puri's face showed marked confusion as he stood outside the car looking left to right and back again.

It made no sense. Vishnu Mishra's village was downstream—about another mile and on the far bank, according to the driver. He would hardly have dumped the body in the water upstream.

Come to think of it, Mishra wouldn't have put the body in the canal at all, Puri reflected. He'd grown up in the area, knew the territory, could have dumped Kamlesh in any number of canyons for the jackals.

74

Mishra was innocent for sure. Someone was trying to frame him. But what had prompted the murderer to put the body in the canal upstream rather than simply dumping it on Mishra's land?

Light, perhaps? Dawn had broken by the time he, and perhaps his associates, reached the area? Fearing he'd be spotted in Mishra's territory, he decided to off-load the body into the water in the hope that it would be carried downstream.

That meant the body had been dropped into the canal at some point between here, where it had been spotted by the boys, and the lock.

Before making his way back up the road, however, he examined the immediate vicinity. It had indeed been badly trampled. No doubt the police were as culpable in its desecration as the general public. He could make out numerous boot treads in the soggy embankment. The sandy shingle on the side of the road was scored with multiple tire tracks.

Had Inspector Gujar come across any clues or evidence, the existence of which he was keeping to himself? Puri thought it most unlikely. Such young, inexperienced bucks couldn't help blurting out everything in front of the cameras. By now any major discoveries, like a murder weapon, would have been all over the news.

Puri set off back along the canal with the gang of boys in tow, on the lookout for shoe or boot impressions on the grassy verge and trampled reeds on the bank sloping down to the canal. But he found nothing, concluding that the body had been dropped into the water from the lock itself.

Something else didn't add up. How had the boys notified the police? There wasn't a public phone for miles.

Puri went to the car and retrieved a packet of toffees from his bag.

"Who likes sweets?" he asked.

"*Me!*"

Grubby hands were soon tearing away the wrappings and shoving toffees into open mouths.

"So which of you found the body?" he asked.

Four hands went up.

"You said it was six o'clock this morning?"

"That's right, Uncle," answered the eldest of the four as he chomped on his toffee.

"How did you know what time it was?"

"We just knew, Uncle."

"So what did you do when you found the body?"

"We called the police."

"From where?"

"On a phone, Uncle." The boy shifted his weight from one leg to the other and tried his best to look bored.

"Which phone did you use?" he asked.

Some of the other boys exchanged nervous furtive glances. But the eldest tried to brazen it out. "The shop."

"Where?"

"In the village."

"Achcha. So the owner will have a record of your call."

The boy gave a shrug. "His equipment doesn't work that well."

Puri shared out the remaining sweets. The children took them a little less eagerly than before, now weary of their benefactor.

"You know there's a reward being offered for the dead woman's mobile phone," he said. "One thousand rupees."

"One thousand!" blurted out one of the youngest.

"On the other hand, if the police came to know someone had hidden the phone from them, who knows what they might do?" continued the detective. "Removing evidence from a crime scene is an offense. They throw people, small boys included, into prison for that."

He took one of Facecream's one-thousand-rupee notes from his pocket. The boys eyed it as if it were a precious gemstone.

"You won't tell the police wallah?" said the eldest.

"Kassam se, no," replied Puri.

The phone was quickly retrieved from where it was hidden on the canal bank, the exchange was made and the eldest boy inspected the note, holding it up to the light to make sure it wasn't a fake. Then with a frown and a quick upward motion of his head, he asked, "Uncle-ji! Aapke paas change nahi hai kya?" ("What, you don't have any change, Uncle?")

There was still some battery power left in the phone and Puri checked the call log. Kamlesh had received a call from the same number every morning at ten o'clock for at least the past couple of weeks. But there was no record of a call yesterday.

The outgoing log showed that between ten thirty A.M. and around seven P.M. last night, Kamlesh had tried calling the number herself some sixty or more times.

He called Facecream. She confirmed that the number was indeed Ram's.

"Thus the following can be concluded," Puri told his operative, who had gone to the nearest market to buy supplies for the school. "Ram bought his mother the phone and programmed his number into it. Being illiterate and all, she did not add any further names or numbers. The sole purpose of this device was for mother and son to remain in contact."

"But then he failed to call her yesterday," said Facecream.

"And his mother got frantic. Over and over she tried his

number. The maximum number of attempts is listed there in the log, actually."

"And fearing the worst, she left the village."

"That is after digging up something from a metal box buried behind the house."

Somewhere, some time later that evening, her hand was stamped with a smiley face, Puri went on to explain. And then she was murdered—brutally and efficiently by a six-foot-tall lefty who'd proceeded to dump her body in the canal.

"Question is, who all would want to frame Vishnu Mishra for murder?"

"I'm sure there must be a long line of people," said Facecream.

Seven

Mummy and Rumpi both had numerous cousins in Jammu, the city being predominantly populated by Punjabi Hindus and Sikhs. They'd spent the better part of the day criss-crossing the city in Jagdish Uncle's faithful 1994 Maruti, which he affectionately referred to as "Sweetie."

The fact that the car was designed to take only two in the front and three in the back hadn't proven an issue. Like any Indian extended family, the Puris were as seasoned as circus clowns at packing themselves en masse into tiny hatchbacks. Their all-time record, on a six-hour drive from Delhi to Chandigarh, was fourteen—four adults, three teenagers, five children and two infants—although admittedly they hadn't quite made it all the way under their own steam, the engine having overheated outside Ambala.

Sweetie accommodated twelve—and that with Chetan occupying the entire front passenger seat, save for a token toddler on his lap, and no one sharing the driver's seat because the door had a way of popping open when the car went over humps. Mummy and Rumpi shared the backseat along with their nephews Abhishek (who had to stick his long neck half out the window) and Harish, a niece, and Jagdish's wife, Sonam Aunty. The space just behind the hand-brake was taken by three-year-old Akhil, who stood. And the twins went in the dickie, where they thrilled at making faces out the back window.

The absence of air-conditioning (the high that day was an even forty-two degrees Celsius), the loose springs in the seats, and the necessity of having to pass Akhil out the window whenever he needed to stop for a pee (opening any of the doors invariably risked someone falling out) had proven the only "nuisances."

Otherwise everyone had "just enjoyed." Jagdish Uncle played old Bollywood classics on his decrepit tape deck and sang along, his voice high-pitched and out of tune; and everyone ribbed Harish, who was twenty-nine and had been turned down by five prospective brides in the past couple of months alone, the main turnoff being his premature hair loss.

There was no schedule to keep as such, no prescribed time at which they were expected at each house. They simply arrived when they arrived. And at each address, without fail, they were warmly greeted and ushered into reception rooms, where couches and armchairs were arranged along the walls and coffee tables groaned with plates of barfi and ladoos.

A decade had passed since Mummy had last been in Jammu, and over chai, chai and more cups of chai, she passed the hours chatting with numerous new wives, husbands, toddlers and babies and distributing envelopes containing money, the rupee variations correlating to the closeness of kinship, yet always containing a single coin on the outside for good luck.

Sadly, there'd been commiserations to convey as well. In three of the nine households, photographs hung on the walls garlanded with strings of marigolds, commemorating aunties and uncles now passed. In a fourth household, Arjan and Poonam, cousins on Rumpi's mother's side, had suffered a tragedy, the loss of their teenage son in a motorcycle accident, and the Puris all joined the parents in offering teary prayers before the family mandir.

Mummy noticed changes of a different nature, too. The city itself had quadrupled in size. There were plenty of new cars on the roads. A couple of shopping malls offered pizza and imported men's shirts from England. Billboards everywhere also presented images of swanky new housing complexes. "Live livelier life" read one advertisement.

It was a mantra that the younger generation seemed to be adopting wholesale. Markedly less parochial than their parents, many were pursuing their higher studies in Delhi or other "metros." They were marrying Punjabis from other cities, albeit within their own castes and gotras. And they were developing a growing awareness of India's place in the world as well as a recognition that other cultures offered different viewpoints. It was even said that the daughter of Harjot Aunty's neighbors had entered into a love marriage with a boy from Karnataka! They were living in London, where he worked for an international bank.

"Very prestigious," everyone agreed.

But some things never changed. Jagdish Uncle was still estranged from his brother. The two hadn't talked for at least twenty years, despite sharing the same haveli, which had been divided by sealing off the connecting doorways. And Sonam Aunty still made the best rajma chawal in Jammu.

At nine P.M., exhausted from all their house visits, the family stood in Raghunath bazaar eating golguppas and kachaloo.

They were planning to return from there to the haveli to

get an early night's sleep—meaning that after sitting around drinking hot chocolate and watching a movie, they would finally turn in at two in the morning.

Mummy hadn't given the events on the train a second thought for hours, but as she finished off her snack, she saw Pranap Dughal walk past. He stopped briefly to look at some tiffins stacked in front of a shop specializing in stainless steel items and then continued on toward the old city.

Unable to resist the temptation to follow, Mummy told the rest of the family that she needed to go to the toilet and slipped away. The busy bazaar, with its crowds of late-night shoppers and lengths of bright cloth displayed in front of the tiny shops, provided her with excellent cover and she was able to maintain a suitable distance from Dughal without being spotted.

She was hoping to catch him in the act of picking someone's pocket and raise the alarm. But although he bumped shoulders with a couple of passersby and had ample opportunity to plunder unzipped handbags and wallets protruding from back pockets, his fingers didn't stray.

Near the Hanuman mandir, where Dughal stopped to ring the temple bell, he entered a pharmacy–cum–dry cleaner's–cum–money changer's.

Mummy followed him inside and, without being noticed by her mark, approached the dry-cleaning counter. She told the assistant that she'd left a shawl the week before and subsequently lost her ticket. He duly asked to know her name and started to check back through his ledger. While she waited, Mummy pretended to powder her nose and, in the reflection of her compact mirror, kept her eye on Dughal, who stood at the counter behind her.

A pharmacist took down a small white cardboard box from the shelves and handed him a blister pack.

"What's the recommended dosage?" Mummy overheard Dughal ask.

"One before sleep," answered the pharmacist.

"One? Must be powerful."

"Very powerful, sir."

"What if the patient is obese?"

"Administer one-quarter of one tablet more, only."

"Give me ten pieces."

The dry cleaner closed the ledger. She must have made a mistake, he said—there was no record of any shawl.

Mummy gave a tut. "It is hanging there, na," she said as she pointed to a rack in the back of the shop. "See in the middle."

The assistant went to look while Mummy waited for Dughal to leave. Then she stepped over to speak with the pharmacist. He was still holding the white cardboard box.

"Those are sleeping tablets, na?" she said.

"Yes, madam, diazepam."

"A prescription is required?"

The pharmacist jiggled his hand as if to say, "What's a prescription between a helpful pharmacist and a customer?"

Mummy made for the door, but the dry cleaner called after her. "Madam, your shawl?"

"I just remembered I collected it some days back," she said.

Dughal took an auto rickshaw to a guesthouse where he and his wife had a room on the ground floor. The couple was due to leave the next day for the Vaishno Devi pilgrimage site, the clerk at the reception told Mummy.

Mummy found it hard to imagine Mrs. Dughal making it to the top of an escalator, let alone the steep mountain trail, and the clerk whispered that he was inclined to agree.

"Madam spent half the afternoon in the restaurant," he confided. "She's got a big appetite—ate four or five dishes, including a whole biryani. And just one hour back, she called to say she was hungry! We sent her butter chicken, three naan and a double helping of kheer!"

A couple of minutes later, a shrill voice penetrated into reception. It was Mrs. Dughal. She was giving her husband yet another browbeating.

Mummy and the clerk listened for a minute or two, both wincing as the language and tone grew progressively more abusive. A crash of dishes—apparently the receptacles in which her second meal had been served—brought her tirade to an abrupt end.

"That's the third time I've heard her abusing him," the clerk commented. "If my wife spoke to me like that I'd . . . well, I don't know why he puts up with it."

Mummy's face showed alarm. "What was that?" she asked.

"Living with a woman like that . . . it would drive you mad," said the clerk.

Maybe mad enough to kill, Mummy thought to herself.

Facecream had returned to the school with supplies and was cleaning the teacher's sleeping quarters when Puri called to update her on the day's dramatic developments. After they talked, she arranged the bedroll she'd purchased in town on the floor and then washed in half a bucket of brackish water drawn from the school's bore well. Feeling refreshed, she then decided to take a walk. Stepping out into the cool night air, she found Atif, the caretaker, sitting by the gate, smoking a bidi.

"You shouldn't go outside the compound at night," he told her as the smell of smoldering tendu leaf wafted over her.

"What could possibly happen to me?" she asked. "It's such a lovely evening. Can you feel that breeze? I won't be long."

She started to open the gate, but he looked genuinely alarmed.

"You don't understand," he said. "The Yadav boys, they drink." He paused. "This isn't a place for an unmarried woman. They shouldn't have sent you."

Something in the distance caught Atif's eye. Headlights had appeared on the lane, lancing the night sky. A vehicle was heading their way.

"More outsiders," he said.

"Have there been others?"

"Some fat man in a cap was here earlier. He was from Delhi. I didn't like the look of him."

"I heard there were some other visitors a couple of days ago," said Facecream, who suppressed a smile.

"Some men came on Friday—gave a couple of the Dalits a thrashing."

"That's terrible! Who were they?"

The caretaker gave a shrug. "They must have been working for Vishnu Mishra. They were looking for one of the Dalit boys—Ram, the son of the midwife who was killed."

By now news of Kamlesh's murder had reached the village and Atif was in no doubt that Vishnu Mishra was guilty.

"I heard that Ram fell in love with his daughter—only he didn't know who her father was. Had he known . . ."

The headlights were close now, lighting up the trees that stood on either side of the lane and casting long, fleeting shadows across the fields. Atif hid behind the concrete gateposts. Following his cue, Facecream stayed out of sight as the vehicle sped past. It was a white sedan.

"Is it the same vehicle that came a few nights ago?" she asked Atif.

85

"No, that one was big and black—and you couldn't see in through the windows."

Facecream wondered if this was the same vehicle that had been spotted outside the Love Commandos safe house in Agra.

"Looks like the car's stopped in the middle of the village," said Atif as he watched the progress of the headlights.

A minute later, he added, "Now it's heading into the Dalit section. Looks like there's going to be more trouble."

Facecream slipped out through the gate and, ignoring Atif's renewed warnings, set off along the lane by the light of the moon. She reached the center of the village within a matter of minutes and, keeping to the shadows, avoided being seen by three young men, who were drinking country-made liquor under the banyan tree. Passing the temple and the sacred bathing pool, she found her way to the clutch of mud houses and the stockade.

The sedan was parked in the rough track that ran between them.

Facecream could see now that it was a hire car with an All India Tourist Permit number painted in yellow on the rear fender. A driver sat behind the wheel, music playing on his stereo.

She took cover behind a low-lying wall. Thirty minutes passed. And then a short, thin man carrying a kerosene lantern and a lathi stepped out of a brick building. He was followed by another disheveled-looking individual who was clearly drunk. Both men had cuts and bruises on their faces.

Behind them, a third man appeared—tall, fifties, salt-and-pepper hair, big bushy moustache, immaculately pressed trousers and expensive brown slip-on leather shoes with tassels.

Facecream stared in disbelief. What was *he* doing here?

She shrank back, making doubly sure she couldn't be spotted, and watched as the visitor got into his vehicle and drove back the way he'd come.

Facecream waited a couple of minutes and then started back herself, anxious to call Puri from the privacy of her room and tell him about this extraordinary development. In the village center, she found the three young men surrounding a young, scruffy-looking boy.

"Hand it over, maaderchod," one of them cursed, and gave the boy a shove that knocked him to the ground.

Facecream didn't hesitate in stepping forward to intervene. "Hey, leave him alone!" she cried as she brushed past the trio and knelt down to check that the boy wasn't hurt.

The boy himself looked as perplexed by her sudden appearance as his persecutors and stared at her, dumbfounded.

"What is this? Who the hell are you?" demanded Bully Number One.

"The new teacher," answered Facecream.

"At the school?" asked Bully Number Two, his words badly slurred.

"Yes, the school. Where else? Now, you three go home and sleep it off."

Facecream stood up and offered the boy her hand. He took it, albeit with reluctance, and got to his feet.

"You're free to go," she told him.

The boy sent his tormentors a quizzical look, as if perhaps they could provide an explanation for this bizarre development, and then picked up his bicycle from the ground. Tentatively, he began to wheel it away. The bullies made no attempt to stop him.

"I don't want you picking on him again," Facecream told

them once the boy had reached a safe distance and taken the track that led to the Dalit part of the village.

"You can't tell us what to do!" bawled Bully Number Three, who could barely stand.

"I told you, I'm the new teacher."

"Do you give *private tuition*?" asked Bully Number One with a grin.

"Yeah, how about some *one-on-one*?" guffawed Bully Number Two.

Facecream didn't deign to answer and started back down the lane toward the school. Although they caterwauled and called out lewd comments, she reached the gates without further incident.

Eight

When Facecream phoned ten minutes later, Puri was sitting in a hole-in-the-wall Chinese restaurant in Lucknow with a young local journalist named Vijay Tewari.

Vijay, he'd been reliably informed by a senior-newspaper-editor friend in Delhi, knew the local beat inside out and had a reputation for trustworthiness. Puri needed him to explain the lay of the land. But he couldn't risk the journalist overhearing his conversation with Facecream, so he stepped out of the restaurant to talk in private.

"By God, don't tell me," said the detective. "You're certain, is it?"

"It was *him,* sir, definitely," said Facecream. "I'd recognize those shoes anywhere."

Puri sighed into the phone. The universe was still conspiring against him. The prayers and offerings hadn't done the trick.

"What all he was doing there?" he asked.

"He spent more than half an hour inside Ram's house," she replied. "I saw him talking with the village chowkidar and the father. I have the number plate of his hire car. Do you want to take it down?"

Facecream waited for a response but none was immediately forthcoming. Boss was taking this worse than she'd feared. Hari Kumar, head of Spycatcher Investigative Services, which had swanky offices in Namaste Towers, was his chief competitor. He also happened to be the one man in the world with the capacity to really get under Vish Puri's skin. She was in a unique position to understand the rivalry between the two men given that she'd worked for both. And the hard truth was that when it came to detective work, Kumar was Puri's equal. A former spy, he'd cracked a number of high-profile cases during his career. The Harpreet Triple Murder and the unmasking of the Coorg Conspiracy had propelled him into the national limelight. True, *India Today* magazine had never featured him on the front cover (an "accomplishment" of Puri's that he never tired of bragging about), but then Kumar was better suited to the pages of glossy men's magazines. The Indian edition of *GQ*, for example, had pictured him smoking one of his trademark Cuban cigars. "Tinker, Tailor, Soldier . . . Spycatcher" read the title, a reference to his role in the capture of the Chinese mole Mannan Kakkar.

Indeed, Puri's rival was an altogether more polished-looking individual. He preferred Italian-style suits and drove a maroon sedan, and his favorite tipple was Sula Cabernet Sauvignon. Hari didn't shun physical exercise and got in at least thirty minutes of brisk walking every day and often one or two rounds of golf. He was also a TV interviewer's dream, with stories of shoot-outs and derring-do and well-honed anecdotes about famous personalities he'd known.

In part this explained why, given the choice between the two, Delhi's "creamy layer" was often inclined to lean toward Spycatcher rather than Most Private Investigators Ltd.

Kumar also benefited in financial terms from the fact that he had few scruples. He'd work for anyone and was not averse to playing dirty. In Puri parlance, he was a "cheeter," by which Puri meant someone not to be trusted.

"You'd like his car's number plate, sir?" Facecream asked him again.

"No need," said Puri. "I can guess where he's putting up. There is only one five-star hotel in town."

"I guess he's probably been hired by Vishnu Mishra to clear his name and find his daughter," said Facecream.

"God help us if he comes to know we two are involved in the case. Just he'll make our life a living hell. Remember the cow-smuggling case? What a headache he gave us. Bloody cheeter."

Puri headed back inside the restaurant to find that the dishes he'd ordered were on the table and that, to his horror, Vijay was already tucking into the hakka noodles and sweet-and-sour chicken.

The journalist's magnanimous gesture for the detective to join him betrayed not the slightest hint of embarrassment at having started without his host. "Don't mind, sir," he said with a full mouth. "I went without my lunch."

Facecream's phone call had not put Puri in the best of moods and his temper boiled to the surface. "What the hell is this, yaar? I invite you and this is how you behave?" he thundered.

Vijay froze, his mouth half-open. Some noodles dangled from his lower lip. The guests at the other tables turned and stared.

"Sorry, sir," he said with a hangdog expression. "Food was getting cold."

Puri sat down opposite him. He took a moment to cool off.

Journalists, especially "local" ones, were a lowly, uncultured bunch who knew no better, he reminded himself. Vijay's clothes looked like they'd been slept in. But at least he had a reputation for honesty. Most Indian hacks wouldn't have known how to spell "impartiality," let alone define the word. The majority were on the payrolls of politicians and bureaucrats.

"This is not a proper way to behave, actually," Puri admonished him, his anger giving way to an avuncular tenor. "Now, tell me about Vishnu Mishra. Who would want to frame him?"

"You think he's innocent, sir?" asked Vijay as he started to shovel food into his mouth again.

"I told you earlier, no, my words are not to be quoted," Puri reminded him. "This conversation must remain totally one hundred percent confidential—top secret, in fact. Tell me what I want to know and all and I'll give you one scoop when the case gets cracked."

He eyed the rapidly disappearing food, concerned that he wouldn't get his fair share, and started to pile as much onto his plate as it would hold.

"In answer to your question, yes, Vishnu Mishra is innocent of this murder, that much is certain," Puri added.

Vijay cocked an eyebrow in his direction. The consensus in the media was that Mishra was guilty. "Sir, he's definitely capable of such a thing," he said.

"No doubt. But he's not a dog to leave his business on his own doorstep."

"Maybe he just wants everyone to believe it was not him so the case will be thrown out."

Puri groaned. And not because he had an entire spring roll jammed into his mouth.

"Why you people are always believing in conspiracy theories?" he scolded. By "you people" he meant the media in general. "A journalist should not be so ready to believe anything he is told. He should keep an open mind, remain objective 'til all facts are known."

Vijay looked unfazed by the lecture and ate on. "You've got proofs, sir?" he asked.

"Believe me, there is no doubt. Someone is trying to frame Mishra. It is someone with political muscle. Now, tell me: Who is out to get him? One of his own people, is it?"

The journalist gave a shake of his head. "They're loyal. Have to be. If they cross him, their family members suffer."

"Who then?"

Vijay leaned forward. "Sir, I, too, have to be careful," he said, his voice low.

"No one will come to know we have spoken," said Puri.

"Fine, sir. Just I would require one beer, also."

"Anything else? Maybe tickets for a cruise?" Puri's voice was thick with sarcasm.

"No, sir, sorry, sir," said Vijay. "But beer goes well with pork, no?"

The detective signaled to the waiter. "Bring *sir* one beer," he said as he watched Vijay clear his plate and help himself to the remaining food.

"Now, you mind answering my question?" asked Puri.

Under his wilting stare, Vijay brought his fork to rest on the plate.

"Sir, the person with the strongest motive for getting Mishra framed is Dr. Bal Pandey."

Puri knew of Dr. Pandey, a former physician and now the vocal leader of Uttar Pradesh's Brahmins. At the last election, he'd made national headlines after railing against the Dalit chief minister Baba Dhobi, about whom he'd said, "Doing laundry is in the blood. Thus he has taken to laundering money."

"Some years back there was a Thakur and Brahmin alliance, so Pandey and Mishra were partners," continued Vijay. "But old caste rivalries got in the way. Pandey claimed Mishra tried to dominate and promoted his own people to the detriment of the Brahmins, so they split up. It is also rumored that Mishra seduced Pandey's mistress. He found out and swore revenge."

"What happened to the girl?"

The journalist gave a shrug. "Vanished."

Puri jotted down some notes. When he looked up, the last spring roll was gone. His guest was also scoffing down the ornamental cabbage-and-carrot bedding.

"You are planning to eat the plate, also?" Puri felt like saying. But he stuck to his line of questioning. "Mishra has other enemies, no?" he asked.

"Plenty, sir. He's been directly responsible for the death of dozens of Dalits over the years."

"So?"

"Framing him in such a way is definitely Dr. Pandey's style. A very cunning individual, very calculating."

"But he could not act alone. Someone high up gave the order for Mishra's arrest."

"Sir, cops can be bought like anything. Also, the current chief of police is himself a Brahmin and from Dr. Pandey's hometown."

Puri's editor friend had been right: Vijay certainly knew his stuff.

"Then tell me this: who does Dr. Pandey's dirty work?" he asked.

"Killings and all?" asked Vijay with nonchalance. "No one has ever been linked to him. But he maintains his own bodyguards. Big fellows."

Puri wondered if there were any members of this outfit

who were six foot one and left-handed. But he didn't want to risk the question and give too much away.

"Dr. Pandey is having any rallies in the coming days?" he asked.

"There is one scheduled for tomorrow, sir. You're thinking of attending?"

"Most definitely. I was thinking of visiting the circus also."

"Circus, sir?"

"There's one in Lucknow at present?"

"Not that I'm aware."

"A traveling fair, perhaps—with rides and all?"

"Why, sir? You're looking for entertainment? I'd be happy to accompany you to a movie."

"And eat all my popcorn," Puri felt like saying, but instead replied, "Good of you. But it is getting late, actually. I should be heading to my bed."

He gave a big yawn and called for the bill.

"You'll keep me updated with the case?" asked Vijay as he finished his beer.

"Most definitely. But before you go, one more thing is there. I've come to know this evening, only, that Vishnu Mishra hired one private detective by the name of Hari Kumar. He is Delhi based, also. Most probably you will find him at the Grand."

Vijay's eyes lit up. "Right, sir, thank you, sir. I'll be sure to chase it up," he said.

"Tip-top, very good. Just remember my name should not appear in the story," said Puri.

He waited until the journalist had gone, ordered another plate of noodles and one of spring rolls, and called Facecream. When he was satisfied she was safe, he put in a call to Rumpi, who'd returned by now to Jagdish Uncle's haveli.

She'd sent his wallet by overnight courier and it was due to reach Lucknow the following afternoon, she told him, before asking whether he was going to be able to join them.

"Most unlikely, my dear. The case is a dark and murky one."

Rumpi detected a distinctive lack of confidence in his voice. "Something wrong, Chubby?" she asked.

Puri hesitated before answering. "Seems Hari is working on the same case," he said.

His words were met with an "Aah," quickly followed by an "Oh, well," and then, "Now, don't let him affect your thinking, Chubby. You're a better man than him by far."

"Problem is Hari is always one to cut any and all corners. Short of murder and blackmail, there are no lines he is not prepared to cross."

"That may be, but your morals have always stood you in good stead. Sounds like you need a good night's sleep."

"Some meter down is required, that is for sure."

"Will you have a quick word with Mummy before you go? I think she's still upset about this morning. She was only trying to help."

"I've been meaning to call her, actually."

Mummy came on the line. She still sounded testy.

"Something is the matter?" he asked.

"One apology and such is in order. Manners are totally lacking!" she said.

Puri was in no mood for a lecture; equally, the last thing he wanted to do was argue.

"Hearties apologies, Mummy-ji," he said. "It was not my intention to sound ungrateful, actually."

"Fine," she said. "Now you have done forwarding of the picture?"

"Picture?"

"Of the pickpocket—one Pranap Dughal."

"I'll pass it on to the concerned persons for sure. I would welcome the opportunity to become acquainted with him."

"This one's a charge-sheeter for sure, Chubby," she said. "He's planning to do murder of his wife, na."

Rumpi's voice cut in. "Now, Mummy-ji, we have no proof of that," she said.

"Just he's going to do drugging and push her down the mountain," Mummy managed to say before Rumpi took the phone back from her.

"What she's saying?" he asked.

"Nothing to worry about, Chubby. It's been a long day. I suggest we all get some rest. Sweet dreams."

And the line went dead.

Nine

The next morning, a Monday, Facecream woke at six and lingered on her bedroll for a few minutes, watching a gecko up on the ceiling. Most people were terrified of these harmless little lizards and had all kinds of superstitious beliefs about how they were portents of bad luck. Many Indians believed that if one crawled over you at night, you would be dead within days. But she admired their agility and patience. Geckos were masterful hunters, hanging motionless from ceilings and walls for hours until insects wandered within reach of their darting tongues.

She watched her roommate catch a mosquito and whispered a thank-you for a deed well done. Then she got up and retrieved her khukuri from beneath her bedroll. As a schoolteacher, she could hardly go around wearing a four-inch steel blade, so she put the weapon at the bottom of her bag for safekeeping.

Outside, she found smoke rising from the kitchen, where the cook was crouched on her haunches stoking a new fire. The paranthas would take "a while," she said without looking up from what she was doing, and so Facecream, who'd forgotten to buy toothpaste, decided to head into the village.

Atif, who was standing by the gate rolling up his prayer mat after the first obligatory namaz of the day, said that he, too, needed something from the shop, and they set off together. He made no mention of her foray of last night, seemingly content to mind his own business, and seeing that the sky was clear again, he lamented the monsoon's no-show. Those without the means to irrigate their fields were growing ever more desperate for the rains. "May Allah in his wisdom grant their wish," he intoned.

Facecream noticed a sour vinegary smell coming from the direction of the river to the east. It caught in the back of her throat. But it soon passed and her attention was drawn to the fields on either side of the lane. She could hear women whispering to one another amid the crops, the word "teacher" being passed down an invisible line. Looking closer, she spotted several pairs of eyes staring out at her from between heads of corn.

A few yards from the periphery of the village proper, they came across three boys engaged in the same activity as the womenfolk, albeit with less regard for their own privacy. Here, Atif suggested a detour so that he could show her his house and they set off east along a narrow pathway. The caretaker soon stopped beneath a neem tree, which he promptly began to climb with the dexterity of a teenager, his sinewy legs scaling up the trunk. When he returned, it was with a young twig snapped from the topmost branches.

"No need for toothpaste," he said as he peeled back the brown skin and handed it to her.

She smiled, working the end against her incisors, and they continued on to the Muslim area of the village. Here the houses were separated from their nearest Hindu neighbors by a no-man's-land some ten meters wide. In spite of this age-old segregation, the Muslims were prospering. Many of them were traders and owned shops in the nearest town, Atif explained.

"My nephew supplies spare parts for tractors," he said with pride. "He has money like none of us has ever known."

Atif led on past an area inhabited by Kumhars, or potters, who, judging by the state of their dilapidated homes, were not faring well in the new Indian economy. Tupperware containers had supplanted clay storage vessels across the country and chai stands were gradually doing away with the traditional biodegradable terra-cotta cup.

"These people have no land and they're not adapting," explained Atif.

Ironically, the same could be said for the village's Brahmin families. "They refuse to do manual work and their fields have been divided up by all their sons, so they're not profitable," he explained. "Also, there are no government jobs reserved for them."

The power of the Thakurs, too, had waned in the area, despite the fact that they remained in possession of roughly 50 percent of all the agricultural land in the state. This had allowed the Yadavs, who'd risen from laborers to landowners in the past half century, to gain dominance. The pradhan ranked amongst their number and had ensured that they were all in possession of highly prized government-issued "Below Poverty Line" cards. The cards entitled them to around thirty-five kilos of cut-price rice a month and five liters of subsidized fuel. Outside one Yadav house that enjoyed such concessions stood a brand-new hatchback with a red ribbon stretched across the hood and plastic covering the seats inside.

"Since they've become wealthy, they treat Dalits like slaves," said Atif. "They don't allow them to own land or even spend time in the middle of the village. And they're still prevented from visiting the temple by the high castes."

"Are the Dalits allowed to vote?" she asked.

"In the state and national elections, yes. The big parties make sure security is in place so their people can get to the polls. Every Dalit votes. But when it comes to village elections, they can't set foot in the booth."

They came across the pradhan himself, Rakesh Yadav, standing outside the village shop with a few hangers-on, smoking a cigarette. He was in his fifties with a chin of graying stubble, bulbous cheeks and abnormally large ears. Atif greeted him with a friendly "Ram, Ram!" and introduced Facecream.

"Welcome, madam," said Yadav, whose gums were stained red with gutka and whose hands and fingers were blemished white, as if he'd been handling strong chemicals. "You are comfortable?"

"I'm excited to be here, sir," she told him, striking an enthusiastic, innocent tone.

"If you need anything, you need only ask," said Yadav with largesse. "I am here to serve."

"Actually, there is one thing, sir," she said. "The children's food: I'm concerned about the quantity. It seems like they're not getting enough. The daal yesterday was very watery. Who's responsible for the supply?"

"That duty falls to me, madam," said Yadav.

"I believe the school should receive one kilo of lentils per day and two kilos of atta, sir," said Facecream.

The pradhan sucked on his cigarette and blew out a plume of smoke. "I will make sure everything is in order, madam, don't worry. That is my work. Now there is one thing from my side. Such a young and beautiful woman as yourself should not be outside after dark."

He'd come to know about the incident last night, she realized. "It's not safe?" she asked.

"Men should not be tempted" was his cryptic reply.

"I saw some young men bullying a boy last night. They knocked him to the ground. I think they'd been drinking."

"Madam, let the school be your concern and I will look to my responsibilities. And please, it is better you don't go wandering around at night. Your safety is my concern."

Facecream set off back to the school in no doubt that if she tried to rectify the food situation, it would put her in direct confrontation with the most powerful man in the village.

About halfway, her thoughts were interrupted by the sound of an auto spluttering past. It was packed with squealing schoolchildren all dressed in the uniform of one of the private schools on the highway—the girls in green salwar kameez, the boys in white shirts and shorts.

A scruffy-looking boy with disheveled hair and tattered clothes followed behind on a bicycle, two wooden blocks attached to the bottom of his feet so that he could reach the pedals. Facecream recognized him as the Dalit kid she'd rescued the night before. He stared back at her without the slightest hint of acknowledgment or recognition and pedaled on.

"Who is he?" Facecream asked Atif.

"A dhobi, I think."

"He's seven, eight maybe? He should be in school."

"I've seen him working at the chai stand on the highway."

"Is there anyone you don't know in the village, Uncle?"

"I see them all passing my gate!"

"Did you see that murdered woman?"

"I did. She came just after dark, walking on her own."

"She was on her way to the highway?"

"Where else?"

"Who could have done such a terrible thing?"

"I told you last night, it's dangerous to be out at night."

"You mean someone from the village might have killed her?"

The question went unanswered as Atif called out to some Muslim neighbors walking toward them.

"Salaam alaikum!" ("Peace be upon you.")

The children began to arrive at seven. Facecream could see right away that she'd inherited a mixed bunch. The majority belonged to the Shudra laborer caste and wore an array of ill-fitting hand-me-downs. There were half a dozen Yadav kids, those whose parents had not escaped the toil of un-skilled labor; two Brahmin boys easily identifiable from the holy threads visible beneath their white cotton shirts as well as their distinctly lighter skin tone; and Facecream counted three Muslim girls in head scarves.

When Facecream, aka Miss Padma Jaiteley—or "Jaiteley Madam," as she came to be known—told all twenty-eight children to gather beneath the banyan tree, they arranged themselves into caste groupings. Schisms became apparent even amongst the Dalits, with the Chamars, who'd tradi-tionally been condemned to collect dead animals and cure skins, automatically separating themselves from the rest.

This was only one of the challenges she faced. There were also big age differences within the group. The youngest of the children was three or four, while the eldest, a Yadav boy, was developing facial hair and was a disruptive influence with no regard for her authority.

And who could blame him? The school's "official" teacher, Mr. P. Joshi, had by all accounts spent his days sitting around drinking tea—that is, if he'd bothered to turn up at all. This served to explain why none of the children—not one—had learned to read or write.

Standing there at the head of the "class," it occurred to Facecream that she might have bitten off more than she could chew. Her task, after all, was to retrace Kamlesh's movements in the hours before her murder. In order to maintain her cover, all she needed to do was take down the attendance record and call it a day. This was as much as they and hundreds of thousands of other children in government schools across the country expected.

But she found the urge to make a difference too strong to resist. How could she live with herself if she didn't try to set a good example? These kids had never been given a chance and she wasn't about to let them down now.

She would need to tread carefully, of course. Sending home the underage children would only create ill will. And if she started lecturing on universal equality, not to mention common humanity, she'd be tossed out of the village on her ear.

There were other means, however.

Once she'd achieved a semblance of order, she told the children to stand up and began to sing the national anthem.

"*Thou art the ruler of the minds of all people, / Dispenser of India's destiny.*"

Taken aback at first, her class hesitantly joined in.

"*The saving of all people waits in thy hand, / Thou dispenser of India's destiny.*

"*Victory, victory, victory to thee,*" they sang more or less in unison.

Puri's hotel in Lucknow was an old British establishment with high ceilings and musty bed coverings. He slept through his alarm and woke with a start at ten past eight. By the time he'd washed and gotten dressed, breakfast had been brought up to his room on a tray. The masala omelet appeared to have been cooked in motor oil, the toast was so white it was hard to imagine it contained any nutrition, and the jam, an alarming bright red, looked like it might glow in the dark.

He took the unprecedented step of pushing the food to

one side, opting only for a cup of tea. Then he reached for the *Lucknow Gazette,* journalist Vijay Tewari's rag.

The headline on page one brought a broad grin to his face. EX-SPOOK IN CITY—SUSPECTED WORKING FOR ACCUSED VISHNU MISHRA.

"Hari Kumar of Spycatcher Private Investigators, Delhi, was last night putting up at Grand Hotel," read the article beneath. "Well-placed sources said Kumar, formerly of Indian intelligence, or RAW, and infamous for busting a Chinese spy ring some years back, is working on behalf of Vishnu Mishra, accused in the murder of a Dalit woman. It is believed the private investigator is working to clear his client's name and locate his absconding daughter, Tulsi. Kumar himself was not available for comment late last night. Repeated calls to his room went unanswered."

Puri clapped his hands together with glee at the thought of Hari being harassed by a pesky journalist. Oh, how that bugger must be wondering who shopped him, he thought with a guffaw before cutting out the article for his scrapbook.

Puri decided to head out of the hotel in search of a proper breakfast. In the elevator, he made a mental list of the tasks ahead of him. Top priority was a call to Tulsi, who was still lying low with the Love Commandos in Agra. Despite having been under her father's guard for the past three months, there was a chance she might be able to shed some light on how Ram had made his money. If not, she would at least be able to provide him with a list of Ram's friends who might be able to help.

After that, Puri needed to call Flush, his young electronics and computer whiz, whom he'd already assigned to hacking into Ram's mobile phone account. And at eleven o'clock, he was due to pick up Tubelight from Lucknow train station and give him a full briefing. Puri was setting him the task of doing "background checking" into Dr. Bal Pandey, the Brahmin politician, and finding out whether any six-foot-one, left-handed killers ranked amongst his coterie.

He reached the lobby, still chuckling to himself about the story he'd planted in the paper about Hari, and took his key to the front desk.

"Sir, it is a great honor to have such a famous detective as your good self staying as a guest in our hotel," said the receptionist. "Anything we can do to make you comfortable. The restaurant is always open."

Puri was used to being recognized, given his occasional appearances on television, and thought nothing of it.

"Just I left some laundry on the bed," he said. "One trouser leg has got mud on it."

"Pleasure, sir."

Puri headed across the lobby toward the front door, but the words "Best of luck with the murder case" stopped him in his tracks.

He turned around slowly and shot the receptionist a quizzical look. How could he possibly know about the investigation?

"Sir, it is in the newspaper—front page!" said the now beaming receptionist, brandishing a copy of the *Uttar Pradesh Herald,* the *Lucknow Gazette*'s competitor.

Puri grabbed it from him. His own image stared out from the front page. Beneath it, the copy read: "Private Eye Vish Puri arrived in Lucknow yesterday morning. His presence here and the murder of a Dalit woman whose body was discovered yesterday in the canal can hardly be considered a coincidence entirely. However, the identity of Mr. Puri's client remains a mystery. His agency, Most Private Investigators Ltd., which was once one of Delhi's premier private detective firms, is said to have hit hard times. Mr. Puri has been scraping the bottom of the barrel when it comes to cases. Most recently he was involved in retrieving a kidnapped pet dog from a Delhi gang, handing over lakhs in ransom. But though Mr. Puri might have entered the twilight of his career, his appetite remains legendary and the city's restaurateurs can expect a brisk trade, according to sources."

The detective mashed the paper between his hands.

"Bloody bastard!" he bawled at the dismayed receptionist before tossing the paper aside and storming out of the lobby.

While he waited for his hire car, Puri paced up and down the car park, kicking loose stones across the tarmac, muttering, "Hard times, is it? I'll give you hard time, by God!" and trying to fathom how Hari had found out he was in Lucknow.

Had someone recognized him at the station or perhaps the hospital?

Another, stronger possibility came to mind: if Hari was working for Vishnu Mishra, the latter would have told him about running into a purported police officer by the name of Lal Krishna, one of Puri's old aliases.

Suddenly, his phone rang. It was Hari. He waited a moment or two, steeling himself before answering in a gruff voice, "Puri this side."

"Aah, there you are!"

"Good morning," he heard himself say in a cordial tone.

"I understand you're in Lucknow. By a strange coincidence, so am I. Why don't you come for breakfast? I'm at the Grand—down in the café."

Puri knew he had no choice but to go.

"I'm very much busy," he said. "So many meetings and all."

"I'll expect you in ten minutes," said Hari.

• • •

To witness Vish Puri and Hari Kumar greeting each other, one would never have guessed they were bitter rivals. Their firm, matey handshake was accompanied by broad smiles and ho-ho laughter that echoed off the marble walls, momentarily drowning out the café's Muzak. Each asked after the other's wife and children and made small talk about the national cricket team's recent loss to England on home soil.

There was no reference made to the stories they'd planted in the newspapers, nor was there the slightest hint of the anger they had both exhibited independently earlier in the morning. When they inquired after each other's business, they both answered in turn, "Couldn't be better," and "World-class," their claims to be delighted studies in faultless speciousness.

This was customary. Neither man had ever raised a word of anger at the other, regardless of what they had to say behind each other's backs. To do so would have been to show weakness and vulnerability. Their infrequent conversations, therefore, were a trial of wits, each trying to provoke and rattle the other with sangfroid. Even their handshake was a tournament of sorts, with neither detective willing to let go before the other.

Standing on either side of Hari's table, the palms of their hands locked together in an increasingly sweaty grasp, they only disengaged when a waiter approached with a couple of menus, therefore giving both men an excuse to call it a tie.

"I've been meaning to ask you where you get your safari suits made," said Hari as they sat down at the table, ensuring that his guest took his seat first. "I've an uncle with a birthday coming up. He goes in for that *style*. But it's not easy to find old-fashioned tailors these days. They're a dying breed."

"A man with taste and refinement, your uncle, evidently," said Puri. "Not one of these flashy fellows who goes in for foreign cuts and all."

"'Flashy' is definitely not a word one would use to describe my uncle. He's almost ninety after all."

"Ninety, is it? Just goes to prove the safari is timeless and eternal."

There was a genial exchange of smiles across the table—the opening round acknowledged by both men as a draw.

The waiter returned and asked to take their order.

Knowing Hari to be a skinflint, at least when it came to spending money on anyone other than himself, Puri was happy to stick him with as large a bill as possible.

"I'll take one full English breakfast," he replied. "Bring me one glass of fresh juice and ready-made tea, also."

"The healthy option for me," said Hari. "A plate of idli and one mint tea."

He dismissed the waiter with a wave of his hand and adjusted the silk handkerchief protruding from the breast pocket of his blazer. The silver buttons on his cuff glinted in the fluorescent spotlights pointing down from the ceiling. Puri could taste his aftershave on his tongue, it was so strong.

"So, Mr. Vishwas Puri, I take it you're not here in Lucknow on vacation," said Hari, who was one of the few people who ever addressed the detective using his full name. "The newspaper article I read suggested you were investigating the murder of that unfortunate lady who washed up in the canal yesterday."

"You should never believe what you read in the papers, Hari—journalists being corrupt and complacent and all."

"Well, you can hardly be taking a vacation. You don't do that."

"I'm indeed making inquiries as to the circumstances of

that poor lady's death. But whatever else was written is a flat-out lie."

Puri felt another rush of anger as the wording of the article came back to him but didn't let it show. "And you, Hari? What are you doing in Lucknow, exactly?" he asked.

"Seeking the truth, what else? That is what we do, the two of us, is it not?"

"In our own different ways, yes, I suppose."

No less than three waiters arrived simultaneously at the table, a testament, if ever there was one, to the abundance of the country's cheap labor. The first bore Hari's mint tea, the second Puri's orange juice and chai, while the third stood and watched. All three then withdrew in perfectly choreographed synergy.

"We're agreed the killer was six foot tall and left-handed?" said Hari as he stirred a sachet of sugar substitute into his tea.

"Six foot and one inch exactly. Totally ruthless, also. The shot was made at point-blank range."

Puri pictured Kamlesh's face again—and that strange, bewildered expression. He almost wished he could ask Hari whether he'd noticed it, too, and what, if anything, he'd made of it.

"Presumably you've visited the village and the canal and come to the conclusion that Vishnu Mishra is innocent?"

"Of the murder—yes, there can be no doubt. But is he capable of such a heinous crime? Undoubtedly. He's not the type I'd want as a client, that is for sure," Puri said pointedly.

"Aaah, but not all of us are possessed of such faultless moral fiber as your good self, Mr. Puri saar. We mere mortals are made of weaker stuff, I'm afraid."

Hari sipped his mint tea, studying his adversary over the top of his cup. "I hear there's been something of a delay in recovering the loot from that jewelry job," he said. "Don't tell me India's number one detective is stumped?"

"A temporary setback, only. We are all prone to facing them from time to time, no? I was thinking of that kidnapping you handled few years back—the Sushil Jha case. Turned out it was your client himself who had the boy locked in the cellar."

Hari gave a nod, as if to say, "Touché." The score remained even.

Puri fortified himself with half a cup of chai, then asked, "You came across the hole in the ground behind Ram's house?" he asked.

"It did not escape my attention," answered Hari.

Nor the smiley stamp on Kamlesh's hand, Puri thought to himself. But was there anything else, anything that he might have overlooked and Hari had spotted? He was a hard one to read. His conceit manifested itself in the self-satisfied smirk that was never quite absent from his face. Behind his lingering, confident gaze, Puri always got the impression that he was mocking him.

"Let us get to the point, shall we?" said Hari. "It's obviously no coincidence that we're both here. We're clearly working on the same case. I propose that we put aside our rivalry and combine our resources. Spycatcher and Most Private Investigators united for once."

A slow grin suffused Puri's features. He didn't buy Hari's pitch for a second. He wasn't interested in cooperation. The man was only out for himself.

"Whether Vishnu Mishra hangs is of no concern to me," he replied.

"And you imagine it is to me?" asked Hari.

Puri felt as if the earth had suddenly dropped away beneath him. He'd got it completely wrong, he realized. Hari wasn't working for Mishra. "No, no, not at all," he stuttered in an attempt to conceal his surprise. But his miscalculation

111

wasn't lost on Hari. He leaned across the table to press home his advantage.

"This thing is bigger than you realize," he said. "There's gold at the end of the rainbow."

"Gold, is it?"

"Twenty-four karat."

Their food arrived at the table, affording Puri some breathing room. If Hari wasn't working for Vishnu Mishra, then what was he up to?

"Why don't you stop all this dancing around and tell me who all you're working for, Hari?" asked Puri once the waiters had again withdrawn.

"You know I can't tell you that—not until I meet Ram in person. But I give you my word, my client has the boy's best interests at heart. He's also willing to offer you a handsome fee should you produce the boy. Not a paisa less than fifty lakhs."

Puri couldn't help but smile again. His competitor's entire approach—the offer of a financial reward, the whole breakfast, in fact—had been leading up to this crucial question. It was designed to determine whether he knew of Ram's whereabouts. And it meant that Hari too had been commissioned to find him.

"You're wasting your time. I might have been born at night, but not last night." Puri started to tuck into his breakfast. "Now, tell me," he said, "you watched the Sri Lanka game? Quite an innings from Laxman, no?"

Hari regarded him with something approaching deference. "I missed it," he said.

"You were on the way from Agra no doubt."

"No doubt."

They made more small talk as they ate and then Hari called for the bill. When it was brought to the table, Puri went through the motions of offering to pay, but his competitor would have none of it.

"You seem to be without your wallet," he said. "You usually keep it in your jacket pocket."

Puri managed to feign surprise. "Must be I left it at the hotel," he replied.

"Really? For a moment there, I thought maybe it was lost or stolen," said Hari.

"No, no, heaven forbid! Nothing like that," said Puri with a loud, nervous guffaw.

Ten

Hari had an advantage. He'd come to the case from a different angle and saw the bigger picture. In other words, he probably understood what Ram had got himself mixed up in. Which meant that he probably also understood how the young Dalit had come by so much money and what had been inside the metal container buried behind the house, Puri surmised.

In poker terms, this would be called a straight flush.

By contrast, he felt like he was holding a pair of threes.

Still, Puri came away from breakfast heartened by one bit of good news: Ram was of some value and with any luck that meant he was still alive.

The bad news was that Hari's involvement added operational complications. Certain security precautions were going to have to be put in place.

From breakfast, he went straight to the nearest STD phone booth and called the office. Hari would be trying to eavesdrop on his phone conversations and he wanted to be sure that his line was secure and that no one else could access his call log.

"Boss, your phone's casing is constructed of nanomaterials to block all RF signals and wave radiation," Flush assured him.

"Translation?" said Puri.

"Means your phone is secure, Boss."

"Tip-top."

"And, Boss—I've downloaded Ram's phone records."

"Wonderful!"

"Thanks, Boss. Only thing is, someone beat us to it."

"Meaning?"

"The numbers have been deleted."

"*Arrey!*"

This smelled of Hari's handiwork.

"There's any way of getting them back?" asked Puri.

"I'll check to see if they're using a RAID-array multiple system, Boss."

"Speak proper English, yaar!"

"Means the data might be replicated on another drive."

"Do it, by God."

Puri returned to his hotel. A search of his room with his RF detector netted two bugs, one in the hotel phone handset and the second in the light socket—both planted by Hari's people during breakfast.

Puri took a certain amount of pleasure in crushing them underfoot and then flushing them down the toilet for good measure.

He made a second sweep and, when he was sure the room was clean, sat down to call Tulsi in Agra. She'd been moved again this morning to a new Love Commandos safe house and sounded worried, for not only Ram's well-being but her father's as well.

"The news said he's been taken to Lucknow jail," she said. "I hope he's OK. I never meant for any of this to happen."

"Your father had nothing to do with the murder of Ram's mother—of that I am certain," said Puri.

"Who could have done such a horrible thing?" asked Tulsi.

"That is exactly and precisely what I am endeavoring to find out."

Ordinarily he would have added, "And Vish Puri never fails." But remembering the evil eye, he stopped himself from doing so just in time.

"Sir, I still don't understand who took Ram. If it wasn't Papa, then who?" she asked.

"All efforts are being made to answer that question, also," he said.

"It's our . . . our anniversary in a couple of days," she said.

"Anniversary?"

"We went on our first date two years ago—to . . . to see the Taj during the full moon," said Tulsi, promptly bursting into tears.

Puri murmured, "Now, now, my dear, God willing you will be reunited," but he sounded wooden and the sobs duly intensified, forcing him to hold the phone away from his ear and wait for her to calm down.

Finally, he heard her clear her nose.

"Beta, some questions are there," said Puri, before going on to explain that Ram had given his parents a considerable amount of money in the past couple of months. Did she have any idea how he might have come by it?

"What money?"

He put it to her that Ram might have got involved in some kind of illegal activity. How else could he have come by so much cash?

But she was adamant that he would never break the law.

"He was desperate, no?" the detective said, pressing her. "His mind was turned to one thing only: starting a new life with his dear lady love. In such circumstances even the most honest of young men can go to the dogs so to speak."

"No, not Ram," Tulsi insisted. "Ram doesn't worry about

money. He says that our love will conquer all obstacles. Nothing can stand in the way if we keep our faith in one another."

Quite the young Dev Anand, this Ram fellow, Puri reflected as he hung up. The girl, who sounded highly impressionable, had fallen for him hook, line and sinker. Had he pulled the wool over her eyes? Puri hoped not for all their sakes. But the detective still had his doubts. Impoverished Dalit students did not simply come by lakhs of rupees by chance.

Tulsi provided a list of Ram's closest friends and their phone numbers and Puri set about calling them one by one. He soon found that he was following a well-trodden path.

"You're the second person to call today," said the first.

"Stop hassling me," said the next.

Only one of Ram's friends, whose name was Brijesh, cooperated.

"I talked to Ram on Friday," he said.

"He sounded relaxed and all?"

"More like worried."

"How he was making money?"

"He used to work for a pizza joint called Yum Yum, but he got fired."

"When exactly?"

"Two months back."

Puri asked Brijesh why he'd lost the job.

"The owner found out he was a Dalit. Bastard said he'd go out of business if his customers knew their food was being delivered by one."

"Ram lied about his identity, is it?"

"How else are you meant to get a job?"

"So how he came by so much of money?"

"What money?"

"Ram built his parents a house. Got them a flat-screen TV, also. Must have cost some lakhs."

"I've no idea," said Brijesh.

"Could be he got into crime—selling drugs and all," suggested the detective.

"Ram? No way. You've ever met him? He's Mr. Clean."

The rest of Facecream's morning at the school went as well as could be expected. She taught rudimentary reading skills for the first hour and then basic geography, pinpointing the village on a map and familiarizing the children with their place in relation to the outside world. She also described some of the other places in India she'd visited, like Assam, where she'd seen one-horned rhinos, and the Brihadeeswara Temple in Tamil Nadu, India's largest.

Keeping the children's attention proved a constant battle. None of them had been taught to sit and listen, let alone concentrate, and she faced frequent interruptions. An example had to be made of a few of the worst troublemakers and she escorted them to the gates and sent them home. This proved especially effective with the poorer kids, for whom lunch constituted the most substantial meal they would receive during their day. In one case, a mother marched her daughter back to the school, promising that she would behave in future. When Facecream expelled a Brahmin boy for bad language and he threatened his father's retribution, she answered cheerily that she'd look forward to his visit.

Once she'd stamped her authority on the group and they began to sense she cared, Facecream found that the majority responded positively. And by organizing group activities that encouraged them to interact with one another, she enjoyed some success in circumventing social divisions.

Cricket proved the most effective tool. It was especially suitable given that only a bat and ball were required and that it wasn't a contact sport. Indeed, no observer seeing the two teams competing against each other and hearing the enthusiastic choruses of "Four!" and "Howzat!" would have guessed these same children had arranged themselves by caste at roll call that morning.

And yet, when it came to lunchtime, the old divisions reasserted themselves. The remaining Brahmin boy, who'd been sent to school with his own packed food, ate separately, while the Muslims were forced to use dishes and utensils brought from home.

Jagdish Uncle had elected not to accompany Mummy and Co. on their ascent to the Vaishno Devi shrine—he suffered from diabetes, high blood pressure and gout. But he insisted on driving them to Katra, the small town at the base of the mountain from where pilgrims embark.

With a pyramid of bags piled onto Sweetie's roof, the entire clan stuffed themselves inside the Maruti, pushing the undercarriage perilously close to the ground. Observers would have been forgiven for imagining that the occupants were refugees fleeing a war zone. And the speed at which Jagdish Uncle took the turns on the winding road that led up into the hills—overtaking other vehicles on blind bends and weaving between the trucks crawling toward the Banihal Pass and the Kashmir Valley—suggested that they were indeed being pursued.

Still, the jostling and spine-jarring bumps did nothing to dampen the family's spirits. They thrilled to the fresh mountain air and the panoramas of pine forests, arid peaks set against a cobalt sky, and boulder-strewn riverbeds that sliced down through terraced paddy fields.

When the Himalayas came into view, their snowcapped

summits rising above the haze like a frozen fortress, Jagdish Uncle pulled over at a scenic spot. Everyone tumbled out, cameras at the ready, and posed for pictures. A soft drinks stand was assaulted, colas and cartons of Mango Frooti were quaffed, and Chetan raided the tiffin packed by Sonam Aunty, who had risen at four A.M. and, apparently concerned that they would all die of starvation during the two-hour journey, cooked them enough paranthas to last four days.

Back behind the wheel, Jagdish Uncle kept the family entertained on the last leg of the journey with the well-worn story of his birth and how the goddess Durga had saved his mother's life.

"The doctor couldn't stop the bleeding," he said. "In those days there weren't the kind of medical facilities we have today. No medicines. People were not so educated. The most the doctor could do was stuff some bandages inside her and hope that the bleeding would stop. My father didn't put his trust in this man. He set off right away for Vaishno Devi to appeal for intervention from the mother goddess. It was the dead of winter. There was snow on the mountain. He climbed to the top, did darshan and came straight back down. He did not sleep or eat one thing. He was gone from the house for four days. There were no phones. Until he came back into the house he didn't know whether Ma was alive or dead. Thankfully, the goddess granted his wish."

The car rounded the final bend and the Vaishno Devi shrine complex came into view, a zigzagging trail etched up the side of the Trikuta mountain.

"Jai Mata Di!" ("Praise be to the Mother!") The cry went up again and again as they descended into the valley, soon reaching the outskirts of Katra.

Mummy had last been here as a young bride on her honeymoon and she remembered nothing more than a hamlet at the base of the mountain. She and Om Chander Puri, together with her in-laws, had slept in tents. They had prepared their meals on campfires and washed in the stream that ran along the bottom of the mountain. Afterward, they'd lain in meadows of wildflowers and soaked in the sunshine.

Save for the rocky escarpments rising around the town, she hardly recognized the place. Vaishno Devi was now the second-most popular pilgrimage site in India with some five million visitors every year. Katra had burgeoned into a bustling town with countless eateries offering every north Indian vegetarian dish. Modern hotels had sprung up with spas, swimming pools and satellite TV. There were banks, hoardings advertising American soft drinks and touts carrying around bags of pink candy floss.

A sign even advertised helicopter rides up to the summit.

"What is this?" Mummy asked, her voice thick with incredulity. "Without pain, what is gain?"

But Jagdish Uncle, despite the story of his mother's miraculous survival, regarded the helicopters with a sense of wonderment.

"In five minutes, only, they're taking you right up to the top!" he enthused. "Can you imagine? No need for all that climbing! Such luxury!"

"I agree with Mummy, taking a helicopter's just cheating," said Rumpi.

"How you can expect blessing from the goddess without sacrifice?" added Mummy.

"Sacrifice is there," rejoined Jagdish Uncle with a chuckle. "The helicopter is costing a fortune!"

"You mean we can't take one?" whined Chetan.

By the time they joined the back of the long queue outside the counter for pilgrim passes, it was already two o'clock and there were hundreds of people ahead of them. At the earliest, they would be able to start their ascent at three thirty, when the heat would be at its worst. The family was therefore left with two options: set off at dusk and reach the summit long after midnight (the trail was well lit) or wait until the crack of dawn.

A debate ensued. Everyone presented their arguments for their preferred choice in loud voices, all talking at once.

Mummy kept well out of it. The Dughals, she'd been reliably informed by her inside man at their guesthouse, had set off from Jammu an hour after the Jagdish Uncle Express. They were due in Katra any minute and were staying in the Regal Hotel.

Tomorrow morning, when they started their ascent, Mummy planned to be right behind them.

In the meantime, she seemed to be developing a nasty headache.

"Just my eyes are paining," she said.

The rest of the family immediately crowded around her, fussing and diagnosing—"must be altitude sickness," "change in weather." All sorts of remedies were offered. Did she want to take an aspirin? An injection? One of Jagdish Uncle's sedatives? Perhaps a head rub with mustard oil would do the trick?

It was enough to give her a *real* headache, Mummy thought to herself as she suggested that perhaps it might be a good idea for her to check into a hotel and get some bed rest.

This sparked fresh debate and a new consensus was soon reached: they would start at dawn.

In the meantime, Jagdish Uncle would take Mummy to a hotel.

"The Britannia is close by," he said.

"Regal Hotel is better, na," said Mummy.

Eleven

Certain he was being watched, Puri decided against collecting Tubelight from the station and arranged to meet him for a late lunch in the depths of Lucknow's Aminabad Bazaar. Famous for its chickan embroidery, the area's labyrinthine alleyways provided the ideal environment in which to lose a tail—or indeed oneself. The detective was swept along with a tide of shoppers, past repositories of curly toed sequined slippers, paper kites, secondhand books and embroidered linen. And although the cries of the merchants and the competing horns of scooters and bicycles made for a jarring dissonance, Puri noticed a refinement in the local manner and language that bespoke the city's courtly heritage. Spotting some grandees seated outside a café discussing the burning issues of the day over a leisurely hookah and looking suitably immune to the rush of life around them, he felt momentarily transported back in time to the courtly Lucknow of kathak performances and ghazals.

Confident that he'd shaken off any would-be shadows, Puri entered Tunde Kebabs and found Tubelight already seated at a table toward the back of the restaurant.

Most Private Investigators Ltd.'s senior operative had spent the night on a hard wooden bench in a third-class train carriage with the crook of his arm serving as a pillow. This had been by choice, air-conditioning being anathema to the former thief. Despite the hot, overcrowded conditions on board, the constant cries of "Chaaaaiiii!" and the numerous arguments that had broken out amongst his fellow passengers—one had led to a knife fight—he had enjoyed a fitful night's sleep.

Still Tubelight was hungry and nodded approvingly when Puri ordered one plate of galauti kebab, a mutton biryani and some sultani daal. This was followed by kulfi topped with rose-scented falooda.

"Boss, nothing's turned up—just dead ends," said Tubelight, in reference to the Jain Jewelry Heist.

"Anything from Tihar?" asked Puri, who'd sent his operative to consult with a notorious jewel thief currently serving time in India's most infamous prison in the hope of finding a lead.

"Nothing, Boss—he's as mystified as the rest of us," said Tubelight. "Hate to admit it, but I'm out of ideas."

"Let us hope something turns up," said the detective, although he didn't sound convinced himself. "Meantime, you brought the file?"

He was referring to the dossiers on Vishnu Mishra and Brahmin leader Dr. Bal Pandey that Elizabeth Rani had compiled yesterday after Puri had called her into the office. Along with various magazine and newspaper articles on the politics of Uttar Pradesh, it included a copy of a confidential report on Pandey compiled by the Intelligence Bureau, India's secretive internal intelligence agency, whose computer system's firewalls were not all they should have been.

"Links him to numerous killings and several rapes," said Tubelight as he laid the file on the table.

"Anything on known criminal associates?"

"Nothing."

"The killer is six foot one, left-handed and totally ruthless. Also, it is entirely possible he was known to the victim. You've anyone local you can work with?"

Tubelight gave a nod.

"Make sure he's not on Hari's payroll."

"Please, Boss. My boys have standards. Anything else?"

Puri told him about the smiley stamp on Kamlesh's hand and how since breakfast with Hari he'd visited a circus on the edge of Lucknow and found that paying customers were indeed branded with indelible ink when they paid their entry fee, but the symbol used was that of a tiger. He'd also visited a traveling theater and two of the city's remaining single-screen cinemas—all without making the breakthrough he was hoping for.

"Try the urinals, the malls also—anywhere a stamp would be required for entry purposes," said Puri.

After lunch, Puri picked up his wallet from the office of the courier company Rumpi had used, and returned to his hotel. He found the receptionist in an agitated state. There had been a visitor in sir's absence.

"A very big man."

"The skin around his eyes was red and all?" asked Puri.

"Yes, sir. That's him! He waited here for one hour. Then left a number. Said you're to call it immediately. It sounds serious, sir," the receptionist added with masterful understatement.

The detective had no wish for any further entanglements with Naga, who'd evidently been released on bail and had tracked him down thanks to Hari's newspaper leak. He decided to change hotels.

Ten minutes later, his car was pulling out of the car park

when a vehicle blocked the exit. It was a police jeep. The occupant was Inspector Gujar.

"Sir, I wish to talk to you," he explained when he came to the window. His tone was considerably more assured than it had been during his arrest of Vishnu Mishra yesterday.

"Official business?" asked the detective.

"Regarding the murder of the Dalit woman. I understand you examined the body yesterday?"

"The concerned doctor was kind enough to accommodate me," said Puri.

Gujar wagged a finger. "Sir, that's against regulations," he said. "Permission was required. You're to accompany me."

"I'm somewhat busy just now, Inspector," said Puri, concerned that Naga might turn up at any minute.

But Inspector Gujar insisted and the detective accepted the order with rueful grace.

Ten minutes later, they were seated in a moribund office fitted with decrepit furniture that bespoke the chronic underfunding of the Uttar Pradesh state police, the largest force in the world under one command.

"I saw you outside Govind village yesterday," said Gujar. "You were speaking with Vishnu Mishra. I want to know what it was about."

"He was asking what all I was doing there," said Puri, his chair creaking under his weight.

"And what did you tell him?"

"That it was none of anyone's business."

"He would not have liked that."

"He did not. In all honesty, Inspector, I do not see a friendship blossoming."

"You mind telling me what you were doing there, sir?"

"That all depends, Inspector."

"On?"

"What all kind of information you're willing to provide in return."

"Sir, you are not in a position to make demands. I could have you arrested for tampering with evidence."

"That is a threat, I take it?"

Gujar knitted his fingers together and placed them on the desk in front of him. "Sir, I don't want tension," he said. "I have asked you a simple question. You are in my jurisdiction and involving yourself in my investigation. Procedure demands that you tell me your intentions and upon whose behalf you are working."

"Understood, Inspector," said Puri with an almost pitying smile. "Your superiors are concerned I will blow a hole in your case and prove Vishnu Mishra innocent."

Gujar's forehead creased into a frown. "Sir, you believe he's innocent?"

"Inspector." Puri sighed in the most patronizing tone he could muster. "Mishra is no saint. Quite the reverse, in fact. But he is being framed—of that I am very much certain."

"He had motive and was in the vicinity. I've witnesses who saw Kamlesh Sunder picked up by his vehicle and driven away."

"Witnesses?"

"Two in all."

"The usual suspects, no doubt?"

Gujar sat haughtily erect. His eyes darted with pique. "Sir, I'll be the one asking the questions. Now, I'm requesting you to tell me why were you visiting the village."

Puri took a moment to weigh his options. Had Gujar been under orders to lock him up on the pretense of tampering with evidence, he would simply have done so. The young inspector was bluffing, in other words. And Puri saw no reason to give in to this lackey's demands.

"I'm under no obligation to reveal the identity of my client—nor the details of my investigation and all," he said.

Gujar started to object, but the detective spoke over him. "*That being said*," he stressed, "allow me to assure you that when the time comes I will endeavor not to make a total fool out of you in front of the national media persons. And now, Inspector, I'll wish you a good day."

Calling him into the station had been the clumsy move of an amateur, Puri reflected as he checked into a new hotel and lay down on the bed to have some meter down. If he'd half a brain, Gujar would have turned up with a bottle of Scotch and made friends before trying to ascertain the detective's game. Under such circumstances, they might have cooperated with each other. God only knew Puri could do with an ally, he reflected. The odds were stacking up against him by the hour. Naga was searching for him. Hari Kumar was breathing down his neck. And now Inspector Gujar's yet-to-be-identified puppeteer was aware that he was on the case. Should that individual decide that Puri posed too great a threat, then there was no telling what might happen. This was Uttar Pradesh after all. According to an article in the morning's paper, there had been nearly five thousand murders in the state last year—and that was just the official figure.

It crossed Puri's mind that he was risking his life for a young man he'd never met and for a cause he didn't believe in. But he quickly gave himself a sharp rebuke, shocked by his own pusillanimity.

"Such a thought is not worthy of you!" he exclaimed.

He had acted out of loyalty and there was no going back. Besides, the case had become much bigger than some silly love affair. It was about justice. And that was always a cause worth fighting for.

Fortified by this thought and feeling somewhat choked up by a swell of emotion, he got off the bed and called downstairs for a cup of chai and a few whole green chilli peppers.

"Make it fast," he ordered.

Room service provided him with three Naga Bhut Jolokias, rated amongst the hottest in the world, and he proceeded to dunk one of them in salt and bite off the end. The result was a pleasing fire in the mouth (for lesser mortals, this would have meant a trip to the hospital), which he quashed with a mouthful of sweet tea.

He finished off two chillies in this way, saving the third for later, and then turned his mind to his next move.

Vijay, the journalist who had eaten everything in sight, had messaged to say that Dr. Bal Pandey's political rally was due to start at eight P.M. It would be a good opportunity to get a close look at the man and try to establish his whereabouts two nights ago.

Puri called Vijay to suggest they go together.

"We would need to eat beforehand," the hack replied.

Four hours of teaching left Facecream exhausted. After the children went home, she lay in her room, intending to close her eyes for just half an hour. When she woke, it was already five o'clock.

Furious with herself, she got ready quickly and set off to try to retrace Kamlesh's steps. Outside the gates, however, she found three Dalit women waiting for her. They needed help, one explained.

"With what?" asked Facecream. This simple question prompted an outpouring of problems: Their families didn't have enough to eat. Their husbands worked as farm laborers, earning just twenty-five rupees a day. Their families were therefore eligible for Below Poverty Line cards, which entitled them to thirty-five kilograms of rice or wheat each month. Getting the cards had proven impossible, however. The application required photographs verified by a gazetted officer or municipal councilor, as well as proof of residence. For this a letter from the village headman was a prerequisite and they dared not even approach Rakesh Yadav.

Were local Dalit political representatives not willing to help them? Facecream asked.

"They do nothing!" cried the women before haranguing her with a litany of complaints against those who professed to be representing their interests.

Facecream listened patiently and then agreed to do what she could to help them. Yet still the grievances came. They had to walk a mile to fetch water from the river. They had been promised one hundred days of work annually under the National Food for Work Programme, only half of which had materialized. One of the women had a pain in her abdomen and wanted medicine. Another claimed her daughter was possessed and needed money for an exorcism. The third had a big green and yellow bruise on her arm.

"I've had it for weeks—since they used the needle," she said.

"What needle?"

"They took some blood," she said.

"Who is 'they'?"

"The doctors who came."

Facecream examined the woman's arm. It was just skin and bone, which was why the bruising was so bad.

"Don't worry, it's nothing serious," she assured her before applying a little antiseptic cream and asking whether the women had known Kamlesh, Ram's mother.

"Of course we knew her. She was our neighbor."

"Who do you think killed her?" she asked.

The answer was unequivocal. "Yadavs!"

"Why do you say that?"

"She had money. They took it from her and killed her."

"How much money?"

"A fortune! Her son has been working in the city. He has a good job."

Facecream sent the women on their way, watching as they walked back to the village, astounded by their ignorance and wondering if they were simply repeating gossip.

The walk to the highway took Facecream thirty minutes. Assuming Kamlesh hadn't been abducted en route, she would have reached the intersection at approximately eight o'clock. So where had she gone from here? The most plausible answer was a bus.

To the west, three hundred kilometers away, lay Agra. But to reach it required a ticket on an "interstate" and they didn't generally stop en route to pick up individual passengers.

Lucknow, which lay to the east, seemed the likelier possibility. This meant Kamlesh would have crossed the road to reach the bus stop next to the chai stand.

Facecream dodged traffic and went to investigate.

The chai stand had open sides and a roof made of bamboo matting lined with blue plastic. All but one of the eight molded plastic tables were occupied. The customers were truck and bus drivers, bar one man with a cage full of chickens.

Facecream took the last available table and ordered a cup of chai from the teenage waiter. A short, chipped glass filled with a liquid the color of mud was soon placed before her and she let it cool as she watched the traffic pass by.

It was a busy spot with private buses pulling up every few minutes. Cocky conductors shouted out the names of destinations and herded people on and off like cattle. Drivers revved their engines like aspiring Formula One champions and then tore away, often with hapless passengers hanging from the doorways for dear life. Three-wheel auto rickshaws puttered up as well, faces peering from the prisonlike bars at the back. In one, Facecream counted at least twenty-five people seated around a cow.

Gandhi had glorified rural living, saying famously, "India is not Calcutta and Bombay. India lives in her seven hundred thousand villages." But cities offered the promise of a society free of caste. In Delhi, Facecream had achieved anonymity. Who would have guessed that she was from an "untouchable" community herself? Not even Vish Puri, it seemed. If he knew, he might understand her affinity for the Love Commandos.

Her attention was drawn from the highway back inside the chai stand, where she noticed the Dalit boy she'd rescued last night sweeping the earthen floor with a reed brush. She smiled, but he didn't reciprocate and went about his work.

"You don't remember me?" she asked when he drew close to her table.

The boy glanced at his employer before answering.

"What are you doing here?" he hissed.

"What's your name?" she asked.

"Why? What's it to you?"

"I thought we could be friends."

This gave him pause. His brow furrowed.

"How old are you?" asked Facecream.

The boy cocked his head to one side. "Nine."

"You should be at school."

"What for?"

"If you learn to read and write, you'll have a better future."

"Who says?"

"Me. I'm your new teacher."

"I have to work," he said, and went back to his sweeping.

"I could talk to your parents."

The boy stopped again. "Look, I don't need your help," he said. "You've already caused me enough trouble."

"I was only trying to—"

"I can take care of myself."

"Do those Yadav boys beat you every night?"

He moved away from her table, driving a small pile of litter and cigarette butts before him.

Another bus pulled up on the road and a couple of locals climbed on board before it took off again. They'd been standing outside the chai stand for four or five minutes in clear view of everyone inside, the boy included.

It stood to reason that he might have seen Kamlesh board a bus or an auto. Perhaps he'd even heard the destination.

Facecream decided to wait until he finished work and walk him back to the village.

Twelve

Mummy's headache miraculously passed by the evening. And by a happy coincidence she and the rest of the family reached the hotel restaurant shortly after the Dughals sat down to eat.

From the corner table occupied by the Puri clan, Mummy was able to keep an eye on the couple, who polished off a goodly portion of the vegetarian buffet before making their way to the veranda to take in some evening air.

Pranap Dughal then pushed his wife's wheelchair to the elevator, which she duly took up to their room, while he exited the hotel.

Seeing him leave, Mummy suddenly felt her headache returning.

"Some altitude sickness is there, na," she said.

"But we're still only seven hundred and fifty meters above sea level," pointed out Chetan.

"You all remain seated," she said, ignoring him. "Bed rest is required."

Mummy stole away and reached the main doors in time to see Pranap Dughal getting into a three-wheeler. Mummy hailed her own and climbed inside.

"Follow that auto," she instructed the driver.

The Regal sat on a hillock less than a mile outside Katra and it took them but five minutes to reach the town. By now it was half past eight and the main drag was packed with pilgrims eating street food and having portraits taken in photo studios that provided tacky replicas of the Vaishno Devi shrine.

Pranap Dughal stopped in front of a small shop with a sign that read YATRA HELICOPTER HIRE.

Mummy, who got her auto driver to park across the street, watched as her mark entered the premises.

He introduced himself to a man sitting inside wearing a pilot's uniform.

The pilot looked like he had been expecting Dughal. Mummy could almost hear him saying, "Yes, absolutely, it's all arranged."

Dughal then produced an envelope from inside his jacket pocket. It contained a thick wad of notes; the pilot counted them and then gave a nod.

There was another brief exchange, a handshake, and then Dughal left.

The pilot watched him go before stuffing the envelope of cash into his trouser pocket.

Facecream waited an hour by the side of the lane.

When the boy spotted her, he didn't look best pleased. "What are you doing here?" he demanded.

"Waiting for you."

"Why?"

"You ask that question a lot."

He reached the spot where she was sitting on a grassy bank and dismounted from his bike, the blocks still strapped to his feet.

"My name's Padma," she said, and offered him a hand.

He studied it before giving it the briefest and limpest of shakes.

"Aren't you going to tell me your name?" she asked.

"It's Deep."

"Deep," she repeated. "That means 'light.'"

"You don't look like a schoolteacher," he said.

"What do schoolteachers generally look like?"

"The last one was fat and ugly."

She stood up. "Will you walk with me? I'm afraid of the dark."

He hesitated. "Why?"

"Don't you ever ask any other question?"

Deep sat down to take off the wooden blocks and slip on his chappals.

"That bike's too big for you," she observed as he pushed it along.

"It belonged to my father."

"Belonged?"

"He died."

"I'm sorry to hear that, Deep."

"It doesn't matter. I live with my uncle."

"Where's your mother?"

"She died as well—when I was born."

They walked on in silence. A sickle moon hung in the sky like a fishhook waiting to entice the mother of all carp.

"What are you doing here?" he asked suddenly.

"Why?" she asked.

He snorted and said in a mocking tone, "Don't you ever ask any other question?"

Facecream grinned. "I told you, I'm a teacher."

"Then why are you carrying a knife?" he asked.

Her grin widened. Deep didn't miss much. "For protection," she answered.

"Can I see it?"

She reached under her shirt, pulled out her khukuri and unsheathed it. The metal glinted in the moonlight.

"Do you always carry it?" he asked.

"Not always. But most of the time."

"Have you ever used it?" he asked.

She pushed it back into the scabbard. "Do the Yadav boys bully you a lot?"

"I usually avoid them."

"Will they be waiting for you tonight?"

"Probably. They're after money."

"You could always stay with me if you like. Just for to-night. You could have a wash. The water's clean. And I'm going to cook a chicken."

"Chicken?" he repeated lightly with an undertone of pure innocence.

At nine P.M., Puri and the journalist, Vijay, arrived at a large white tent pitched on a dusty field just outside Lucknow. Inside, an audience of Brahmins five hundred strong was en-grossed by a performance. Three bare-chested pandits sat on a stage. With saffron scarves draped over their shoulders and white tilaks on their foreheads, the priests blew conch shells and chanted Vedic hymns dating back some 3,500 years.

Nothing spoke more of Brahmin exclusivity than this spectacle, Puri reflected with disdain. As a member of the Kshatriya warrior caste, he took umbrage with the represen-tation of the mythical warrior-saint Parasurama, celebrated by Brahmins for slaughtering Kshatriyas with his silver axe.

Feeling suddenly like a spy in enemy territory, he stom-ached it nonetheless—even suffering the cries of "Jai Par-asurama!" ("Hail Parasurama!") that greeted the Brahmin politician Dr. Bal Pandey as he took to the stage.

In a long white kurta and collarless waistcoat, the bald, bespectacled, pharisaic politician saluted the audience with a pious namaste. A welcoming committee of overeager local bigwigs then decked him with preposterously large marigold garlands. A frenzy of camera flashes lit up their grins. Dr. Pandey was also presented with a silver axe, which he held aloft to the delight of the audience before taking his place on a replica throne in the middle of the stage.

A warm-up speaker approached the microphone and began the long, laborious process of welcoming Dr. Pandey and various other Brahmin dignitaries, waxing lyrical about their positions and achievements.

Puri did his best to filter out the crawling speech while he appraised Dr. Pandey. The man's gaze and his manner were calculating. The detective sensed he was a man who could rationalize anything to further himself and his cause. This perception was validated when Pandey eventually took to the podium and spoke. A capable orator, his speech was peppered with eloquent phrases and the odd line of classical scripture.

But the rhetoric was poisonous. The Brahmins were the marginalized of society, he thundered. Affirmative action had robbed them of jobs and education. For once, though, his ire wasn't directed at Chief Minister Baba Dhobi. Instead, he railed against the Yadav community—the ex-laborers now prospering and upsetting the traditional order. Terming them a "menace" and a "scourge," Dr. Pandey singled them out as a threat to the security and well-being of Uttar Pradesh's Brahmins.

The tirade left the press pack, Vijay included, baffled. Dr. Pandey had fought the last election as part of an alliance with the Yadavs. Where did that now place him and the Brahmin vote?

Vijay and his colleagues fell over one another trying to put those questions to Dr. Pandey as he left the stage. But he refused to comment, making only a cryptic remark about "adapting to the times, the circumstances and political realities."

Just one question caught his attention. It came as he reached his sedan and the door opened for him.

"Sir, what all were your whereabouts night before last?"

Dr. Pandey turned to identify the source and his gaze met Puri's. A flicker of recognition showed on his face. And then he was gone amidst a cavalcade of police vehicles, sirens and flashing blue emergency lights.

The detective stood watching the motorcade vanish into the night and became aware of a man standing to his right. The scent of his aftershave betrayed his identity.

"Good evening, Hari," he said.

"Mr. Vish Puri saar. You enjoyed the entertainment?"

"Not especially. You?"

"These Brahmins take themselves so seriously. Give me Baba Dhobi any day. At least the man knows a good joke or two."

"He is equally divisive."

"No more so than any of the others."

Hari started toward the parking area. "How is that investigation coming along, by the way?" he asked over his shoulder.

"Couldn't be better," said Puri. "World-class, in fact."

Facecream and Deep reached the school to find two more Dalit women waiting outside the gates. Like the others who'd visited in the afternoon, they wanted help with fundamental problems in their lives. One also had bruising on her arm, like the other woman earlier, and wanted "the medicine."

Facecream inspected the brown and yellow discoloration. It wasn't serious, but she fetched her tube of antiseptic cream nonetheless. As she applied a little, she asked the woman why she'd been injected.

"They took blood," she said.

"Who did?"

"Some outsiders."

The vagueness of the statement sparked Facecream's curiosity. "What outsiders?" she asked.

The woman could only tell her that they'd spoken "city" Hindi and given every Dalit who'd donated blood one hundred rupees.

Facecream asked Deep whether he knew anything more about it.

"Sure. They said they were doing tests for disease," he replied.

"Did you give them blood?"

"Of course," he said with a smile. "I got a hundred rupees, too!"

"Did they tell you what they wanted with it?"

No one had an answer. But then Deep had a brainwave.

"A few days before they came, a notice was nailed to the trunk of the banyan tree, the one next to the shop in the middle of the village," he said. "I think it's still there."

"Show me," said Facecream.

"I can't—the Yadav boys."

"Fine, we'll go later, after they've passed out."

Thirteen

Mummy went to bed knowing that she wasn't going to be able to keep an eye on Pranap Dughal any longer. He was taking a helicopter and would cover the distance up to the top of the Trikuta mountain in a matter of minutes, while she was committed to doing the pilgrimage the "proper" way: on foot.

That left her with one option: to inform Inspector Malhotra of the Jammu police of her suspicions. If he didn't take the matter seriously and act to stop Dughal from murdering his wife, then it would be on his conscience and not hers.

When she woke the following morning at five o'clock and saw that it was still dark, however, Mummy decided it was far too early to call him.

She did the decent thing and waited half an hour.

"Inspector sahib, I woke you?" she said when he answered his mobile phone with a croak.

"Who is this?"

"I'm Vish Puri's Mummy-ji this side," she said without a trace of apology. "Something urgent is there."

"What . . . what time is it?"

"Morning time, naturally. Now kindly listen. That

Pranap Dughal—the motu on the train, you remember? Just he's planning to murder his wife. She's abusing him and making his life totally miserable. Under such circumstance, any one of us might do consideration of the same. But murder is murder, na? It is not right at all. Thus we cannot simply stand by and do nothing. Now, what I want to tell you—"

Malhotra cleared his throat again. "Madam, let me understand one thing," he said, still sounding drowsy. "You're referring to the same individual whom you falsely accused of stealing your son's wallet?"

"Not falsely in fact, Inspector, if you please. Just he returned the wallet in the wee hours. He's a cunning one. That is why my suspicions were first getting aroused. So I did surveillance in Jammu and witnessed him buying so many of sleeping tablets."

"Surveillance?"

"Correct. Just he intends to do intoxication of his wife and deposit her over the mountain edge."

There was silence on the other line, prompting Mummy to say, "Hello? Hello? Inspector? You're awake?"

"Yes, madam, believe me, I am very much awake."

"You'll give the matter top priority?" Her request sounded more like an order.

"Rest assured, madam, your call has been duly noted."

"Very good, Inspector. Thank you, na, and God bless. Such a weight it has been on my mind I can't tell you." She paused for breath and then continued. "One thing, also. Dughal is taking one heli—"

Malhotra interrupted with the words, "Good night, madam," and the line went dead.

Mummy scowled at the phone as if the instrument itself had somehow failed her and returned the receiver to the cradle. She couldn't help but wonder if Inspector Malhotra hadn't been "tulli" the night before.

"Sounded totally out of it," she said with a disapproving tut.

For once, all the Puris were ready on time. Mummy, Rumpi, Chetan and the other family members gathered at six in the hotel lobby, eager to begin their ascent. They found the shops and eateries along the town's main drag shuttered. Sweepers armed with jharus were tidying away the detritus from the night before. Crows perched on overhead wires, ever vigilant for tidbits of edible refuse. Street dogs who'd battled over territory all night turned tail at the approach of the more dominant species.

Mummy relished the thrill that comes from being up before everyone else, of seeing the world as it is before the great director in the sky yells, "Action!" Yet upon entering the town square, this sense of privilege quickly gave way to one of fraternity. Hundreds of pilgrims, or yatris, who'd slept in the open overnight, were rolling up sleeping bags and bedrolls in a flurry of excitement. Many wore red and gold bandanas, and as they set off for the entrance to the mountain—youngsters raised aloft on shoulders, elderly uncles and aunties striding forth with walking sticks—euphoric cries of "Maan aap bulandi!" ("The Mother herself calls!") echoed along the narrow street leading to the mountain pathway.

Mummy was heartened to see that the pilgrimage remained predominantly a family affair. The Puris were one of hundreds of families three or four generations strong, many of them singing and joking and helping one another along. She spotted honeymooning couples, the brides wearing henna designs on their hands, bunches of red, white and gold bangles on their wrists, and fresh daubs of sindoor in the parting of their hair. In spite of all the talk about the Westernization of Indian culture, countless young Hindus dressed in jeans and T-shirts, who appeared as caught up in the ritualism as the most pious sanyassis, thronged the way. There was even a group of widows from a village near Bhopal in central India who'd pooled their resources, hired a bus and traveled more than a thousand miles to be here.

It came as a relief, too, to find that the mountain path was paved. And for those unable to manage the climb of their own volition (this included numerous aunties with bad hips who wobbled), there were small horses, decked in bright, multicolored bridles and saddles, available, with a keeper leading them on.

It was also possible to be carried up in a sedan chair— although Mummy found something repugnant in the sight of people, some of them obese, being borne upon the shoulders of porters who were being paid at most a few hundred rupees a day.

Thirty minutes into the climb, however, and with the scale of the challenge now dawning on him, the idea of being carried suddenly struck Chetan as an extremely appealing proposition.

"I want to go in one!"

The answer from Rumpi was an emphatic no.

"But I'm paining!"

"So are we—from all your whining! Now, we're walking and that's that."

"Pleeeeeease!" begged Chetan, who began to drag his feet.

At this point, Mummy intervened. "Such a nautanki! Always stuffing your face with sweeties and some such," she scolded him.

Chetan was indeed halfway through a packet of chips. A masala moustache had formed on his upper lip.

"Gaad, what a pain, yaar!" he complained. "What's the big deal about walking, anyway? Why do we have to suffer?"

Mummy, who very rarely lost her temper, turned on him. "That is daal in your brains or what?" she cried. "Call this suffering? During partition time, Om Chander Puri did walking for three weeks total across all Punjab and Haryana. Thousands were slaughtered along the way itself. Only thanks to the God he escaped in one piece with his life and reached Dilli. That is proper suffering!"

Chetan's face turned ashen. He looked on the verge of tears, but Mummy didn't soften.

"I am seventy plus," she continued. "See me doing sweating or complaining? Just I'm walking double your speed. Now come. Don't do feet dragging."

"But my knees really do hurt, Mummy-ji," said the boy.

"No surprise, na? What with all your sitting all day playing Nintendo and all. So much of boredom is turning you into a ladoo. Just consider: today you are a yatri. Some pride should be there. Your thinking, also, should be on reaching the goddess and doing inward reflection—nothing more."

A suitably chastened Chetan followed behind.

"Sorry, Mummy-ji," he mumbled, and tried his best to keep up.

An hour later, with the sun now beating down on them, everyone was ready for a break. They sat in the shade of a stall quenching their thirst with bottles of nimboo pani, while looking down on the rooftops of Katra far below. They could make out their hotel, trace the route of the road snaking back toward Jammu, even spot cars and trucks passing one another on the bends.

A whirring sound filled the air like a mosquito at night and then a helicopter appeared above the town. They watched it rising higher and higher until it was but a speck amidst the colossal mountain range. Finally it disappeared from sight.

Another helicopter followed—and before long, there were four or five coming and going at regular intervals.

The Dughals would surely be on one of them, Mummy reflected. Inspector Malhotra had probably ignored her warning, leaving Pranap Dughal free to conspire with Weasel Face to arrange his wife's accident. With thousands of pilgrims clamoring to gain access to the shrine, no one would suspect foul play. Such "mishaps" were known to happen all the time. Only yesterday an elderly pilgrim had tripped and fallen one hundred feet down into a ravine, "succumbing to fatal injuries on the spot," according to the local newspaper Mummy had read in the hotel.

She wondered what part Weasel Face was going to play in the whole sordid business. Maybe he'd loosen a railing? Or arrange to spike Mrs. Dughal's food?

But as Mummy thought on it some more, she began to wonder if perhaps she hadn't jumped to the wrong conclusion. Pranap Dughal was clearly a conniving, intelligent man. He had no need of an accomplice to do away with his wife. It would be sheer idiocy to involve someone else.

He and Weasel Face were planning something else entirely.

Where then did the sleeping tablets fit in? And what was inside those heavy bags?

Mummy was so absorbed in thought that she nearly missed Mrs. Dughal passing by on a sedan chair with no less than six porters struggling to keep her aloft.

The woman was fast asleep with her triple chin bobbing up and down in time with the rhythmic march of her bearers.

Pranap Dughal followed in his own sedan chair. Looking relaxed and chatting on his mobile phone, he didn't appear to spot the Puris, who were finishing up their drinks.

"Challo," said Mummy, getting quickly to her feet. "It is getting very much late."

"But we've only had five minutes' rest!" protested Rumpi.

"You are right. Let us continue on horse."

"Horses! Mummy-ji? You were saying we had to walk!"

"They are for you people, na. So slow you are, always doing dillydally," said Mummy, and went in search of a ride.

Fourteen

Puri had been woken at two in the morning by Facecream, who'd informed him that an Agra-based organization called the Institute for Cellular and Molecular Biology (ICMB) had taken blood samples from Dalits in the village of Govind nearly three months ago—and that Ram had been present at the time.

Although Puri deemed this a strong lead, there was nothing he could do about it in the middle of the night, and so he'd gone back to sleep.

At five o'clock, he'd checked out of his Lucknow hotel and, with the same hire car and driver, started along the highway to Agra.

An hour later, he'd called Elizabeth Rani, whom he'd ordered into the office to do some research on the "wifee."

Now, at a few minutes to eight, and with at least another hour's drive ahead of him, Puri was speaking to his secretary as she sat at her desk in the office back in Delhi.

"On the home page of their website it says ICMB is 'on the front line of modern biology,'" said Elizabeth Rani. "It goes on, 'We promote new techniques in the interdisciplinary areas of biology to collect, collate and disseminate information relevant to biological research.'"

"Meaning what, exactly?"

Elizabeth Rani read from another page: " 'Molecular analysis of human genetic disorders and chromosome biology.'"

"Any contact is there?" he asked.

The sound of her mouse clicking was audible down the line. Then she mumbled something unintelligible.

"What is wrong, Madam Rani?"

"Sir, I was just looking at the list of those notables who serve on the institute's advisory board. It includes retired netas, generals and ambassadors. A very high-powered list. The staff includes half a dozen PhDs also."

She paused. "This is interesting, sir," she continued. "It says here that they're conducting the most comprehensive mapping of the Indian genome so far undertaken."

"Indian genome? What is that? Some kind of dwarf."

Elizabeth Rani searched for a definition. " 'Genome: the haploid set of chromosomes in a gamete of a microorganism, or in each cell of a multicellular organism,'" she read.

Puri responded with a vexed "Arrey, my brain has gone for a toss."

Fortunately the dictionary also provided a layman's definition: "the complete set of genes or genetic material present in a cell of an organism."

"DNA and all," said Puri, who knew a certain amount on the subject given his familiarity with forensics. "Anything more is there, Madam Rani?" he asked.

"One thing, sir. Seems a doctor employed at this ICMB was killed in a car accident just a few days back."

"His name?"

"*She*, sir—Dr. Anju Basu. There's an article in the *Times*—

says her car skidded off a bridge near Agra into the Yamuna."

Puri made a note of this as his secretary went on.

"One thing is strange, sir," she commented. "There's no information available about this organization. No articles have been written about their work in any journals. The staff is not quoted anywhere that I can see. None of its research is published online. And another thing, sir—only an e-mail address is provided."

Puri was quiet for a moment and then said, "Let us shake the tree and see what all falls down."

"Sir?"

"Madam Rani, please be good enough to send them one e-mail message on my behalf. Make mention that I have been in the village of Govind and spoken to certain Dalits with bruises on their arms. Provide my identity and mobile number and request an interview with the director at the earliest opportunity. Meanwhile I'll endeavor to find out their location."

Puri spent the next half an hour calling various contacts in the world of medicine to ask if any of them knew of the Indian Institute for Cellular and Molecular Biology, and was eventually given an Agra post office box listed in a medical directory.

Deep spent the night on the floor of Facecream's room, his hardened, streetwise demeanor melting into innocence in slumber. He slept on his front the way children do, his legs splayed and arms flopped by his sides.

Over breakfast, he was quiet.

Facecream asked if anything was the matter.

"You're not a teacher, are you, ma'am?" he said.

She put her food to one side. "No, I'm not," she admitted.

"What then? Police?"

"I'm looking for Ram Sunder. Someone abducted him and I'm trying to find out what happened."

Deep didn't look surprised. But then nothing seemed to faze him. "You think he's still alive?" he asked, his tone faintly mocking.

"Until it's proven otherwise I have to keep looking."

"Why?"

"Because I promised to help him. And he's my friend."

The boy lapsed into silent thought as if the concept of friendship was new to him. Half of his breakfast remained in his bowl. He began to spoon it into his mouth again.

"I've got to get to work," he said.

Facecream couldn't help but smile to herself as she watched him eat. She'd been a lot like the boy at that age—old beyond her years with a tough exterior born of an equally rough, unforgiving childhood and desperate never to show the slightest sign of vulnerability.

"Deep, I need your help," she said. "I have to find out if Ram's mother, Kamlesh, got on a bus—and where she went. It's very important. At the chai stand, you see all the buses leaving and know all the conductors. You hear all the talk as well."

"Is that why you're being nice to me? Giving me chicken, walking with me, so I'll tell you what you want to know?"

"I admit I came to see you hoping to get information. But I like you, Deep. I want to help you."

"Like the children who come to school?"

"Yes."

"When you get what you want, you'll leave."

"I'm not like that. I don't make promises I can't keep."

"You've told them you're going to give them better food and proper teaching."

"I'll do everything I can to make sure those things happen."

The boy finished eating in silence, cleared away his bowl, and went to rinse out his mouth.

Facecream followed him to the washbasin.

"If I can find out what happened to Kamlesh, there's a chance, just a chance, that we might be able to find Ram—assuming he's still alive."

"What if I tell you what you want to know and someone finds out? You'll be gone and then what? I'm the one who will have to face the consequences."

"I'll make sure nothing happens to you—I promise."

Deep found his bike and strapped on his wooden blocks.

Facecream appealed again for his help. But she was forced to watch him ride off through the gates like a mother who, despite her best intentions, felt misunderstood.

Upon reaching Agra, Puri headed straight for the main post office, where, in the canteen around the back of the building, he managed to persuade one of the employees to indulge in a little felonious activity.

Escorted into a dusty filing room, Puri spent an hour searching through the card indexing system of PO box numbers, which had suffered the ravages of heat, humidity, monsoon floods, rodents, termites and pesticide—not to mention the usual dust and the odd chai spillage. By a minor miracle, he found ICMB's card and was able to decipher the spidery handwriting.

At midday he was back beyond the Agra city limits, driving through a so-called Special Economic Zone. It was one of dozens set up across the country and comprised hundreds of acres of formerly agricultural land that had been forcibly purchased by the government and sold to industry at a handsome profit. Much of it lay fallow, with large empty plots surrounded by brick walls and signs warning trespassers to keep out. Along the borders of the tarmac roads that crisscrossed this forlorn landscape, countless piles of broken concrete, bricks and plaster had been dumped from other construction sites. They passed the odd factory, processing plant and storage depot where trucks were being loaded and off-loaded.

And then, like a mirage, the ICMB building came into view—a three-story cube of blue reflective glass.

It was surrounded by twenty-foot-high walls topped with razor wire, turrets mounted with CCTV cameras, a double set of gates with a raised anticrash barrier in between, and uniformed security personnel.

The only sign read NO ENTRY.

Puri got out of his car and was approaching the gate when his phone rang. A young woman introduced herself as the assistant to Dr. Arnab Sengupta, ICMB's head of research.

"His diary is full. The earliest he can see you is Tuesday of next week," she said.

"I'm outside the gates now, actually," Puri responded.

"Outside where?"

"Your facility," he said. "It is a big blue glass construction, no?"

There was a stunned silence. The assistant mumbled something about having to call him back and hung up.

Puri returned to the car to sit in the air-conditioning while he waited. His tree-shaking strategy seemed to be working. The fact that the assistant had called him suggested that whoever was in charge at ICMB wanted to get a look at him, find out what his game was. He'd certainly proven his tenacity by turning up at their door. But from here on, he was going to have to improvise, jugaad being his watchword.

He passed the next ten minutes staring out the window.

The odd pye-dog scurried past. A man sitting perfectly per-pendicular on a straight-bar bicycle came and went. A couple of hundred yards away, four laborers worked in the baking sun, digging a ditch. A couple of tents were pitched nearby, the roofs made of blue plastic. Puri guessed this was where the laborers slept at night. A woman and some children squatted outside the entrance of one, cooking on a couple of bricks and some chunks of coal. What must it be like to be so destitute, he found himself wondering suddenly. There was surely nothing noble about poverty. And yet the wealthy often ended up worse off—blinded by their conceit.

The sound of his phone ringing broke into his thoughts.

"Dr. Sengupta will see you," said the assistant. "I'm send-ing someone out to collect you."

Passing through the reception and the windowless corridor beyond was like entering a science fiction spaceship. The walls were a futuristic silver. Spotlights dappled the carpet-ing in recurrent circles. Automatic doors swished open and closed with precision.

Finally a conventional wooden door opened into a large, modern office. It could have been located anywhere in the world. The only natural feature was a potted plant, and even that looked like it might not last long beyond the confines of its fabricated environment.

As for Dr. Sengupta himself, Puri would have guessed that he was Bengali even without knowing his last name. His ethnicity could be read from his bone structure, dusky skin and bookish demeanor. Was there ever a "Bong" doc-tor, academic or intellectual, who *didn't* wear glasses?

"Come in, Mr. Puri," said Dr. Sengupta, his tone brisk and awkward. "You'll take tea, coffee, water?"

"Nothing."

154

Dr. Sengupta wore a white laboratory coat over a shirt and tie with a couple of pens sticking out of his breast pocket. The diplomas framed on the wall bespoke a lifetime in academia and research, the dustbin brimming with paper coffee cups of a workaholic nature. Not exactly the social type, Puri surmised, noting the absence of a wedding ring despite his age, which he put at around forty.

The female assistant, who'd escorted Puri from reception and lingered in the doorway for further instruction, pulled the door shut.

"I understand you found us all on your own?" said Dr. Sengupta as Puri placed a copy of his card on the desk and sat down. "Would you mind telling me how you managed that?"

"Will and way, sir—will and way," said Puri.

"I'm not sure I understand."

"A trade secret if you like."

"I see," said Dr. Sengupta with impatience. "Well, I suppose we all have them—trade secrets. It's just that we have gone to considerable lengths to remain anonymous."

"I would certainly say so, sir. There is not even so much as one sign outside your facility."

"I suppose that makes you suspicious?"

"It is certainly unusual, is it not?"

"Our research is extremely sensitive, Mr. Puri. We have to take our security seriously."

"You've been threatened, is it, sir?"

"We deal with genetics, Mr. Puri, and by default that's about people's identities. I don't need to tell you that identity—or at least people's perceived notions of their identities—can be a thorny issue in India to say the least. Our findings are highly controversial. They answer definitively, once and for all, who we are and where we came from. Potentially that poses a threat to certain sections of society. When it comes to caste and Hindu identity, there are numerous vested interests. But then science always threatens preconceived notions amongst the narrow-minded."

There was a hint of the evangelical in Dr. Sengupta's voice.

"You are on something of a crusade, is it, sir?" asked the detective.

"We are a research institute, Mr. Puri. But I would say this: India will never progress, never join the rest of the civilized world, until we are rid of the caste system once and for all. It is utterly divisive, breeds corruption in our political system and ensures that tens of millions of Indians remain mired in poverty and ignorance—a great albatross around our collective necks. So, yes, it is my sincerest hope that our research will change the way society regards itself."

"You've no argument from me on that count, sir," said Puri, who wasn't sure what an albatross was but decided not to ask. "But I fail to understand how your research will change things."

"Mr. Puri, what is caste?" asked Dr. Sengupta, although the question was clearly rhetorical. "A hereditary transmission of a style of life that often includes an occupation, ritual status in a hierarchy and customary interaction and exclusion based on cultural notions of purity and pollution. We are born into it, in other words. I, for example, am a Vaidya Brahmin. We are one of the elite classes of Bengal—physicians by tradition. If you believe in fairy tales, I'm descended from Pandit Budhsen, a notable Vedic scholar. That chain is believed to be unbroken, lending us a perceived purity. However, an analysis of my own genetic sequencing proves that although my forebears have long remained endogamous—that is to say they have married within their own community—I'm the product of two genetically divergent and heterogeneous populations that mixed in ancient times: in lay terms, Indo-Europeans and Dravidians."

"The concept of racial purity is thus proven false," ventured Puri.

"As is the entire basis of the hierarchical structure of caste."

"Mind-blowing," murmured the detective, who could certainly see why such findings would prove controversial.

"You see, Mr. Puri, India is quite unique. The range of genetic diversity is up to four times higher here than it is in, say, Europe. Yet for the best part of three millennia, there's been little mixing between communities. Time and again we're finding people from different castes, religions and tribes living in close proximity to one another—sometimes separated by a matter of meters—who've never intermarried. You might liken this phenomenon to pools of water high up on a beach, separated from one another and the tide."

Puri took out his notebook and scribbled a few lines. Then he stopped, frowned and rubbed his forehead. "I'm getting confusion," he said.

Dr. Sengupta checked his watch. "Yes, Mr. Puri," he breathed.

"You say you are mapping the population's DNA, but for the purposes of knowledge, only, or you are seeking some profit, also?"

"Our principal activity here at ICMB is the study of genetic disorders."

"Disorders, sir?"

"Mr. Puri, I'm not sure I have time to explain the whole science to you. But genetic disorders are caused by sequence variation in genes and chromosomes. Some are inherited, others are caused by new mutations. Some types of recessive gene disorders confer an advantage in certain environments."

There was a knock on the door and Dr. Sengupta greeted it with marked relief. "Come!"

A tall, broad-shouldered foreign gentleman with combed-back flaxen hair appeared. He was wearing a flannel suit and a sharp, blue-striped shirt. "Justus Bergstrom, ICMB director," was how he introduced himself in an accent reminiscent of the old newsreaders on Radio Moscow—a kind of cross between American and Eastern European.

"My apologies, I was in another meeting," he said as he shook Puri by the hand. "I hope Dr. Sengupta here has cleared up any preconceived notions you might have formed?"

"Preconceived notions, sir?" asked Puri.

"That we might be exploiting people," said Bergstrom, who hovered to one side of the desk. "You've been in one of the villages where we've been working, I understand."

"In one such village, sir."

"Our team was there some three months ago, I believe?" Bergstrom looked to Dr. Sengupta for verification of this and the Bengali gave a nod.

"So what exactly is your concern, um, sorry, Mr."—he looked at the detective's business card—"Mr. Poori."

"A poori is a type of fried bread, puffed and all. I'm a Puri, actually," said the detective.

"My apologies. My Swedish accent. And these Indian names, you know." He emitted a stabbing laugh. Dr. Sengupta smiled in concert.

"It is my understanding you paid some Dalits one hundred rupees in return for a sample of their blood and asked them to sign some kind of release form," stated Puri.

"Perfectly standard practice—all within the guidelines set out by your health ministry, I can assure you," replied Bergstrom.

"But with such DNA samples your organization could benefit to the tune of tens of millions of dollars—hundreds possibly—through the genetic research you're conducting, no?"

Bergstrom met this statement with a quizzical smile, as if he regarded it as pitifully naïve. "Why don't we take a little walk, you and I," he said. "There's something I'd like you to see. Perhaps then this thing will become a little clearer."

Bergstrom went and held the door open. "Please, Mr. Puri," he said, one arm held out toward him.

The detective put away his notebook and pen, stood from his chair and thanked Dr. Sengupta for his time.

"Pleasure," he said with the most perfunctory of handshakes.

Puri moved toward the door but stopped halfway across the office. "By the way, my deepest condolences," he said.

"Condolences?"

"For your loss. I understand one of your faculty was killed on Thursday, only."

Dr. Sengupta nodded sadly. "Yes, poor Anju," he said. "A terrible loss for all of us. I still can't quite believe what happened."

"A car crash?"

"She lost control of the wheel and spun off the road," he added.

"She was a brilliant scientist and will be sorely missed," said Bergstrom in a dry, corporate tone. "Now, if you'd like to follow me, Mr. Puri."

The Swede led the detective to an elevator. This took them up to the second floor, every movement monitored by dome cameras fixed to the ceilings. Puri found himself standing behind the glass wall of a large laboratory. It looked like something out of a James Bond set with a cast of anonymous men and women in identical white coats, masks and rubber gloves. Some of them were peering into microscopes. One took samples out of a large refrigerator.

"Take a guess as to how much this facility cost to build," said Bergstrom.

"Some millions of rupees I would imagine."

"Fifty million dollars, Mr. Puri. Everything you see here is state-of-the-art. The laboratory is air sealed. Only recently, after all the failures on the national grid, we had to build our own power plant providing an uninterrupted supply twenty-four hours a day, seven days a week. I can't tell you how challenging it's been to set up this kind of research facility here in India. The business environment is extraordinarily discouraging."

"Your investment comes from where exactly?"

"International equity firms mostly. Some Indian money also."

"All looking for a healthy return no doubt."

"If you're asking whether they'll profit, the answer is that I jolly well hope so. Millions of Indians will also benefit from the drugs that will be developed thanks to our research, I might add. So when you accuse us of taking advantage of ignorant villagers, you would do well to keep in mind that we're working to improve their lives and those of their children and their children's children."

"Sir, I've not accused you people of anything," said Puri, who'd stomached about as much corporate rhetoric as he could take for one day. "It is my sworn duty to investigate the case inside and out, leaving no stone unturned."

"And what is this case you're investigating?"

"I'm endeavoring to locate a certain young Dalit by name of Ram Sunder, who was forcibly abducted from where he was staying in Agra. I am endeavoring, also, to find out who brutally murdered his mother."

Bergstrom's face revealed startled dismay.

"And you think there's some connection with ICMB?"

"Sir, their native place is Govind, near to Lucknow, from where your organization took blood samples some three months back."

"We've taken blood from a hundred or more villages."

"Sir, as I previously intimated, I am simply following up any and all leads."

The frown etched across Bergstrom's forehead set. "I fail to understand what it is that you hoped to achieve by coming here today, Mr. Puri," he said.

"It would help if you could tell me whether you took any blood from this Ram Sunder."

"That's completely out of the question. We're not at liberty to share the details of our research with anyone. The identities of our subjects must remain strictly confidential."

He strode over to the elevator and pressed the call button. When the doors opened, he told the security guard inside to escort the detective to the front gate.

Puri stepped inside.

"Let me also assure you that our lawyers in Delhi will deal vehemently with anyone who suggests any wrong conduct on our part and we will take our complaints to the very pinnacle of government," said Bergstrom.

His words were punctuated with a ping as the elevator doors closed.

Puri drove away, wondering if he'd erred in admitting the real purpose of his visit and whether Bergstrom's indignation had been genuine. It seemed to have been. But then he didn't know how to read Swedish people. Perhaps they were all brilliant actors.

He couldn't even be sure that there was a connection between Ram Sunder's disappearance, his mother's murder and ICMB. The fact that their team visited Govind three months ago and their facility was in Agra, just a few miles from the university, might have been a wild coincidence.

Was he barking up the wrong tree?

Somehow Puri doubted it.

"I want round-the-clock surveillance of this facility," he told Tubelight over the phone. "Send two of your boys to Agra without delay. Tell them to keep all eyes and ears peeled."

Next he put Flush to work trying to hack into the ICMB computer system. "Leave no computer chip unturned."

Finally he called Elizabeth Rani and asked her to "do background checking" on Dr. Arnab Sengupta and the gora, Justus Bergstrom.

That left him free to find out more about the death of their colleague.

"What's her name?" asked Facecream when Puri called to update her on his end of the investigation.

"Anju Basu."

"Another Bengali?"

"And a PhD, also. I tell you these people are such intellectual brainy types. Must be all that fish they eat, yaar."

Fifteen

"The report says the car, an Indica, skidded off the road," said Puri's contact in the Agra police department when they spoke on the phone soon after Puri was ejected from ICMB. "Dr. Basu sustained a head injury and drowned."

"What time the accident occurred, exactly?" asked the detective.

"Two in the morning—last Thursday."

"Any sign of foul play?"

Puri knew he was wasting his breath with such a fundamental question. On average, fourteen people died and fifty-seven others were injured on the roads of India every hour. Even if the police had wanted to investigate each incident, there wasn't the manpower to do so. Uttar Pradesh alone was short of nearly a quarter of a million civil and armed police. And its serving officers were essentially uniformed bribe takers. Most raked in several lakhs per month from truck drivers alone, a goodly percentage of which ended up in the pockets of their superiors and political masters.

Puri put the odds of the scene of Dr. Basu's accident being professionally investigated at about ten billion to one, give or take the odd billion.

"That's an accident-prone zone" was the predictable response from his contact. "Cars are always overtaking and turning turtle."

Puri thanked him, ended the call and told his driver to take him directly to the bridge.

It spanned the Yamuna River beyond the Babarpur Reserved Forest, a few miles to the northwest of Agra. A quarter of the way across, a section of the barrier was missing.

It took the detective little more than three minutes to conclude that the "accident" had been nothing of the sort.

Such was his incredulity that he found himself sharing his reasoning with his driver. The fact that the sum total of the man's English vocabulary was "left side," "right side" and "backside" mattered little. Puri was hardly seeking a second opinion.

"Number one, there is no way a little Indica could tear through the metal—must have been a truck at least," he said. "Second, no red paint is in evidence on the severed section. Nonetheless a buildup of rust is there. Thus we can conclude the damage was done some time back, only."

The driver looked on nonplussed as Puri stepped away from the barrier and indicated the black skid marks on the asphalt.

"These are by no means fresh," he said. "Most probably they were made some weeks or months back, also. Without one shadow of a doubt, their thickness indicates the wheels belonged to a truck—in all likelihood the one that plowed through the barrier in the first place."

Puri took a step backward. "What all a young PhD female was doing at two in the morning on a road leading through a forested reserve into the middle of nowhere?"

The driver recognized this as a question but could only offer a shrug in return.

"Getting knocked on the head, placed behind the wheel and pushed off the bridge—that is what," Puri answered.

The two men stood looking down into the churning, polluted waters of the Yamuna below, grimacing at the stink.

"Murder most foul, that is for sure," said Puri.

But was there a connection between Dr. Basu's murder, Ram's abduction and his mother's murder? Puri went over the sequence of events again in his mind. Dr. Basu was killed in the early hours of Thursday morning. The next day someone thrashed Ram's father. On Saturday, Ram was abducted and that very evening, his mother was brutally murdered.

All this three months after ICMB took blood samples from Dalits in Govind village.

Was Dr. Basu part of the team that went there? Perhaps she'd known Ram.

Puri decided to go and take a look around her apartment. According to his police contact, she'd lived in a fancy new complex on the other side of Agra.

Posing as a wannabe buyer—"A dicky bird told me one apartment is lying vacant"—Puri quickly ingratiated himself with the manager of Royal Luxury Apartments, which promised "Inspirational Living!"

He soon learned that Dr. Basu had "not gone the married way" and that she was "a wonderful humanitarian."

The manager was then persuaded to show Puri her apartment.

When he opened the door, he let out a gasp, clasped his hands to his head and exclaimed, "What the hell has happened?"

Puri peered over the manager's shoulder. The place looked like it had been hit by a tornado—the floor littered with papers, upturned potted plants and a blizzard of upholstery and feathers.

"Seems there has been a break-in," the detective said in a calm, measured tone.

The manager stepped inside, being careful not to tread on any of the scattered possessions, dismay writ large across his face.

"When was the last time you entered the premises exactly?" asked Puri.

At his feet lay a teddy bear that had been mercilessly ripped apart.

"The day before yesterday. I just don't understand how someone could have got inside."

"Who has a key?"

"I've one. Dr. Basu's father has another."

"Dr. Basu herself had one at the time of her death, no?"

"Must be."

Puri suggested to the manager that he go and call the police, knowing full well that they'd take hours, possibly days, to turn up.

"You don't mind keeping guard until I return?"

"Not at all."

The manager hurried back to his office while the detective examined the lock. There were a couple of fresh scratches etched into the brass. Someone had picked it recently, someone who knew what they were doing—like Hari, for example.

Such finesse didn't tally with the state of the apartment, however, and certainly not with the way Hari did things. Thugs had torn the place apart and to get inside they must surely have had a key.

Perhaps two different parties had broken into the apartment, Puri surmised as he moved from room to room, eyes scanning the floor.

Whatever they'd been looking for was small enough to be concealed in the battery casing of a TV remote control or a makeup compact. A data key, perhaps?

He found his way into Dr. Basu's study, where even the computer mouse had been pulled apart. Black pollution marks on the wall indicated that the shelves above the desk had held a set of box files. These were nowhere to be found. A shiny patch of parquet floor suggested that a computer tower was missing, too.

He picked up some of the books lying on the floor. English fiction set in India, mostly: Rushdie, Lahiri, Desai. There were a few textbooks lying around as well. Beneath the window there were also a couple of dozen business cards scattered about.

Resting one hand on the windowsill to support his weight, Puri kneeled down to gather them up.

He was struggling to get himself upright again when he heard the general manager call out his assumed name. Slipping the cards into his trouser pocket, he stepped back into the sitting room, his face still flush from the physical exertion.

"A sudden call of nature was there" was how he explained his presence in Dr. Basu's study.

"I called the police," said the manager. "My boss is on his way. It would be better if he didn't find you here. I'm not sure how I would explain."

"Tip-top and best of luck," said Puri as he made a quick exit.

Once his car had pulled out of the Royal Luxury Apartments gilded gates, Puri searched through the business cards. Most of them were in pristine condition and bore the names and associations of scientists, pharmaceutical company representatives and research fellows. He could imagine them being handed to Dr. Basu at conferences, symposiums and business meetings. They had then been placed in her purse before being brought home and transferred into a clear plastic box that he'd spotted lying upturned under the window of her study.

There were seven other cards in which she appeared to have taken greater interest. These had been given to her in altogether different circumstances. One was stained with beer; another had been handled by greasy fingertips and the words "call me" written on the back; the corners of the others were all bent.

They had something else in common as well: they all belonged to fellow Bengalis.

Dr. Basu had been looking for a prospective groom, it seemed.

Puri felt inside his pocket and took out the last card. It belonged to a "consultant" with a marriage brokerage called Shaadiwaadi.in. That sealed his theory.

Turning it over, he found another card stuck to the back. Carefully, he peeled it away. It bore the name of a Delhi lawyer, R. V. Jindal. Last Monday's date was written on the front together with a time: "3:00."

Puri couldn't help but smile to himself. Hari—assuming it was he who had picked the lock—had missed Jindal's card.

"Your loss is Vish Puri's gain, old pal," he said with a chuckle. His luck was looking up; perhaps the evil eye no longer had its gaze fixed on him.

"Bhai sahib, you've an All India permit?" he asked his driver.

The man gave a nod.

"Dilli, challo. No delay," said Puri, who wanted to go and meet this lawyer, Jindal, in person.

• • •

Facecream spent the morning teaching and, after ensuring that the children received a healthy meal paid for out of her own pocket, walked from the school up to the highway, where she caught a bus to Lucknow.

When she returned in the late afternoon, she went straight to the chai stand. As she entered, the owner gave her a dirty look.

"If you're looking for your rat-catcher friend, he doesn't work here anymore," he said, scowling.

"What happened?"

"I don't want any trouble. Just go—and don't come back."

"Tell me where he went!"

"I said get out!"

Facecream searched for Deep on the main road but couldn't find him anywhere. Fearing the worst, she hailed an auto and drove back to the school.

A welcome committee was waiting for her outside the gates—the village pradhan, Rakesh Yadav, and two goons.

"You've been in Lucknow," said Yadav as she got out of the auto and paid the driver. His mouth was full of gutka, his lips blood red. The crazed look in his eyes suggested he'd had a little too much of the stuff. He added, "You were seen at DAR."

DAR stood for Department of Administrative Reforms. It was the government office where the public was entitled to file Right to Information (RTI) applications. Facecream had gone there to request last year's records for the distribution of food rations in the village. Apparently someone had tipped off Yadav.

"What of it?" she asked.

"I want you to go back tomorrow and withdraw your application," he said.

"Or?"

169

The goons moved closer.

"Or that pretty face of yours will get messed up," said Yadav.

"Call off the monkeys," Facecream ordered.

"Or?"

"They'll get hurt."

"Think you're some kind of hero?" Yadav guffawed, gutka juice running down his stubbly chin.

One of the goons, who had white blemishes on his hands just like his boss, lunged at her, but Facecream blocked him, twisted his arm and flipped him onto his back. The second fared no better, falling to the ground, clutching his vitals and howling in pain.

Yadav looked on in amazement.

"Now get lost—and if you come here again, I won't be so nice," said Facecream.

The goons picked themselves up off the ground, dazed, and stumbled away.

Yadav, however, offered an ominous parting shot. "You are just one girl on your own," he said. "Think you can beat me? I can bring an army if necessary. And there is nobody here who will raise a finger to protect you!"

He turned and hurried back to the village, giving the two goons a shove.

Facecream watched them for a while, furious with herself for letting things get so out of hand, and then entered the gates. She found Deep sitting beneath the banyan tree. He had a bloody nose and a cut lip. His grubby face was stained with tears.

"It's all your fault," he said. "We were spotted together last night. The pradhan came and found me at work. He wanted to know what we were doing in the village. I refused to tell him. So he thrashed me and then sir fired me."

"I know. I went to the chai stand. I'm so sorry."

"I should never have helped you. Now what am I going to do?"

Facecream kneeled next to him. "You needn't worry, Deep. I'm going to look after you now," she said.

His eyes were fixed on the ground. "Just give me money for a ticket. I'll go to Delhi or Mumbai. Find work there," he said.

"I told you I'll look after you and I will," she said, a hand placed on his knee. "Now, let's get you cleaned up. And then have something to eat." Facecream stood and offered her hand. "Come."

She washed Deep's face and tended to his lip and nose. To calm his nerves, she gave him a couple of sips of aaila from the small bottle she'd brought with her. Then she suggested he help her prepare dinner in the kitchen. She'd bought some vegetables in Lucknow, and as Deep sat in the corner of the kitchen with his knees huddled against him, she set about making a simple tarkari curry.

Atif the caretaker appeared in the doorway while she was chopping the green chillies. He lingered for a while in silence and then said, "I have children, grandchildren."

"I understand, I don't want trouble for you," said Facecream. "But before you go there's one thing I need to know. On the night Kamlesh was killed, did you see the Yadavs follow her out of the village?"

Atif shook his head. "No one followed her. They didn't do that thing."

"Do you know who did?"

"It wasn't anyone in the village," he said before turning and walking away.

Facecream lit a fire. Young twigs began to crackle in the flames.

"I know which bus she took," said Deep. "The bus conductor is my friend."

Facecream stopped what she was doing. "If you help me you'll have to leave the village for good," she cautioned him, her face half lit by the flames. "Are you ready to come with me to Delhi? You'll have to go to school and study. And you'll have to work as well."

"Work as what?"

"Helping me from time to time."

"Where would I live?"

"With me—if you behave yourself."

Deep grinned. "I'd like that," he said.

"Good. Now bring some bowls. First we're going to eat. And then you can tell me everything."

An hour later, Facecream and Deep climbed over the back wall of the school and made their way along a series of paths that led across the fields to the highway. They reached the back of the chai stand unseen and watched the buses and autos come and go.

Forty minutes later, Deep spotted the private bus Kamlesh Sunder had boarded on Saturday night. He and Facecream broke cover and scrambled on board, squeezing in amongst the passengers standing in the aisle.

The bus lurched forward, its stereo pumping out the theme tune to *Oye Lucky! Lucky Oye!*

"Are we going to Lucknow?" asked Facecream after Deep had spoken with his friend the conductor.

"She got off near the center of the city."

"Where exactly?"

The boy looked suddenly apprehensive. "Are you sure you want to know?" he asked.

Sixteen

Soon after Puri set off on the new Yamuna Expressway for Delhi, he realized he was being followed by a black SUV with tinted windows matching the description of the vehicle in which Ram had been abducted.

It had an untraceable number plate and a sticker at the top right of the windscreen printed with a unique code. He'd seen such stickers before: they served as notice to the police that the occupants were politically connected, meaning the vehicle wasn't to be stopped under any circumstances.

That the SUV made little attempt to conceal itself and simply shadowed the detective's vehicle at a respectable distance suggested three possibilities: the occupants weren't very good at surveillance, they were trying to intimidate him, or their intentions were altogether more sinister.

Perhaps they'd arranged for an accident up ahead? Collisions happened all the time. Indeed, in the last seconds as his life flashed behind his eyes, Puri might well find himself at a loss to know whether he'd met his end by his faceless enemy's design or whether he'd just been the victim of some idiot with kamikaze tendencies.

He considered stopping at the next petrol station or

resort-type place where there would be people around. But the expressway had opened only a few weeks earlier and none had yet been built. The detective therefore put his seat belt on, retrieved his pistol from his bag and warned his driver that they were being followed.

Puri soon wished that he hadn't said anything.

The driver, who looked terrified, couldn't keep his eyes off his rearview mirror (he didn't have side ones—they'd been shorn off during several close shaves) and stopped paying the requisite amount of attention to the road ahead. Given the numerous obstacles—including a herd of goats, an oncoming truck that had taken to the wrong side of the road and several homemade jugaad tractors that didn't differentiate between the slow and fast lanes despite moving at the speed of a petrol lawn mower—this resulted in four or five near misses. And when, ten miles into the journey, the SUV suddenly closed the distance between them, the driver looked like he was about to have a heart attack.

Puri, too, could feel his heart pounding like a dhol drum. As he cocked the trigger on his pistol and tried to keep one eye on the road ahead and the other on the vehicle behind, his hands shook badly.

If it came to it, he would aim for the tires and hope that his driver held his nerve and didn't lose control of the wheel, Puri decided.

In any event, the danger passed.

The SUV soon slowed and stopped to make a U-turn.

Puri watched it start back for Agra, puzzling over what had caused the occupants to break off their pursuit—and indeed whom they were working for. It wasn't Hari. Nor Vishnu Mishra. Perhaps ICMB?

But there was no profit to be gained in speculating. Tube-light's boys were already on their way to set up round-the-clock surveillance of the facility, so he would soon know either way.

Puri put his revolver back in his bag, yet kept his seat belt on, given that his driver's nerves seemed a little strained. He then took out the Shaadiwaadi.in business card he'd found in Dr. Basu's apartment and dialed the number.

A helpful manager soon came on the line and confirmed that Dr. Basu had been a client of his.

"And a contented one at that," he added. "She was getting engaged to a certain gentleman on our books. In fact, she had dinner with him that very night."

"Sir, it is of the utmost importance that I speak with this individual right away," stated Puri, and went on to explain his purpose for calling.

But the manager said he couldn't help. "There are privacy issues," he said.

"Sir, under normal circumstances I would respect your wishes. But understand this: Dr. Basu was murdered."

"Murdered?"

"Correct."

"By who?"

"That is my sworn duty to find out."

There was a long pause. "The best I can do is ask him to call you."

"Sooner the better."

It was almost dark by the time Puri reached Delhi. After paying the driver, who seemed positively relieved to be seeing the back of him, the detective traversed the busy pavement at the front of Khan Market. He stepped over the sleeping street dogs, scowled at the newest designer sunglasses shop to have replaced one of the old mummy-and-papa stores, almost fell into an open drain that was being excavated manually, and greeted Zahir, the blind shopkeeper, who welcomed him back with his customary good humor.

Elizabeth Rani was waiting upstairs in the small reception. She greeted him with the phrase "Sir, I'm afraid your rotis have gone stale."

This was code for "The office is bugged," and Puri responded with "Then we had better feed them to the crows, Madam Rani," to indicate that he had understood her.

He followed this up with "Kindly fetch some kathi rolls with extra chutney."

Elizabeth Rani shot him a puzzled look before realizing that the order contained no hidden meaning and promptly dispatched Door Stop, the office boy, to the market.

Entering his office, Puri found the walls bare, his secretary having put away all his accolades, including his signed and personalized Kenny G album cover and the photograph of him in his younger years posing next to Indira Gandhi. He went and washed his face in his "executive" bathroom. Then he called Rumpi.

"You made it, haan? Wonderful! How was the climb? You took horses, is it? But Mummy was determined to walk every foot of the way. Well, her years are fast advancing, I suppose. All well otherwise, my dear? Pardon? Chetan made it without collapsing, is it? Pukka? That is a bloody miracle if ever there was one!"

His next call was to a retired army batchmate and fellow member of the Gymkhana Club whom everyone called Pappi. Puri asked if he was busy and said that he had some work for him.

"That is assuming your wife hasn't got you on one of those bloody diets, you bugger."

A burst of raucous laughter came down the line.

"Tip-top. See you tomorrow ten o'clock. Usual place."

Elizabeth Rani stepped into the office and placed a file in front of him containing a short biography of Justus Bergstrom, the ICMB director. One section, which Puri's secretary had taken the trouble to highlight, provided details of his work in Ecuador, where he'd been accused of stealing DNA from a tribe living deep within the Amazon. In an attached news report Bergstrom was referred to as a "vampire" and a "racist." The Indigenous Peoples Council on Biocolonialism had called for his prosecution for crimes against humanity.

Puri put the report aside, turned on the TV and then headed into the communications room, which was protected by jamming equipment.

He found Flush working on a laptop.

"Tell me," said the detective.

"There's an IF beam pointed at your office window. State-of-the-art."

For once, Puri understood his brilliant young operative's lingo. IF stood for "infrared." It was his understanding that such beams were bounced off panes of glass, which acted as sound conductors and picked up the vibrations of people's voices.

"It's coming from where exactly?"

"A new Volkswagen van parked outside. Tinted windows."

"Untraceable number plate, is it?"

"Right, Boss."

"That is why the SUV turned around—they planned to pick up my trail this side," Puri said to himself. "Anything more is there?" he asked.

"I'm working on accessing the ICMB mainframe—sorry, computer system. But it's going to take some time."

"How much time?"

"Days, could be weeks, Boss. Decoding the system's going to take a lot of hair."

"Hair?"

"Never mind, Boss—hacker term. Basically, whoever built that system knew what they were doing."

Puri sighed. "Tell me some other progress is there."

"Yes and no. I got hold of Dr. Anju Basu's mobile phone records."

"Wonderful!"

"Just one problem."

"Don't tell me."

"Someone tampered with the records, erasing all the numbers dialed and received."

The detective groaned.

"See here," Flush continued as he ran his finger down the printout. "They're all gone."

"Arrey! What's the good news?"

"They failed to delete the call time figures at the bottom of the page." He pointed. "See here—it lists the total talk times of the five most popular numbers."

"Numbers are missing."

"They were deleted, also."

Puri's face was impassive. "Get to the point, yaar."

Flush reached for another printout. "This is Ram's phone record, Boss. His account was tampered with, also."

"That I know."

"See here at the bottom of the page. His total talk time is there also for his most popular five numbers."

The detective looked down at the top figure. It read: "03 hr 52 mins."

He felt a pang of excitement as he looked again at Dr. Basu's record. The number matched.

"By God, that cannot be a coincidence!" exclaimed Puri,

and gave his operative a slap on the back. "Tip-top work, yaar!" he added. "Now there can be no doubt. There was a connection between these two. Dots are starting to connect!"

They celebrated by scoffing down the kathi rolls brought by Door Stop.

Puri promptly sent the office boy back to the market for two more, as well as some sticky jalebis to share around.

Mummy and the family had maintained a constant pace throughout the afternoon, stopping only for lunch and a couple of saddle breaks. The Dughals had never been more than five minutes ahead, reaching the summit with a scant three-minute lead. With the sun setting over an ocean of frozen peaks stretching toward the horizon, the Puris and their faithful mounts finally found themselves being led along a series of narrow alleys that wound through a complex of buildings perched on the side of the mountain. Temples and restaurants were nestled with guesthouses and dhabas. Despite the presence of electricity and the occasional blaring TV, the place retained a distinctly medieval atmosphere. The sounds of worship, of yatris chanting and singing, and of bells pealing pervaded the place.

Mummy ensured that the Puris checked into the same guesthouse as the Dughals, which meant that they all had to share a single room.

The family deposited their bags, freshened up, and promptly set off again to reach the cave complex where their prebooked darshan tickets guaranteed them entry to the shrine at eight o'clock.

They joined a long queue that snaked up a series of steep steps and, over the next hour, inched slowly upward. The entrance to the cave was ornate and buzzing with excitement as hundreds of pilgrims waited to go inside. A curtain of plastic flowers hung around the mouth and a pair of golden lions stood sentinel on either side.

From her honeymoon, Mummy remembered a narrow entrance through which she'd had to squeeze herself in her bridal finery. But a larger tunnel now led to the sanctum inside the mountain. The chiming of tiny cymbals and the flickering light cast by flaming jyotis, or divine lamps, greeted them as they approached the shrine itself, flanked by a crush of other pilgrims. Lying within an alcove, they found three small rock formations representing shakti, the concept of divine, feminine creative power, each adorned with dazzling crowns and surrounded by a bed of red cloth with gold braid. Strings of marigolds and bunches of plastic mangoes and oranges hung from the rock ceiling above.

Each pilgrim was given but a few precious seconds in front of the sacred spot—barely enough time to seek the mother goddess's blessings before making a cash donation to a priest holding a brass tray. Mummy was the last to stand before the shrine, palms pressed together, her covered head bowed in obeisance. With a long line of yatris pressing impatiently behind her, she stepped aside and placed a five-hundred-rupee note on top of the pile lying thick upon the tray.

It was only then, by the light of the diyas burning in the cave, that she took note of the priest. He was dressed from top to bottom in red—tunic, dhoti, turban. But she recognized him instantly. It was Weasel Face.

Concealing her surprise, she left the cave bereft of the sense of fulfillment she'd experienced, albeit momentarily, while standing before the mother goddess.

"What's the matter, Mummy-ji?" asked Rumpi when she saw her troubled expression.

"It was him—from the train," she replied.

"Oh please, not this again."

They stopped halfway down the steps. The rest of the family had gone on ahead.

"He's a priest. Means he knows the place inside out."

"Mummy-ji, please, I'm exhausted and sore from all that riding. All I want to do is sleep," said Rumpi.

But her mother-in-law's mind was elsewhere. She'd spotted Weasel Face again, coming down the steps from the shrine. He and another priest were carrying two canvas sacks. The jingle-jangle sound these made was unmistakable: they were filled with coins.

"That is it!" Mummy exclaimed suddenly. "Dughal is planning to do robbery of the shrine! Imagine how much of cash the temple takes each and every day. Must be lakhs and lakhs at least."

Suddenly it all made sense. Weasel Face was the inside man. He'd provide Dughal with access to the temple coffers. They'd loot as much as they could carry and escape on the chartered helicopter.

Rumpi listened patiently to her explanation and then said, "Mummy-ji, I'm sure you're right. God only knows you have a nose for such things. But all I care about now is sleep. Let's rest 'til morning and then—I promise—I'll do whatever I can to help."

At about the same time that Rumpi and the rest of the family (bar Mummy) were settling down for a fitful night's sleep, Facecream and Deep's bus crawled through Lucknow's evening traffic.

They got down from the bus outside an ordinary office block with four floors and air-conditioning units jutting from windows.

Only it was no ordinary building. Fixed to the railings were big portraits of Uttar Pradesh chief minister Baba

Dhobi. Above the entrance was a sign spelling out the name of his political party.

"She came here—to his political headquarters?" asked Facecream as they stood on the pavement.

"Baba Dhobi was here that night," said Deep. "One evening a week he sits here and people come to tell him their problems and ask for help."

Sirens sounded down the street and a cavalcade of vehicles appeared moving toward them. Like any Indian government cavalcade, it swept along at high speed with total disregard for everything in its path. The lead car, an Ambassador, was packed with peons and secretaries, two of whom leant out the window signaling wildly for people to get out of the way. Behind them rode two more Ambassadors packed with special protection officers, the barrels of their machine guns protruding from open windows. Then came a couple of police jeeps with whirring red beacons on their rooftops, four motorbike outriders, a black BMW, and finally another couple of Ambassadors with yet more functionaries gesticulating as if any further warning of their approach were needed.

Security guards bustled Facecream and Deep down the pavement as the cavalcade screeched to a halt in front of the building. The special protection officers got out and took position around the BMW. A back door was opened and Facecream immediately recognized the figure who stepped out. Dressed in a simple white dhoti with tufts of hair growing from his ears, Baba Dhobi was dwarfed by the officers. Yet they had to hurry to keep up with him as he strode purposefully toward the building. The bevy of secretaries and peons all clutching files, clipboards and briefcases followed behind, leaving the police and drivers to their idle banter and packets of Gold Flake cigarettes.

"How do you know Kamlesh got inside?" Facecream asked Deep after the street had returned to normal.

His answer was drowned out by passing traffic. But Facecream didn't ask him to repeat himself. Something had caught her attention—something that sent a chill down her spine to the tips of her toes.

Discreetly, she pulled out her khukuri and handed it to the boy. Then she told him to wait and approached the building. At the entrance, a security guard waved a metal-detector wand in front of her. It emitted a beep a couple of times. A female security guard gave her a pat-down. Facecream was cleared to enter and stepped up to a small desk. A bored-looking functionary sat with a phone and a thick visitors ledger before him. Facecream told him that she wanted to make a donation to the party.

"Fourth floor, room seventeen," he said with impatience, before writing down her name and designation.

Then he said, "Show me your hand."

Facecream reached out with her right one. The man pressed a rubber stamp onto the skin.

She'd been branded: a smiley face in black indelible ink.

Seventeen

Tubelight's boys Shashi and Zia had opted for ragpicker disguises and, having purchased an old wooden barrow from a bemused kabari wallah in an Agra slum, set up camp on an undeveloped plot of land across from the entrance to the ICMB compound. The guards paid them no heed, even when the two passed the gates in their rags, asking if they had any plastic or paper that needed hauling away. The duo proceeded to collect all the trash that lay scattered across the plot and make piles of it outside the primitive tarpaulin tent they'd erected.

"What is this place Swi-dan?" Shashi asked Zia once they were settled around a fire with their spotting scope, disguised inside a cardboard roll, trained on the gates.

Zia rolled his eyes. "It's a country, you idiot."

"Where?"

"Find out yourself."

"Ha, I knew it, you don't know!"

"I know that it's a country, which is more than you."

The two didn't speak for a minute or so. Through the scope, Zia watched the guards standing around, chatting and laughing. He noted that there were five in all.

"So what do you call a Swi-dan person?" asked Shashi.

"Listen, yaar, we've been here only one hour and already I'm getting sick of your questions," complained Zia.

"Please, oh Baba, share with me your wisdom!"

Zia sighed. "Someone from Swi-dan is a Swi-dan-i. Like those from Pakistan are Pakistan-i, those from Kashmir are Kashmir-i," he said with confidence.

"Like Angrez are Angrezi?"

"Right."

"So these Swi-dan-i, they're goras?"

"Pure Aryan."

"They play cricket?"

"Of course."

"What do they eat?"

"What do all goras eat, yaar? Bland things—ham-bugg-ar, boiled subzi."

A vehicle was leaving the ICMB compound. Its headlights pierced the gap between the gates like sun through a forest canopy. A sedan appeared. Zia read the number plate and checked it with the one listed on Most Private Investigators' copy of the national car owners' database. It was a Skoda belonging to Dr. Sengupta, the head of research.

"That's the Bong scientist," he said. "I'll take him. Watch for the Swi-dan-i—and don't forget to write down the number plates of other vehicles coming and going. Note the time, too. It's ten thirty."

"Ten-four."

"No, *ten thirty*, idiot!" cursed Zia.

He jumped onto one of the two Vespa scooters they'd parked out of sight and sped off in pursuit. When the geneticist stopped at a red light, the operative pulled up behind his car and attached a homemade magnetic GPS tracking device to the bottom of the rear bumper. The operative was then

able to follow from a safe distance and, twenty minutes later, stopped unnoticed outside Dr. Sengupta's house.

The door was opened by a frail, gray-haired lady in a sari.

"Sorry I'm late, Maa. I got caught up at work," Zia heard the Bong say as he removed his shoes and stooped down to touch her feet.

Mummy couldn't have hoped for a better room. It was on the ground floor of the guesthouse five doors down from the Dughals. The corridor running between them provided the only way of reaching the reception and entrance beyond. There was no other exit.

While the rest of the family slept, Mummy kept vigil, watching for any movement in the corridor through a gap in the door. The Vaishno Devi shrine was open to worshippers around the clock and a number of guests came and went in the middle of the night. An elderly couple set off around eleven thirty and returned an hour and a half later. At one A.M. a young woman wearing a backpack made her way down the corridor and was gone approximately two hours. And at five o'clock a bleary-eyed family of six emerged from the adjacent room and staggered past the Puris' door, yawning and rubbing their eyes.

Mummy had to wait all night, until six thirty in fact, for a glimpse of Pranap Dughal. And then all he did was walk the short distance to reception.

By turning up her hearing aid full volume, Mummy overheard him telling the clerk on duty that he and his wife would be checking out at seven and that they'd need a few porters. After that, he stepped into the street to smoke a cigarette and, five minutes later, returned to his room.

Mummy caught a snatch of Mrs. Dughal's scolding voice before the door closed.

A few minutes later, Rumpi awoke. "Mummy-ji, don't tell me you've been sitting there all night," she said.

Her mother-in-law gave a sheepish nod. It was beginning to look as if she'd got the wrong end of the stick again.

"Perhaps he met that priest on the train by chance and was just getting some friendly advice on how to carry out the pilgrimage," suggested Rumpi.

"Could be," conceded Mummy.

"It's also entirely possible that he bought those sleeping tablets to make sure that his wife sleeps soundly. I wouldn't want to be woken by her in the middle of the night."

"Also true."

"Then why don't you come and lie down? You look exhausted."

The thought of sleep felt suddenly irresistible. "You are right," said Mummy-ji. "Bed rest is required. Just I'll sleep for one hour or so. What is the harm?"

She started to unpack her nightie but was distracted by the sound of porters in the lane and looked out the window. The Dughals' bags were already being loaded onto a pack mule.

"Must be getting senile, na," Mummy commented as she lay down and closed her eyes.

Mummy wasn't the only Puri to have gone without sleep. Facecream's disturbing revelation about Kamlesh going to see Baba Dhobi had kept her boss up all night.

Puri had tried everything to put himself under: a few Patiala pegs, counting the stars, even reading a mind-numbingly tedious account by a senior journalist about his experiences covering Indian politics over the past forty years.

Finally, at first light, he gave up, woke the servant girl and got her to make him a cup of chai, and then took it up onto the flat roof of his house.

Standing there watching the sun break over Delhi's southern suburbs, he met the dawn with a grim countenance. It was true that nothing was proven yet. For all he knew, Kamlesh had entered Baba Dhobi's party headquarters, failed to meet with him and then been sent on her way. Some time later, she could have been picked up off the street and murdered by someone else who'd sought to put the blame on Vishnu Mishra. But the expression on her dead face said otherwise.

Puri could read it clearly now. It had been engendered by betrayal. A Dalit who'd been oppressed all her life, treated worse than the stray dogs in the village, had gone to see the one person in the world she believed she could trust. She'd asked Baba Dhobi, the self-proclaimed messiah of the Dalits, for help. Yet within a few hours Kamlesh Sunder, an innocent midwife, had been brutally murdered. How had Chanakya put it?

"There is poison in the fang of the serpent, in the mouth of the fly and in the sting of a scorpion; but the wicked man is saturated with it."

Had the yet-to-be-identified item buried behind her house sealed her fate? If so, what was it? And why would she have taken it to Baba Dhobi?

Puri stopped himself from speculating any further and turned his attention to his chilli plants. The squall four days earlier had deposited a layer of sand and grime on the leaves, and he went about cleaning them with a spray bottle of water. He found the process soothing. Indeed, by the time he got round to affixing tiny bamboo splints to the stems that had been damaged in the high winds, he found that the despondency he'd struggled with all night had begun to dissipate.

Something else, though, was gnawing at him: that conversation with Dr. Sengupta at ICMB. It seemed simply incredible that from a single drop of blood scientists could tell you more about yourself than you had ever known. It was almost as if they could look into your soul.

Puri understood why such genetic scrutiny would put many Indians off. He himself was immensely proud of being from the Kshatriya warrior caste, a pedigree that was an intrinsic part of his identity. What if he found out there was nothing to it? That far from bravely fighting for their way of life, once upon a time his ancestors had been simple buffalo herders? Puri certainly wouldn't want other people knowing such a thing.

He could think of others for whom caste was sacred. Take a Brahmin politician like Dr. Pandey, for example. His entire persona was founded on the exploitation of caste, of pitting himself and his supporters against the lower castes whom, if his rhetoric was to be believed, were out to steal their jobs. What if it emerged that he was actually one of *them*, his own blood tainted by, say, lowly Jat genes?

Were caste secrets the key? Was someone trying to cover up a genetic revelation that Dr. Basu had stumbled across?

Puri picked a couple of ripe Scotch bonnets for his breakfast and made his way back downstairs. Sleep would come easily to him now, but it was fast approaching seven o'clock and he needed to head into central Delhi. He took a quick bucket bath and donned a gray safari suit and matching cap, then set off in his Ambassador.

Following behind were the Volkswagen van that had been parked outside Khan Market last night and a black sedan with tinted windows and Uttar Pradesh plates. Puri suspected this belonged to Vishnu Mishra's goon Naga. Evidently he'd managed to get hold of the detective's residential address and now seemed to be taking a nonviolent approach, presumably hoping that Puri would lead him to either Ram or Tulsi.

"How do you want me to drive, Boss?" asked Handbrake.

"Normal driving," said the detective, who was acting under the assumption that Hari's people were keeping tabs on him as well.

Normal driving meant driving like everyone else—in other words, winding through traffic without signaling, straddling two lanes at once, flashing "dippers" at any car that dared to get in the way, honking incessantly, jumping queues at red lights and wherever possible blocking everyone behind trying to go straight ahead.

Anything that varied from this—like responsible "lane driving"—might raise the suspicions of those tailing him, Puri reasoned. And for now at least, he was happy to play Pied Piper.

His first stop was the R. K. Puram government administrative complex, where he found Lakshman in his usual spot under the banyan tree making paranthas in his makeshift kitchen. He ordered two of the aloo variety, which he quickly devoured with a goodly helping of garlic pickle.

Tubelight called while he was eating to tell him about a breakthrough in Agra. His boys had spotted a black SUV with tinted windows leaving the compound.

"Same number plate as the one that followed you, Boss."

Puri didn't sound in the least surprised. "Seems I went and shook the right tree for sure," he said. "How about Dr. Pandey? Any dirty linen?"

Tubelight gave a sigh. "Boss, where to begin?" he said. "Pandey's into everything. He's got companies registered even in the names of his drivers and maids. They say the mattresses in his home are all stuffed with cash."

"Any person in his company fits the profile of the killer?"

"There's no one so tall, Boss. Plus, Pandey is smart. He'd use a professional."

"A contractor?"

"Probably an Afridi. Those people are tall. But, Boss, no one in that community will talk."

Puri lapsed into prolonged thought. In light of Facecream's revelation about Ram's mother having gone to see Chief Minister Baba Dhobi, any further investigation into Dr. Pandey seemed unwarranted. There could surely be no connection between the two. One Dalit, the other Brahmin, they were sworn political enemies.

Tubelight's time would be better spent in Agra.

"Let us focus on this ICMB," said Puri. "I want to know how many sugars that gora director has in his coffee. Same goes for the head of research, Dr. Sengupta. Something was there in his eyes—something . . . wrong."

Twenty minutes later, with the white Volkswagen and the black sedan still tailing him, Puri's Ambassador pulled up outside the toilet complex at Sarojini Nagar bus depot. It was operated by Sulabh, a charity, and unlike the pitiful public toilets "maintained" by the Delhi civic authorities, the place was clean.

Inside, the detective found one of the two cubicles free. Sitting down on the toilet, he began to hum one of his favorite old Raj Kapoor songs, "Mera Joota Hai Japani."

A man's voice responded. "All OK?"

It was Pappi. He was sitting in the other cubicle.

"World-class. Your good self?"

"Thirsty. You owe me a drink, you bugger."

"Definitely. Once the case is gotten over. Best of luck, haan."

The man who stepped out of the toilet complex could have been Puri's identical twin. Their faces were uncannily similar, they were the same height and build, and it would have taken a sharp-eyed observer indeed to notice the minor difference in the curl of Pappi's moustache, the paler dye of his safari suit or the fact that his aviator shades were replicas rather than genuine Ray-Bans.

As he crossed the pavement and approached the Ambassador, Pappi mimicked the detective's walk, pitching slightly to his right each time his left foot made contact with the ground. He waited for Handbrake to open the door for him, glanced up and down the street and then sat on the left-hand side of the backseat.

In order to leave his audience in absolutely no doubt that it was Vish Puri whom they were pursuing, Pappi then drove to the nearest Tibb's and ordered a chicken frankie. From there, he planned to lead Puri's tails on a merry dance around South Delhi.

The real detective remained in his cubicle for a few minutes out of necessity. Once he'd washed his hands and paid the janitor, he stepped onto the street and hailed an auto. His destination was Nizamuddin East, a so-called colony of South Delhi. But just in case one of Hari's people had got wise to the switch, he told the driver to take him to INA Market. There, he wove a path through the labyrinth of ramshackle stalls, stepping over live chickens and open drains and ignoring touts offering everything from cans of imported baked beans and Iranian pistachios to cheap bras. He then headed down into the Delhi metro and took the train one stop to Jor Bagh. From there, he hired a taxi from the nearby stand.

He was about halfway to his destination when his phone rang. It was an Agra number.

"This is Satyajit Dasgupta. I got a message from Shaadi-waadi saying I should call you—regarding Anju?"

He was referring to Dr. Basu.

"You two were going the marriage way, I understand?" asked Puri.

"Yes, that's right."

"How long you had known her, might I ask?"

"A few weeks."

Nothing untypical about two people getting married so quickly even amongst the educated elite, reflected Puri. "It is my understanding you were with her the night she met her death," he said.

"Do you mind telling me what this is about? The man at Shaadiwaadi said you believe it *wasn't* an accident?"

"I do not believe—I know for certain."

"You're saying Anju was murdered?"

"Correct."

"What makes you say that?"

Puri explained his reasoning and asked whether Dasgupta knew of anyone who would want to murder her.

"I can't think of anyone," he said. "She was such a warm, caring person."

"Dr. Basu was content with her working situation, is it?"

"Well, no, not entirely. She was leaving her job, in fact. I think there were personal issues."

"She mentioned any one individual?"

"She wouldn't have discussed that sort of thing. We'd only met a few times."

"A marriage of convenience, so to speak?"

"I don't see the relevance of that question."

Puri felt like pointing out that it was entirely relevant. Dasgupta might well have killed Dr. Basu himself, and that made the nature of their relationship relevant. But he let it go for now.

"What all were your movements the night she died?"

"We had dinner at Silk Route."

"What time exactly?"

"I got there at nine."

"And Dr. Basu?"

"She was already at the table."

"What time you left?"

"Almost eleven, I think."

"She drove herself, is it?"

"That's right."

"She had some drink?"

"Drink? Anju was strictly teetotal."

Puri thanked him for his time and was about to hang up when Dasgupta suddenly remembered something.

"When I arrived at the restaurant, she was sitting with someone—a young man," he said. "He got up and left after I arrived."

"You saw what he looked like, what all he was wearing?"

Dasgupta proceeded to provide an exact description of Ram Sunder. He then asked Puri whether he thought the young man could be the murderer.

"In point of fact, no. But it is entirely possible he knows the identity of the killer," answered the detective.

"You mean you haven't spoken with him?"

"He's missing, in fact."

"Since when?"

"Saturday."

"But I saw him last night."

"Pardon?" Puri felt stunned.

"I went to see a movie and he was outside hanging around. He was wearing a baseball cap, but it was definitely the same guy."

The detective didn't know whether to celebrate or scold himself for being a damn fool.

"Which theater exactly?" he asked.

"Sanjay Cinema."

"Sanjay Cinema! Of course! Tulsi said they were regulars!" Puri almost howled.

He thanked Dasgupta profusely, hung up the phone and gave himself a light slap on the forehead. How could he have been so slow on the uptake? Ram had escaped his abductors and gone to ground. Everyone else—Hari, ICMB, no doubt Vishnu Mishra, too—had figured it out. No doubt they all imagined that Ram was his client and were hoping he'd lead them to him.

Puri felt the lack of sleep suddenly catching up with him and made an unscheduled stop at one of the posh, over-priced coffee shops that had sprung up all over Delhi in the past few years. He downed two double "expressos" and felt the caffeine revitalize his system as assuredly as the magic potion in *Asterix*. It was then that he realized his advantage. He was holding a trump card—the Queen of Hearts. And that might—just might—give him the edge.

Rumpi burst into the room.

"Mummy-ji, wake up! You were right!"

She knelt down next to her mother-in-law and took her by the arms. "Can you hear me? I said you were right. And he's getting away!"

The rest of the family stirred from their slumber.

"Who's getting away?" Chetan yawned from his pillow.

"The shrine's been looted exactly as Mummy predicted!" Rumpi gave her mother-in-law another shake. "You've got to wake up. I'm sorry! I should have listened to you."

Her mother-in-law's eyes flickered open. "What is that you said?"

Rumpi repeated her news and this time Mummy sat up. "But the whole night long Dughal was very much present in his room," she said.

"It can't be a coincidence, it just can't," said Rumpi.

Mummy stepped into the bathroom to change into her

clothes. "What time it is?" she asked when she emerged, now fully alert to the crisis.

"Quarter to eight."

"Must be he is planning to abscond by helicopter!"

She and Rumpi hurried out of the guesthouse and made their way up the hill. It took them ten minutes to reach the helipad. They found the Dughals, together with their porters and baggage, waiting on the far side of the landing area.

Mummy and Rumpi attempted to reach them but were prevented from doing so by two security guards, who pointed up at the sky at a helicopter that was preparing to land.

The downward thrust of its blades forced the ladies to turn away and put their backs to the wind, their chunnis beating against their shoulders like flags caught in a gale. Shielding their eyes, they watched over their shoulders as the helicopter touched down, the door opened—and out stepped none other than Inspector Malhotra of the Jammu force.

Much to Mummy and Rumpi's delight, he, together with three jawans, made a beeline for the Dughals. He interrogated them for a few minutes and their bags were searched. Even the contents of Mrs. Dughal's handbag were given a thorough inspection. Nothing untoward was discovered, however. No bundles of notes, coins or gold. Just packets of diet candy bars (the jawans ripped open each and every one) and dozens of blister strips of weight-loss pills.

By the time the helicopter blades had come to a stop and Mummy and Rumpi were able to circumnavigate the helipad, Inspector Malhotra had excused the couple.

"But, Inspector, I'm telling you he's the one," protested Mummy. "He was working with one pandit. The other one on the train. I witnessed them doing discussion of the robbery plan and such."

Before Malhotra could reply, Pranap Dughal himself objected.

"Inspector, I've had enough of this woman's accusations," he said. "First she accuses me of stealing her son's wallet. Now of robbing the temple."

"She's out of her mind!" screeched Mrs. Dughal. "She's been following us wherever we go!"

"That's right—even watching us through the gap in her door. I want to make an official complaint!"

"Is this true, madam?" asked Malhotra.

Mummy held her head a little straighter. "Responsibility is on my shoulders, na," she said in a defiant tone.

The inspector placed his hand on the back of her arm and gently led her away. "Madam, I will not tolerate interference with police business," he said once they were out of earshot of the Dughals. "I request you to return to your guesthouse."

"But Dughal did hiring of one helicopter. Just he'll be getting away."

"Rest assured, madam, I have closed all airspace. Like everyone else, including your good self, the Dughals will have to leave on foot."

Malhotra signaled to his jawans and they all marched off in the direction of the shrine.

The porters repacked the Dughals' belongings and the couples' caravan started down the mountain path.

Rumpi watched them leave with a puzzled frown.

"I told you this Dughal is a clever one," said Mummy.

"But if he didn't leave his room all night and he doesn't have the loot, then surely he wasn't involved."

"Definitely he is involved."

"Then where's the money?"

"Just we must find out, na—and the clock is doing tick-tock."

Eighteen

After their success in tracing Kamlesh's last steps, Facecream and Deep had spent Tuesday night in a cheap hotel in Lucknow.

They returned to the school at seven A.M. and found the gates wide open.

Papers and activity books were scattered across the compound. Facecream's clothes, bedding and suitcase lay in a blackened, smoldering pile beneath the banyan tree. In the classroom, they found all the chairs upended. The packets of chalk had been crushed, the pieces of slate snapped in two.

The kitchen had fared no better, with all the pots and utensils pulled off their shelves and the clay water-storage vessel smashed to pieces. The food Facecream had bought—rice, oil, ghee, pulses—was all gone.

"They'll be back," said Deep. "And if they find you here, they'll kill you."

Facecream knew he was right, that the smart thing to do was to gather up any belongings that had survived and turn right around and flee. Puri wanted her back in Lucknow, where there was still a killer to track down. But she couldn't bring herself to go without at least saying good-bye. She'd raised the expectations of the children, and even some of their parents.

Keeping Deep here, however, was far too risky.

"I want you to take your bike, go up the lane and wait for me next to that little bridge over the irrigation channel," she told him. "You know the one? Good. Keep out of sight. If I don't join you in two hours, you're to take my phone and call this number here." She showed him Puri's entry on her mobile. "That's my boss. Explain to him what's happened and he'll send help. Here's some money."

"I want to stay—you might need me," said Deep.

"You've helped enough. Now do as I say."

The boy shifted his weight from one leg to the other and pouted.

"I said go!" she ordered.

He gave a slow, heavy nod and walked over to where his bike lay on its side. It had escaped any serious damage at the hands of the Yadav goons. After straightening out the handlebars, he strapped on his blocks.

"Please hurry," he said, addressing her for the first time as "didi"—"sister."

"Keep yourself hidden," she said. "I'll join you soon."

Facecream watched him go and then set to work. Having dowsed her smoldering belongings with a bucket of water, she set about collecting up all the pieces of paper. It took twenty minutes to straighten out the classroom and make a tidy pile of the broken slates and chalk.

By eight o'clock, she was ready to greet her students and sat waiting beneath the banyan tree. But not a single child appeared—nor any women seeking her advice or help. Rakesh Yadav had warned them off.

She'd been beaten; it was time to face it. The odds were insurmountable. Facecream tied up her few remaining belong-

ings in a bundle and left the compound, her eyes brimming
with tears. Without looking back, she started up the lane to
find Deep. But after less than a hundred yards, she stopped
suddenly. To the right, a path led through the fields. She hesitated for a moment, struggling with her convictions. Then she
turned off the lane and hid her bundle beneath some straw.
With her khukuri sticking out of the front of her belt, she
searched for a way down to the river. She was going to skirt
around the village to reach the Dalit ghetto. She'd have her
say. Then it was up to them.

Delhi's arbitrary zoning laws prevented businesses from
operating in residential areas, yet the authorities turned a
blind eye to doctors, architects and lawyers operating out
of basements. Some of the city's top advocates were to be
found working underground, a phenomenon that had always struck Puri as ironic and, in many cases, appropriate.

Ramesh Jindal's address was in B Block, Nizamuddin
East, which boasted well-tended gardens used exclusively
by the residents. Bordered on the north by the magnificent sixteenth-century tomb of the Mughal emperor Hum-
ayun, and the Nizamuddin railway station to the east, it was
termed a "posh" or "upscale" colony with the odd foreign
correspondent sprinkled amidst a predominantly aging Punjabi population.

Puri found a house number on the outside of the building but no sign indicating that Jindal's chambers lay within.
Through a letterbox window at the foot of the building,
however, he spied shelves lined with bound leather tomes
and a couple of young men in black trousers and white shirts
who looked a bit like human penguins.

Passing through a dirty ground-level parking area and
stepping over a mangy cur that lay curled up on a doormat,

the detective descended a narrow stairwell. The door at the bottom opened into a small, brightly lit reception that was conventionally furnished. A pretty young receptionist's eyes appeared over a marble countertop.

Puri didn't have an appointment, he explained, but wished to speak with Jindal on a "most important and pressing matter, actually."

"It is regarding the death of Dr. Anju Basu," he added.

The receptionist promptly picked up a phone and, reading the detective's name from his card, communicated his request.

"Sir asked you please wait" was the verdict.

The fact that she'd provided no indication whether the wait would be ten minutes or until nightfall neither surprised nor fazed him. Information was never a commodity readily shared in India, least of all by receptionists. Puri was just grateful that she hadn't sent him packing and, having settled himself into one of the comfortable chairs in front of her desk, set his mind to figuring out how best to tackle Jindal. He'd learned from a couple of contacts that he was a top criminal lawyer and had defended some especially unsavory characters in his time, including the son of a cabinet minister charged with shooting dead a young socialite woman at a function. In recent years he'd also had some success with public litigation cases. He was currently arguing before the Supreme Court on behalf of a village of tribals in Odisha who claimed a steel plant had poisoned the local water supply.

Was it this expertise that had brought Dr. Basu to his door—that is, assuming their meeting had gone ahead? Puri knew now that she'd been planning to leave ICMB. Had she also been planning on blowing the whistle on their practices? Was that what had got her killed? And Ram abducted?

"Mere speculation, Vish Puri, saar!" the detective admonished himself.

Still, he needed to tread carefully. Jindal might have sold Dr. Basu out. The idea of a criminal lawyer being duplicitous was hardly beyond the realm of imagination, or indeed experience.

"Casting nets into unfamiliar waters runs the risk of catching hungry piranhas," he reminded himself.

Jindal's office was no bigger than five meters across but the split air conditioner unit was working full blast. Puri, who'd waited just forty-five minutes before being shown inside, felt as if he'd stepped into a freezer. The lawyer himself looked like he'd been frozen solid behind his desk. His hands, which resembled claws, were resting on their backs, the fingers curled inward. Shocks of white ran along the tops of his moustache and eyebrows like dustings of snow. When he turned his head to appraise his visitor, his shoulders barely moved. The detective could have sworn he heard the man's neck give a creak.

"Forgive me if I don't stand up," said Jindal, who looked to be Puri's senior by some twenty years, which put him in his early seventies. "I suffer from acute arthritis."

The detective felt like saying, "Hardly surprising given how bloody thanda it is in here." But instead he thanked Jindal for making time to see him, placed his business card on the desk and, having pulled up a chair, wrapped his safari jacket tight around him.

"'Most Private Investigators, confidentiality is our watchword,'" read the lawyer from Puri's card in a stultified monotone.

Ordinarily before getting down to business, it was customary in Delhi to try to establish social or work-related links between the two parties. Typically Jindal, being the host, might ask where his visitor had grown up and what school he'd attended. Puri might then make reference to his membership in the Gymkhana Club and, by and by, some link would be found that would help break the ice and possibly establish some measure of trust.

The lawyer, however, dispensed with the preliminaries and simply asked, "And you are here because of . . . ?"

Puri suspected that he had little regard for private detectives, but the man's demeanor was abstruse.

"I'm investigating the death of Dr. Anju Basu, sir," he answered.

"On whose behalf?"

Puri skirted the question, adding, "Sir, I believe she was murdered."

Jindal's features displayed as much surprise as they appeared capable of, his left eyebrow arching upward a couple of millimeters before settling back down again. "I see," he said. "And why are you telling me?"

Puri took out the copy of Jindal's business card and pushed it across the desk. "I found this in her apartment," he said. "Last Monday's date is written on the back in fountain pen—one with a fine nib like the Montblanc lying there on your blotting pad. The writing is somewhat spidery in nature. Now that I see your arthritic hands it explains exactly and precisely why."

A subtle change came over Jindal's expression. The detective couldn't tell whether it was derived from admiration or unease.

"It would appear you are swimming in dangerous waters, Mr. Puri—if, as you say, Dr. Basu was murdered," said the lawyer.

"That is something to which I am well accustomed. Danger is my ally."

"You neglected to name your client."

"In this case I am simply a concerned citizen of India. My time is being given freely."

"In my experience, nothing is ever given entirely freely, Mr. Puri. You will surely be looking to derive some gain from this affair."

"Sir, no financial gain will come my way, let me assure you."

Jindal brought the tips of his twisted fingers together. He looked like an ancient chess master contemplating his next move. "If it's information you want, Mr. Puri, I'm likely to disappoint you," he said.

"Dr. Basu was your client, sir?"

"I'm not at liberty to say."

"But you met with her, is it?"

Jindal's answer was preceded by a nod of the head. "I did. On two occasions."

Progress. "You mind telling me what all you discussed?" asked the detective.

"Again, I'm not at liberty to say."

Puri felt like he was playing twenty questions. "She required help?" he asked.

"Advice."

"Regarding the nature of her research?"

"Mr. Puri, I am not empowered to divulge the details of our conversation."

The detective frowned. Something didn't make sense here. If Dr. Basu was deceased, then there was no reason for Jindal to be so secretive. Unless . . .

"Sir, was Dr. Basu by chance accompanied by a young man by the name of Ram Sunder?"

Jindal looked the detective directly in the eye. "She was."

Ram Sunder had sat here in this very office. *He* was Jindal's client.

"You've heard from him since, sir?"

"I have not."

"You were expecting to hear from him, is it?"

"I was."

"When exactly?"

The lawyer considered the question for a moment. "Towards the end of last week," he said.

Dr. Basu had been killed in the early hours of Thursday. Ram had been abducted on Saturday. In between, he hadn't been in touch with Jindal. That suggested that the young Dalit didn't trust his lawyer—suspected him of betraying their confidence.

Puri tried a different tack. "Some question is there you wish to put to me, sir?" he asked.

Jindal's enigmatic eyes dwelled on Puri. "I do have one question to put to you," he said. "You said you believe Dr. Basu was murdered. Do you have evidence to corroborate your assertion?"

"Circumstantial evidence, only," admitted Puri before going on to explain why he believed the "accident" had been nothing of the sort.

"Her apartment was ransacked also," he added.

"I take it you mean broken into and searched?"

"Correct."

"Did you report this crime to the police?"

"The building manager did so."

"This was when?"

"Yesterday morning, only."

Jindal reached for an untouched glass of water that sat on a coaster on his desk. He wrapped one hand around it, brought it to his lips and took a sip.

"Another question has occurred to me, if you will allow me," he said as he replaced the glass.

"Pleasure, sir."

"Were you followed on your way here, Mr. Puri?"

"I took certain precautions, sir."

"Very sensible. I believe it would be in both our interests to keep this conversation between ourselves. Are we in agreement?"

"Most certainly, sir."

"Good." Jindal looked at the clock on the wall. "And now I must wish you a good day, Mr. Puri. I have another appointment."

The detective stood from his chair but lingered before Jindal's desk. The lawyer didn't strike him as the type to betray a client's trust. He was scrupulous in his dealings and evidently concerned for his own safety.

Puri decided to take a chance.

"One more question is there," he said. "You are doubtless aware Ram Sunder is missing?"

"Yes, I believe I read as much in today's newspaper," answered Jindal.

"Sir, it is imperative that I locate him without delay. Other parties are searching for him, also. It is no exaggeration to say that he is facing the gravest of dangers. His mother was murdered on Saturday, only. Therefore, should you be in possession of any means of contacting him, I respectfully request you to do so on my behalf."

"If Mr. Sunder contacts me, I will relay your message. But as I indicated earlier, he hasn't tried to reach me these past few days."

This seemed as much cooperation as he could expect and Puri thanked him for his time and left.

He reached the top of the stairs, emerging into the warm outside air. He stopped, suddenly struck by an alarming thought: Could Hari be working for the lawyer? Had he inadvertently shown him his hand?

206

Facecream covered her head in a chunni that had survived Yadav's wanton vandalism and took a wide circle through the fields until she reached the riverbank. A diminished brook meandered down the middle of wide, sandy beds dotted with rust-colored boulders. Downstream, amidst a rippling haze of heat, she could make out a few trucks super-imposed against a bridge and what appeared to be an army of ants, some digging, others walking back and forth with pans of shale balanced on their heads.

A well-worn path led along the bank through the abundant tropical vegetation. With every other step Facecream disturbed some form of fauna. Butterflies with wings as richly patterned as Persian carpets fluttered into the air. A mongoose scurried through the undergrowth. Further on, a family of monkeys objected to her presence, screeching at her from up in a tree.

A breeze brought with it the same sour vinegary smell she'd detected on her first morning in the village. It got stronger as she drew nearer to a small brick building that had been constructed amidst a copse of trees, effectively camouflaging it from the air or indeed the nearest road.

Facecream crossed some well-worn tire tracks leading to the riverbank and then ducked down out of sight. She'd spotted a couple of men standing outside the building. They were both wearing white masks over the lower half of their faces, but she recognized one of them as Rakesh Yadav. He and the other man talked for a couple of minutes, their words too hard to make out. Then Yadav walked off in the direction of the village, while the other man put on a pair of plastic goggles and went inside.

Facecream stole forward to get a closer look. There were a few rusty barrels stacked against an outside wall. They had leaked something corrosive onto the ground. She knew what the smell was now—acetic anhydride. That explained why Yadav and one of his goons had blemishes on their hands. Even from ten meters, Facecream could feel a burning at the back of her throat.

Keeping low, she stole past the building unseen and continued along the path. Half a mile farther on, she spied five or six women crouched by a pool of water in the middle of the riverbank. Recognizing two of them as Dalit mothers with children enrolled at the school, she strode across the sand toward them.

"Why did you not bring your children this morning?" demanded Facecream, her anger suddenly spilling out.

The women carried on with their washing, eyes downcast.

"Answer me," she insisted.

"We were told the school is closed," said one of the women, whose name was Poonam.

"You were threatened?"

She replied with a jiggle of her head and then went back to scrubbing a shirt.

Facecream stood over them in silence for a few seconds. The rhythmic sound of their washing echoed the grinding poverty in which they were trapped.

"You came to me for help," said Facecream. "But I cannot help you unless you are willing to make some effort yourself."

"It's not safe for you to remain in the village," said Poonam.

"I know. I'm leaving. But I can still help you if you are willing."

She took a business card from her pocket and handed it to her.

"Here, take this. It's an address in Lucknow. Go there and ask for Kukreja Madam. Tell her I sent you. She knows about your case. She will give you the help and advice you need."

Poonam took the card and slipped it inside her sari blouse and continued with her washing.

Facecream lingered for just a few more seconds, then turned and followed her tracks back across the sand.

Puri needed a stiff drink. Fortunately, he was headed to the Gymkhana Club, the one place in Delhi where members were served throughout the day, indeed the one place in the hectic, burgeoning capital that offered a certain tranquillity and civility sorely lacking in today's crass society, assuming you didn't run into the harridan wife of Col. P. V. S. Gill (Retd.), of course.

Puri was soon standing in reception checking the typed notices pinned to the bulletin board. A new one had gone up since the detective had last checked. It appealed to male members not to clear their noses into the basins of the cloakroom while other members were present. Keeping this in mind, and praying that the rubber soles of his orthopedic shoes wouldn't attract the attention of Mrs. Col. P. V. S. Gill (Retd.), who was no doubt lurking somewhere about the club just waiting for an opportunity to catch him on some alleged violation of club rules, he proceeded to the Terrace Bar.

He found Dr. Subhrojit Ghosh already seated at a table in one corner. His friend greeted him with the words, "Chubby, you look terrible. When was the last time you slept?"

"I did not enjoy one wink last night, actually," admitted Puri as they embraced.

"Want to tell me about it?"

For a split second, the detective felt like pouring his heart out. The truth was that the Love Commandos case was teetering on the brink. Unless he could locate Ram ahead of Hari and whoever else was out there scouring Uttar Pradesh for him, there was little hope that he would ever get to the bottom of the affair. But worse, he'd just been informed that he had been removed from the Jain Jewelry Heist case. His now-former client, Mr. Rajesh of First National Hindustan Insurance Corporation, had called the office to say that he'd hired another private detective to take over the investigation. Most Private Investigators was "history," he'd said.

Still, Puri wasn't one to "crib" when he was down.

"Good of you—later maybe," he told his friend, and then called over the waiter.

"Make mine a small one—I'm in surgery later," said Dr. Ghosh, as Puri ordered himself a "double-peg whiskey" and a plate of chilli-cheese toast.

"Shouldn't you be at Vaishno Devi?" asked Dr. Ghosh, once the waiter had completed the usual requisite form filling and chit counting.

"So much of work is there," said Puri.

"That sounds familiar. When was the last time you had an off?"

"Please, no lectures, Shubho-dada."

"You're right. What was I thinking? You're a hopeless case. Now, tell me about Mummy. I hear she locked some intruder in the cupboard?"

"Some total Charlie came to the house with a fake ID— one of those scamster types. So Mummy-ji welcomed him in with a smile, showed him the whereabouts of the meter and locked him under the stairs."

"Marvelous! And is it true she's up for some award?"

"As if she needs any further encouragement. God only knows what's going on at Vaishno Devi. Rumpi was tight-lipped when I talked to her a while back."

Their drinks arrived. Puri raised his glass, took a big gulp and let out a long, satisfied sigh. The chilli-cheese toast was quick to follow and he attacked it like a man who hadn't eaten for weeks.

"Now I want to know what's going on with you, Chubby," said Dr. Ghosh, who stuck with the salted cashews. "I've never seen you so fed up. Something's eating you."

"Nothing I can't handle, Shubho-dada," Puri answered with a wave of his hand.

"We all need a shoulder to cry on, Chubby. Tell me. Perhaps I can help."

The detective sighed. "You've seen the Vishnu Mishra case on TV?" he asked.

"The Thakur accused of murdering the Dalit woman?"

"Her son is missing, also."

"Wasn't he trying to elope with Mishra's daughter?"

"Correct," said Puri. "A Dalit boy and a Thakur girl. What the world is coming to, I ask you?"

Dr. Ghosh regarded him with almost pitying eyes. "Come now, Chubby, times are changing. You sound like a Thakur yourself."

"I'm not one to discriminate against caste."

"Then what have you got against two people coming together?"

"Let them come together provided their parents and family are in agreement."

Dr. Ghosh scoffed. "And since when are elders all so wise? Just look at our leading politicians. Hardly one below seventy. And arrogant beyond all measure."

"You believe youngsters can do better?"

"They could hardly do worse. You know my views on the subject, Chubby. The family model is too stifling. Our young people are not taught to think for themselves. That's why you've got this paralysis. We could do with a bit of revolution."

"I'm in no doubt that our politicians are a bunch of crooks. But it is the family that binds India together—the values we share, of common decency and community, that stops it from falling apart. I, for one, am against anything that threatens it."

"And caste? Does that bind us all together, Chubby?"

They both fell silent for a minute or so, each lost in his own thoughts. When Puri spoke again there was not the slightest hint of animosity in his voice, a testament to the high regard in which he held Dr. Ghosh and the value he placed on their friendship.

"Talking of caste, I wanted to pick your brains so to speak," he said.

"Anything, Chubby."

Puri told him about his visit to ICMB and the work they were doing.

"They're taking blood samples from illiterate village types, paying them one hundred rupees, only, and getting their thumbprints on some consent form."

"Well, that's clearly unethical. But to be honest, even with the best intentions in the world, it's very hard to police. Indigenous communities from South America to Australia have been exploited."

"Seems communities who've intermarried over generations offer rich pickings, is it?"

"Amongst groups who've remained endogamous over long periods, mutations occur in the genes, Chubby. This can create disadvantages and weaknesses, but it can also prove an advantage. Sickle-cell anemia is a good example. Those who carry the recessive gene have been found to have a very high resistance to malaria. So, yes, once we find these mutations in the genes and the chromosomes, there's the possibility of developing treatments."

Puri sat forward in his chair, placing his drink on the table in front of him as if he needed his hands free to think.

"Let us imagine I take the blood sample of a certain young man and find something worthwhile in his DNA and I want to do further tests and all . . . ," he said, his eyes almost feverish.

"Are you asking how much blood would you need?" asked Dr. Ghosh.

Puri gave an eager, childlike nod.

"Well, that would depend on how many tests you were carrying out. But I would imagine a number of samples would be necessary for comparisons."

"And if your laboratory lost power over many hours during load shedding?"

"Your samples would be ruined."

The detective took out his notebook and flicked back to the notes he'd made after his conversation with the Swedish director, Bergstrom.

"After all the failures on the national grid, we had to build our own power plant."

"That's why they needed Ram," concluded Puri. "He was giving them blood and in return they were paying him for his services."

Nineteen

The Vaishno Devi treasury was housed in a building a short distance from the shrine complex. It contained a vault into which daily contributions were placed after all the coins and notes had been sorted, counted and bagged. From what Mummy and Rumpi could gather from a priest to whom they spoke, the vault was watched over at night by a lone security guard employed by a private firm. This security guard, who was obese but had previously been considered reliable, had fallen asleep. A thief—Inspector Malhotra apparently believed the job had been the work of just one—had then entered the building via a skylight and shinnied down a rope.

The priest also told them that the vault's combination lock had been opened with the use of sophisticated safecracking equipment, including a diamond-tipped drill that had been discarded at the scene. The thief had then escaped with an undisclosed sum.

"Must be that Weasel Face priest was the one doing drugging of the security guard using sleeping tablets," said Mummy as she and Rumpi stood outside the treasury watching the police come and go.

"How do you know he's not the thief?" asked Rumpi.

"Why he would do climbing in through the roof?"

"But he could have the loot."

"Doubt it. Remember he was on duty inside the shrine."

Rumpi made a face. "You're absolutely sure you didn't doze off last night, Mummy-ji? Perhaps just for a few minutes?"

"Don't be silly, beta."

"And there's no way Dughal could have climbed out the window?"

"You've seen his size, is it?"

"Well, then surely we should find your Weasel Face and find out what he knows."

"Hardly he is going to tell us how Dughal decamped with the loot."

"So what are we going to do?"

"Watch and wait. And trust to the God."

Mummy's fatalism paid off about an hour later when Inspector Malhotra and his jawans suddenly emerged from inside the treasury and made off down the hill. Mummy and Rumpi followed at a distance. The police wallahs soon arrived at their guesthouse and entered. The manager was waiting for them. He was holding a rucksack and a mountaineer's climbing rope.

"We found it under the bed in room seven, sir," the clerk told Malhotra as Mummy and Rumpi entered the guesthouse and loitered on the edge of the reception, eavesdropping on the conversation.

"And where's the occupant?" asked the inspector.

"Gone, sir."

"When?"

The clerk gave a shrug.

"Describe her to me."

215

"Young—I'd say thirties, dark hair, athletic type."

"When did you last see her?"

"Last night when she checked in, sir."

"What time?"

The clerk thought for a minute, then answered, "Around nine, nine thirty. I can't be sure. We were very busy. One hundred percent occupancy."

Malhotra asked to see the register and the clerk duly pointed out the entry made by the aforementioned guest. "That one: Gauri Nanda, a Delhi address is given," he said.

"And you haven't seen her this morning?" asked Malhotra.

"No, sir, she must have gone."

"Where's the night clerk?"

"Sleeping."

"Where?"

"Upstairs."

"Fetch him."

The young man was sent for and appeared a few minutes later bleary-eyed and with his trousers on back to front.

"The woman in room seven—Gauri Nanda. You remember her?" asked Malhotra.

The night clerk gave a petrified nod.

"Did she leave the guesthouse at all last night?"

"I . . . I don't re-remember," he stuttered.

Mummy piped up. "Inspector, I witnessed her leaving," she said.

Recognizing her voice, Malhotra turned slowly around with a look of fatalistic resignation. "Mrs. Puri," he said, injecting a sense of inevitability into his voice.

"Yes, Inspector. I'm a guest here, also."

"And you saw this young woman—Gauri Nanda."

"Correct."

"And she left her room in the middle of the night?"

"One o'clock, exactly and precisely."

"Was she wearing this pack?"

"Correct."

"And you saw her return, madam?"

"After three o'clock give or take."

"Did you see her leave again this morning?"

"Negative, Inspector. Beyond six thirty I was taking bed rest. So tired I was."

Malhotra thanked her, his graciousness tinged with faint bemusement, and then asked the manager to show him Gauri Nanda's room. He spent less than five minutes inside and left without making any significant discoveries.

"Suspect is female, thirties, going by name of Gauri Nanda. I want any female matching her description held at the bottom of the mountain for questioning," he could be heard saying into his walkie-talkie as he and his jawans swept back through reception.

When they were gone, Mummy approached the manager.

"Kindly tell me when exactly this Gauri Nanda made her room booking?"

The manager checked his computer. "One month back, madam," he said.

"Kindly do checking of another reservation. Name of Dughal," Mummy said.

He obliged her, quickly confirming that it had been made on the same day.

"They were made within half an hour of one another in fact," he added.

Mummy stepped away from the desk.

"You think she was Dughal's accomplice?" asked Rumpi.

"No doubt about it at all."

"You mean Dughal was just the mastermind?"

"Could be," answered Mummy, although there was a degree of uncertainty in her voice.

She made her way down the corridor and found the door to Gauri Nanda's room open. There was a cleaner inside sweeping the floor. Apart from the rucksack, he said he'd found nothing else out of the ordinary. Mummy had a look around herself and came across nothing either. She then asked to see the Dughals' room, which was yet to be cleaned. Inside, it was a mess, with sweets wrappers, empty Coke bottles and takeaway boxes scattered around the place.

When Mummy stepped into the bathroom, something crunched beneath her chappals. Kneeling down, she found some sand scattered across the floor. There were more traces in the shower around the plughole.

"It must have got into his shoes coming up the mountain," suggested Rumpi.

"He wasn't doing walking, na," pointed out Mummy.

They wandered back down the corridor and stopped on the steps of the guesthouse. Some pilgrims who'd made the ascent overnight passed them, elated at having reached the summit. A couple of sedan chairs appeared, both occupied by overweight Punjabis whose expressions showed none of the sense of achievement exhibited by the pilgrims on foot.

Seeing them and the porters who bore their weight triggered a question in Rumpi's mind. It left her lips, however, as a statement.

"You'd think the Dughals would have taken a helicopter up the mountain, seeing as they chartered one to go back down again. It really can't be that comfortable sitting in those chairs for hours on end."

Mummy sent Rumpi a puzzled look, her eyebrows knitted together. "What is that you said?"

"I was just saying that it seems odd—"

"Odd! That is it! He wanted whole world to see them! Just it is a smoke screen!"

"What do you mean a smoke screen?"

Mummy pulled her by the arm. "Come. We are doing checkout."

"Checkout, Mummy-ji? What about the others?"

"Two horses are required, also."

"You want to go after the Dughals? But we'll never catch them in time."

"Don't do tension, na. Someone will be waiting down below, also."

"Who?"

"He knows every person from here to Jammu."

"Not Jagdish Uncle! He can't possibly handle this kind of thing."

"It is a simple thing, na."

"Simple for you maybe, Mummy-ji."

Twenty

Tulsi, who was wearing the same kurta and jeans she'd worn to her finals five days ago, squeezed through the gap in the wall that skirted Agra's Mehtab Bagh, the Moonlight Garden. Officially, the place closed after sunset, yet as a trespasser she was in good company. Many of the city's courting couples came here to while away their evenings free from the prying, disapproving eyes of family and neighbors. The guards rarely turned them away and weren't averse to donations of a few rupees. However, their collusion came with the strict understanding that only the most innocent of canoodling would be tolerated.

For a young woman to come here on her own after dark was unheard of, however, and Tulsi was fortunate that the guard recognized her and remembered Ram, whom he asked after with some fondness.

"You haven't seen him?" she asked, her voice trembling with expectation.

"Not for a long time."

"If he comes tonight, please tell him I'll be waiting in the usual place."

Tulsi made her way between the rows of flower beds, fighting back tears as the scent of the roses triggered memories of their first date.

Ram hadn't been able to afford the trendy coffee shops where she and her friends usually hung out. But when he'd come to pick her up from her dormitory on his old, battered scooter, he'd promised her "something magical that no amount of money in the world can buy!"

Outside the entrance to the Moonlight Garden he'd bought her a choco bar and Tulsi was struck by the consideration he'd shown the vendor. No one in her family or circle of friends would have deigned to talk to a common man in such a familiar—and humane—way. Nor would any of them have shown such relish for a simple ice lolly.

When Ram had talked about how many people in his village went to bed hungry every night, she'd begun to appreciate why.

"My mother's worked as a midwife all her life, delivering babies of all castes and religions, and yet she is considered to be polluted, an outcast," he told her when Tulsi asked about his parents.

There was not a trace of bitterness in him, however. The Dalits of his village did little to help themselves, in his opinion. His father spent any money that came to him on drink; "the rest of them just complain and interfere in one another's business," he said.

By the time he'd led her through the gap in the wall, Tulsi probably would have followed him anywhere.

As they walked through the garden beyond, she caught glimpses of couples wrapped in each other's arms, their whispers punctuated by the odd burst of giggles, and she reached for Ram's hand.

And then it appeared—a vision. Rising up from the riverbed, with its white marble radiating light like an angel, the

Taj Mahal's flawless beauty outshone even the moon above.

Tulsi had never seen the monument at night, nor viewed it from this side of the Yamuna, where its reflection was mirrored in the water. As she and Ram sat on the wall above the river and he quoted Ghalib, she'd never felt happier.

Tonight, her desolation was compounded by the sight of another couple occupying their favorite spot—she lying with her head in his lap, her long hair cascading down, almost touching the earth.

Tulsi kept a respectful distance and leaned against the wall, suspense gnawing at her vitals like the worst hunger.

According to the private detective, Vish Puri, who'd called again just a few hours ago, someone had reported seeing Ram last night outside Sanjay Cinema.

If this was true—and Puri had cautioned her that it could possibly be a case of mistaken identity—then Ram was looking for her and it stood to reason that he'd come to the Mehtab Bagh tonight on their "first-date anniversary."

"You're the only one he can trust," the detective had told her. "Ram has come to believe everyone else has betrayed him. No doubt, that includes the Love Commandos. It was from their safe house he was taken, after all. Most probably he's tried to get a message to you somehow to rendezvous."

"Of course—the wall!" she'd exclaimed.

"What wall?"

"At the university! We used to leave messages there for each other. I could go and check!" she'd suggested.

Puri had warned against this. "Under no circumstances do so, young madam. Your father's people are searching for you high and low. They are watching me, also."

It was at that point in the conversation that Tulsi wondered if perhaps she'd been unwise to call her mother that morning and whether she should come clean about having done so. But she decided against it. She'd taken precautions after all—using an STD booth several blocks away from the Love Commandos safe house. And she'd kept the call short as they always did in the movies in case someone was trying to trace the number. Her mother had made it patently easy to do so. All she'd done was sob and accuse her daughter of bringing shame on the family.

Tulsi surveyed the Moonlight Garden again and then turned around and looked out over the broad sandbank leading to the river below. A rowing boat was struggling upstream, sluggish ripples emanating from its bow in the ethereal moonlight. Giant bats swooped from the sky, skimming the water. She noticed a figure move across the window of the stone chhatri at the far end of the wall—no doubt a lovebird taking in the view of the Taj. From somewhere off in the garden came a whistle—the security guard beginning his rounds.

Another twenty minutes passed. By now it was almost eight o'clock. Behind her, the rowing boat had offloaded a couple of foreign tourists and they were furiously clicking away at the Taj. A young couple—he in jeans and a T-shirt, she in traditional kurta pajama—had perched themselves at the top of the stairs leading down to the river. They were cooing at each other. It made her sick with envy.

Tulsi checked her watch for the umpteenth time. When she looked up, she spotted a male figure hurrying out of the tree line to her left. He started toward her. Although he was wearing a baseball cap with the bill covering the top half of his face, she recognized him immediately as Ram and her heart leapt.

From inside the stone chhatri where he'd been waiting and watching for the past hour, Puri saw the young couple embrace. He wasted not a moment in breaking cover and approaching them as quickly as his short legs and uneven gait would allow.

Spotting him coming toward them, Ram reacted with alarm. "Who are you?" he demanded with a hunted look. Taking Tulsi by the arm, he began to back away.

"It's OK," she said. "He's been helping me. He's a private detective."

"A jasoos?"

"I've been assisting the Love Commandos—Vish Puri, Most Private Investigators, at your service."

"Laxmi sent you?"

"She hired me to find you."

"I don't trust her—I don't trust anyone."

"Ram, listen to me, I'm sure Laxmi had nothing to do with you being taken," said Tulsi. "I was there when she realized you were gone. She was devastated."

He held her by both arms. "Listen, we can't trust anyone anymore," he said with a certain tenderness. "Try to understand: they killed my mother. After they've got what they want from me, they'll kill me, too. We've got to get as far away from here as possible."

"If you run now, you'll be running all your life," said Puri. "I can help you. Give you a safe place to stay."

"That's what Laxmi said."

"It is different now. I can offer you total protection and help you get justice—for your mother and Dr. Basu, also."

"What do you know about that?" Ram demanded.

"I know she was murdered. I know Dr. Basu was trying to help you. I met with your lawyer, Jindal, also."

Ram was still holding Tulsi by the arm, but he'd stopped backing away.

"I really believe Mr. Puri's on our side. Please listen to him," said Tulsi.

Ram, who was a good foot taller than her, looked down into his fiancée's eyes. His features softened.

"That's what got Dr. Basu killed—helping me," he said. "I don't want anyone else I care about to get hurt. Especially you."

"How was she helping you?" asked Puri.

Ram met the detective's gaze. He hesitated before answering. "She shared some information with me," he said.

"ICMB's research?"

The young man gave a nod. "And she said she could help my mother finally get justice as well."

"Justice? From who exactly?"

A sharp sound came from somewhere beyond the tree line. The noise startled Ram and he spun around.

A second later, a young couple walking hand in hand came into view. One of them had stood on a twig. The interruption had put Ram back on edge.

"You can't protect me from these people, they're too powerful," he told the detective before focusing his attention on Tulsi again. "Now, listen, my darling," he continued, "I want you to come with me. We have to get away from here as fast as possible. Do you trust me? Are you ready to come away with me?"

"Of course."

"Then let's go. I've got a bike waiting." Ram took her by the hand and led her back toward the trees.

"Wait, you're making a mistake!" Puri called out. But his protest fell on deaf ears. Tulsi sent him a grateful look over her shoulder and then the couple vanished into the shadows.

"Bloody fool," mumbled Puri as he signaled to Tubelight, who was watching his back.

The operative was by his side in seconds.

"Go after them, yaar. Meantime I'll get back to the car and watch the road."

They set off in opposite directions. But a moment later, the air was rent by a scream. It was Tulsi. Tubelight stopped, trying to get her bearings. Puri reached inside his jacket to remove his pistol from its holster. He gave it a couple of hard tugs but it wouldn't come out.

A second later, Ram and Tulsi came running out of the trees.

In pursuit were two Nepali-looking men wearing smart, Western-style suits and ties. One of them had sustained a fresh head injury and was struggling to keep up.

"This way!" shouted Puri.

Unfortunately the sight of Tubelight bearing down on them caused the couple to change course for the stairs leading down to the river.

Ram and Tulsi found their exit blocked, however, by a big thug wielding a knife. It was Naga.

"Staaaap, baaaaastaaard!" he bawled, and lunged forward.

The couple turned left and sprinted along the wall toward the chhatri. Naga gave chase. Behind him came the young man who'd been cooing with his girlfriend at the top of the stairs and then, at his heels, the two Nepali types.

Puri finally managed to get his pistol free from its holster, pointed it in the air and fired off two rounds. The cracks echoed off the Taj and clattered through the trees. Dozens of crows took to the sky amidst a chorus of caws and beating wings. A third shot stopped everyone in their tracks.

"Hands in the air!" instructed Puri as he leveled his pistol at them. "I want to see ten fingers."

Four sets of hands went up in the air while Ram and Tulsi made good their escape.

"Want me to go after them, Boss?" asked Tubelight.

"Better I go," replied the detective. "You keep these fellows company."

Puri handed his operative the pistol and started toward the entrance. He soon spotted Ram and Tulsi a good forty seconds ahead of him.

Sweating and out of breath, the detective squeezed through the gap in the wall and stumbled out onto the main road. Tulsi was standing next to a white sedan, pounding on the back window, screaming, "Let him go! Let him go!"

Hari Kumar was sitting in the front passenger seat of the car.

He sent Puri a winning smile as the sedan pulled away and Tulsi crumpled to the ground in a fit of sobs.

The detective looked for his Ambassador and spotted Handbrake some way off. He was standing in a ditch with a flashlight searching for his keys.

The black SUV with tinted windows raced past in pursuit of Hari.

When Tubelight appeared seconds later nursing his head and saying that he'd been taken by surprise and that the pistol was missing, Puri felt like crumpling to the ground himself.

The visit to the temple, the offerings to Shiva, the beads—none of it had worked.

"Nazar lag gayi," he groaned. The case had gone for a toss.

Twenty-one

Puri was "totally, absolutely, without doubt, one hundred and ten percent certain" that he hadn't been followed during the drive back to Agra from Delhi.

"Some individual or other gave the game away, that much is certain," he thundered after Handbrake located the keys in the ditch where Hari had thrown them.

It soon became clear who the weak link was.

"I'm so sorry, Mr. Puri, I messed up everything," sobbed Tulsi, who, by now, was seated next to him in the Ambassador.

"Don't tell me—you called your mother, is it?" said the detective, his tone thick with exasperation.

Tulsi emitted a long "Yeeeeeeeesssssssss," followed by "It . . . it . . . it's aalll myyyyy faaaaault!"

Providing comfort to bawling females was not his forte at the best of times—and now was definitely not the best of times. In defeat, the detective was livid. The last thing he felt like doing was offering solace to the person who'd blown the case out of the water and—worse—handed victory to Hari.

"I . . . I . . . feeeeel sooooo baaaaad!"

Puri cringed. He felt like saying, "And so you should,

228

child! I warned you not to contact anyone!" But a reproachful look from Tubelight stayed his temper. He lapsed into a sulk for a few minutes and, realizing that he might have been a little hard on the girl, gave her a gentle pat on the shoulder.

"No need to cry, beta," he said in a perfunctory tone. "I understand, actually. So much pressure was there. What with your father in jail on charges of murder and all."

This provoked yet more tears. At this rate she'll need to be taken to hospital and rehydrated, Puri thought to himself. He tried another pat. "Any one of us would have done the same," he said. "For days now you've been in isolation. Such loneliness was there."

The sobbing gradually abated. "I *have* been so lonely and worried," Tulsi said between sniffles.

Puri had a half bottle of Royal Challenge in his overnight bag. He tugged it out, unscrewed the cap and poured a little whiskey into a plastic cup.

"For medicinal purposes, only," he explained, and handed it to her.

She glugged it back and grimaced.

"Better?" Puri asked, after taking a swig himself directly from the bottle.

Tulsi gave a slow nod and stared out the window in silence.

They were caught in Agra's rush hour. Traffic roiled around them, brake lights blinking in the darkness like red-eyed demons. The intense impatience verging on hysteria demonstrated by many of the drivers suggested that they were all rushing dying patients or pregnant wives to hospital rather than simply heading home.

Puri found himself wishing he had a magic wand to make it all stop. He needed a few minutes to think, to process everything that had happened. He didn't even know where he was headed. Most of all he needed something to eat.

He heard Tulsi ask him, "Who were all those people chasing us?" but ignored her.

However, when she said "I just don't understand how they found us," Puri couldn't help but guffaw. "That much was simple, actually," he said. "They were tapping your parents' home phone and thus traced the call. Had you not called your mother, Ram would now be safe and sound."

Tulsi's chin began to tremble and the tears flowed down her already mascara-stained cheeks again.

Puri threw up his hands in exasperation. "What is the point in crying over so much spilt milk, I ask you? The situation is most grave. If we are to get your boyfriend back in one piece—which will be a miracle, I might say—I will need all my considerable wits about me."

His phone rang. The screen lit up with Hari's name.

"Arrey," he cursed under his breath. "That is all I need."

His adversary was calling to gloat. Ignoring him would show weakness. He took a deep breath and answered. "Puri this side," he said as nonchalantly as he could manage given the circumstances.

"Good evening, saar!" Hari sounded like he had a cigar in his mouth. Truck horns blared in the background. He was on a highway. "I wanted to apologize for not stopping to chat. I'm sure you understand."

"Now you've turned kidnapper, is it?" asked Puri.

"Come now, saar, don't be naïve. You would do exactly the same if you were in my shoes."

"Italian loafers are hardly my style."

Hari guffawed. "That's for sure," he said. "Now listen. I wouldn't want there to be any hard feelings. We're both professionals. Chalk it up to experience."

Puri was growing weary of the badinage. "Hari, you're making a grave mistake," he said.

"Mistake? There is no need for sour grapes."

"You are putting that young man's life in jeopardy."

"Not at all. I was hired to find him and that is what I have done."

"And his mother. Have you forgotten what happened to her?"

"My client had nothing to do with her murder."

"And who is your client exactly, Hari? Mind telling me once and for all, seeing as you are the winner?"

"Sorry, saar, no can do. I can't have you gate-crashing the party."

"Listen to me, Hari, just this once. My people traced Ram's mother's last footsteps. She took one private bus to Baba Dhobi's party headquarters in Lucknow. He was very much present at the time. Hours later, only, she was murdered."

Hari was silent on the other end of the line.

"Hari, you know me. I would not lie about such a thing. Believe me, Ram's blood will be on your hands," said Puri, and hung up.

Spotting a family-style restaurant, he ordered Handbrake to stop. The driver found a spot in the car park and the detective clambered out of the car.

"Come," he told Tulsi, poking his hefty frame back into the car. "It is going to be a long night. Let us eat first."

"But shouldn't we be looking for Ram?" she asked.

"For that we would require directions," said the detective.

Tulsi watched him pass through the door of the restaurant.

"How can he eat at a time like this?" she asked Tubelight.

The operative shrugged. "One time, Boss ate a chicken frankie after watching a hanging," he said by way of an explanation.

The restaurant was packed with families gathered around molded plastic tables making short work of dosas and plates of chaat. Puri ordered three veg thalis and three cups of chai, went and washed his hands and face in the sink outside the toilets, and joined Tubelight and Tulsi at the table where they'd seated themselves. He then set about eating the mango pickle in the little receptacle in the middle of the table. When the food arrived, he devoured the papad with the gusto of Cookie Monster on *Sesame Street*—or rather his Indian cousin, Biscuit Badshah.

Stuffing himself was perhaps an odd reaction to the evening's events. But Puri had only eaten three vegetable samosas since breakfast and couldn't think straight on an empty stomach. To make matters worse, he was exhausted from lack of sleep and his mind was railing against Hari. There wasn't a Punjabi insult he hadn't thought of since seeing his competitor's smug, self-satisfied expression in the car window.

By the time he'd cleared his plate, however, the storm had begun to abate. And once he'd polished off a second helping of daal makhani and gobbled up two gulab jamuns, Puri found that he could think clearly again.

Over a second cup of tea, he sat dissecting the evening's events, trying to figure out who'd been who in the Moonlight Garden.

Naga he knew about—although Puri had to admit that he'd underestimated the goon.

The boyfriend and girlfriend on the steps had been a couple of Hari's undercover operatives—no doubt about it at all.

As for the two Nepali types, they'd worn impeccable, perfectly tailored suits and earpieces. Not your garden-variety goondas.

Could they have been Gurkhas? he wondered.

It wasn't beyond the realm of possibility; there were a number of them working in the private security business in India nowadays. With their British army training and Hindi language skills, they were highly sought after as bodyguards for the rich and famous.

Were they part of an internal security outfit maintained by ICMB? Had they been the ones trailing him in the SUV?

Those questions would have to wait. Far more important was Ram's strange reference to his mother seeking justice with Dr. Basu's help.

"*She said she could help my mother finally get justice as well*" had been his exact words.

Justice for what? From whom?

A sudden urge to share his thoughts came over him, and without the slightest preamble, Puri started to talk out loud.

"Three months back, give or take, a certain medical research institute sent a team to Ram's native place," he said, drawing curious stares from both Tubelight and Tulsi, to whom this news was a revelation. "There they took blood samples from numerous Dalits, Ram included. Some weeks later, one of three things occurred. Number one, ICMB contacted Ram. Or second, Ram contacted ICMB. Or third, Dr. Basu contacted Ram or vice versa." He paused for a moment. "Actually, that is four possibilities."

Both Tubelight and Tulsi looked lost, but he carried on regardless.

"Whatever the case, Ram received two things. Number one, moola—a couple of lakhs at least. Second, information—

this being supplied directly by Dr. Basu, seems without the knowledge of her employers."

"What *was* this research?" interjected Tulsi.

Puri held up a hand. "Kindly wait, beta. I would explain in due course," he said before taking a moment to collect his thoughts. "Last week, only, Dr. Basu met her death," he continued. "Though the scene was arranged and our Indian police played their part to perfection, there is no doubt in my mind she was murdered. Ram said he was of the same opinion, also."

"That's right! He said he thought Dr. Basu had been killed because she'd helped him!" exclaimed Tulsi, whose comment was met with a withering stare, prompting her to mumble an apology.

"*To continue,*" said Puri. "Soon after, Ram returned to his native place, Govind village. He did so at some considerable risk to himself given that Vishnu Mishra was on the lookout for his good self. By now he was scared and cautious. Not even the Love Commandos came to know of his dealings with Dr. Basu. Just he was hoping he would be reunited with his ladylove and get away once and for all."

The detective took a quick sip of his tea. "The question you're wondering is, who grabbed him from the Love Commando safe house?" he said.

Tulsi gave a nod.

"Answer is, goons working for ICMB. They got hold of Dr. Basu's phone records, thus they secured Ram's mobile number, located its signal and picked him up."

Tulsi raised a hand like a child in class trying to get her teacher's attention.

"One minute, only," said Puri. "Allow me first to explain the chain of events. Dr. Basu provided Ram with the ICMB's findings. Ram in turn took them to his village. Thus

one copy got buried behind his house, most probably for safekeeping, only. Finally, his mother dug it up and took it with her on the bus to Lucknow. There she entered the party headquarters of no less a person than the chief minister of Uttar Pradesh, Baba Dhobi, someone she trusted given their common Dalit background and her loyal support as a constituent."

Tubelight couldn't help but blurt out, "Boss, was he there?"

"He was," said Puri with a nod.

His operative gave a long, low whistle.

"I don't understand—are you saying Baba Dhobi had something to do with Ram's mother's murder?" asked Tulsi.

"That I cannot say for sure, but every great detective must on occasion trust his gut and mine tells me Baba Dhobi or some person connected with him played some part in robbing Kamlesh of her life."

"But, Boss, what's the connection between Baba Dhobi and ICMB?" asked Tubelight.

"That is the ten-crore question, no?" said Puri. "Clearly some piece of the puzzle is so far missing."

He addressed Tulsi: "I want you to think back, beta. Ram said Dr. Basu was helping his mother seek justice. That means anything to you—anything at all?"

Tulsi blinked a couple of times. "Ram talked about his mother a lot. He was very close to her. She made sure he got a good education, got him admission in a good school," she said.

"Any grievances were there?"

"He often talked about how she'd been treated badly. You know—being a midwife, delivering babies. She was considered polluted. Ram found that sickening—as anyone would. He talked about changing things." She paused. "I seem to remember him saying that she worked in a hospital—I think this was before he was born. He told me once that she was fired."

Puri put down his tea. "You remember the hospital name?" he asked.

Tulsi looked up at the ceiling as if the answer might be written on the suspended ceiling panels. "Yes, it was Lucknow General. We passed by it one day and he pointed it out."

"Ram mentioned why she'd been let go?"

"No, but he said that she kept on receiving her salary. I think it was about four thousand rupees a month. Ram said it was just enough for his parents to live on. He said that was why his father didn't bother working."

Tubelight sent Puri a quizzical look. "Boss, why she'd get her salary all these years if she was fired?"

But the detective didn't answer. He simply took out his phone, dialed a number and said into the mouthpiece, "Madam Rani, some information is required. Hello, hello? You can hear me?"

Puri's next question wasn't audible to the others thanks to the din coming from the neighboring tables, which forced him to leave the restaurant for the car park.

When Tubelight and Tulsi caught up with him a few minutes later after settling the bill, they heard him say, "So he was general administrator of the hospital from 1987 to 1993. Check one thing further, Madam Rani. Any record is there of Kamlesh Sunder? She served as a midwife at Lucknow General during that time, also."

He waited until his secretary came back on the line. "Nothing? As I expected," said Puri before thanking her and hanging up.

"They were both working there," he told the others.

"*Who?*" asked Tulsi.

But Puri was dialing another number. He put the phone back to his ear, gestured to Tubelight to wait and then said, "Hello, Mr. Jindal, sir? Haan-ji. Vish Puri this side. We met this morning, only. I would need a word, sir."

The detective listened for a moment and then said, "Yes, sir, it is past nine o'clock, actually."

And then: "My apologies to your good wife, but the matter is most urgent. A matter of life or death, we can say. Concerning Ram Sunder. I traced him to Agra and met with him this evening, only. After, he was chased and unfortunately abducted before my very eyes. It is my belief that Ram will be handed over to the very same individual who murdered his mother few days back. If you would be good enough to confirm one detail, then perhaps his murder can be avoided."

As Puri listened to Jindal, he began to grind his teeth in frustration.

"Sir, I am fully aware of your responsibilities, just as I am aware of my own, also," he said. "A young man's life hangs in the balance. I respectfully request that you kindly allow me one question, only. Then at least I will know for sure that I am not barking up a wrong tree."

Jindal's answer was lengthy, but Puri listened patiently.

"Sir, you have made your position perfectly clear," he said. "However, one question is there. Did Dr. Basu provide Ram Sunder with DNA evidence concerning the identity of his real father?"

Again Puri was forced to listen to a lengthy exposition.

"Sir, kindly consider my request and keep firmly in mind that your client's life is in severe jeopardy" were his final words before he hung up and got into the car.

Tulsi followed him onto the backseat. "Mr. Puri, will you please tell me what's going on? Where are we going now?"

"We two—that is, you and my good self—are driving to Lucknow directly."

"And me, Boss?" asked Tubelight.

"You're to remain here in Agra to watch our backs."

"ICMB?" asked Tubelight.

"Without doubt they too wish to lay their hands on Ram. And there is the matter of Dr. Basu's murder, also."

"Think there are two killers, Boss?"

"Most definitely. But I'm in no doubt that the two murders are connected inasmuch as Dr. Basu was murdered for lending assistance to Ram."

"And Hari, Boss. Who's he working for?"

"Come on—that has become obvious, no?"

Twenty minutes later, Puri received an SMS. He read the message with marked relief.

"Thank the God he has come to his senses," he said.

Twenty-two

Jagdish Uncle was an avid reader of Hindi crime fiction. His favorite author was Surender Mohan Pathak, whose best-selling title was *The 65 Lakh Heist*. Whenever Pathak's latest hit the railway stands, where such pulp fiction titles were available for the princely sum of sixty rupees, he would be the first at Jammu Station to purchase his copy. Because Sonam Aunty didn't approve of his reading such "trrraash," he would take it with him to the Jammu Club, where, between hands of cards and generous glasses of Old Monk rum, he'd treat himself to the latest adventures of the thief-cum-hero Vimal.

Another of Jagdish Uncle's characteristics was that he was fiercely loyal to family and generous to a fault. Whenever his sister traveled back to India from America, he insisted on driving ten hours to Delhi airport in order to bring her "home."

When one of his American nieces came to work in Delhi, he found her an apartment and, after negotiating the rent, conspired with the landlord to pay half the amount without her knowledge.

All of this went to explain why, when Mummy called

him in the afternoon from halfway down the mountain and asked that he engage in a little discreet surveillance work, he jumped at the chance.

"Have no fear, ji! I will be like a chameleon—invisible to the naked eye. No one will see me!" he declared in a movie-trailer voice-over tone.

"Kindly don't do time-waste," Mummy implored him in the knowledge that Jagdish Uncle was also fond of banter and jokes and often engaged with total strangers in the street. "Situation is serious."

"I will try my level best," he assured her. "But with so many of people, how I'll spot these Dughals?"

"She you cannot miss—size of a buffalo," said Mummy.

By eight P.M., Jagdish Uncle was in position at the bottom of the mountain, from where he could see the queue of pilgrims backed up along the pathway behind the special security checkpoint that had been set up.

Although he'd donned a baseball cap and black wraparound sunglasses, a number of locals saw through Jagdish Uncle's disguise and stopped to chat. He was crestfallen at being so easily unmasked. Yet being a self-declared "socially minded person" with a reputation for enjoying a good gossip, he could hardly ignore them.

On a couple of occasions, the temptation to reveal that he was engaged in "top secret work" proved too hard to resist.

The mocking laughter that his claim provoked from a Jammu taxi wallah resulted in Jagdish Uncle blurting out that he was on the lookout for the thieves who'd robbed the Vaishno Devi shrine.

"Go ahead, make fun, but I will be the one smiling when the reward is mine!" he declared.

When the Dughals finally appeared at ten P.M., Jagdish Uncle was talking with a candy floss seller who said that he'd heard that ten million rupees had been stolen from the shrine.

Had the couple not stuck out so prominently from the crowd, they would have slipped by Mummy's man. And had the same Jammu taxi wallah not reappeared at the very moment that the couple was being helped into the back of a large Toyota four-by-four and called out in a mocking voice, "Oi, detective sahib, you'll need a big cell to contain those two!" then perhaps Jagdish Uncle might have gone unnoticed as well.

Pranap Dughal, however, turned, caught Jagdish Uncle's eye, and then climbed into the vehicle.

The Toyota promptly pulled away, the driver flashing his dippers and honking at the dozens of pilgrims and touts milling about on the road.

Fearing that he might have been spotted, Jagdish Uncle deemed it wise to take off his sunglasses and baseball cap before setting off in pursuit in Sweetie. Just like his fictional hero, Vimal, he was also careful to keep his distance as he followed the vehicle along the bypass that skirted Katra town. This became increasingly challenging when they joined the main road to Jammu and started to wind down through the hills. Despite the hour, the traffic was still heavy, and when the Dughals' vehicle got stuck behind three trucks, Jagdish Uncle soon found himself only a couple of cars behind.

It was at this point that Mummy called for an update.

"I'm in pursuit, ji," he assured her. "Target is in my sight. Everything is going to plan."

He saw no need to mention his earlier indiscretion or the blather-mouthed taxi driver's faux pas. No harm seemed to have been done.

"The traffic is quite heavy. We will reach Jammu in one hour fifteen minutes," he reported.

When they reached the next bend, the Toyota managed

to overtake two of the three trucks, narrowly missing an oncoming bus and almost forcing a motorcyclist off the edge of the precipice.

Jagdish Uncle, who'd driven this stretch of road countless times, saw nothing unusual in this maneuver, even in the pitch dark, and after another half a mile, he managed to also pass the two trucks without sustaining so much as a nick on the car's bodywork, although, admittedly, he passed within millimeters of a sedan.

On the next bend, the Toyota cleared the last truck, and not to be outdone, Jagdish Uncle quickly caught up. But when Pranap Dughal turned around in his seat and glared back at him, he knew for sure he'd been rumbled and that he and Sweetie were in for a daring chase. Indeed, on the next open stretch the Toyota accelerated away, and Jagdish Uncle slipped her into fourth and floored the accelerator.

He rounded the next bend at forty, nimbly overtaking an Ambassador.

A queue of cars stuck behind a tractor belching out a cloud of thick diesel fumes proved no obstacle either, and Jagdish Uncle and Sweetie proved yet again how accommodating oncoming traffic could be.

It was a beautiful thing, the synthesis between man and machine, he reflected as the Toyota appeared in his sights once again.

Still, there was no accounting for nature.

Jagdish Uncle had but a second's warning to brace himself before a small boulder vanished beneath his wheels and there was an almighty crunch.

Sweetie swerved violently to the left and Jagdish Uncle slammed on the brakes, grinding to a halt inches from the edge of a two-hundred-meter drop beyond.

Out of the corner of his eye, he noticed the Toyota racing on and two of his wheels rolling after them down the hill.

Tubelight and Zia were sitting outside their ragpicker tent on the plot across from ICMB playing cards around a cow-dung fire.

It had been nearly an hour since the SUV with the tinted windows had returned with its front smashed in—the result of a head-on collision.

Fifteen minutes later, Dr. Sengupta, the head of research, had left work and Shashi had set off after him on his Vespa.

The operative had soon realized that he wasn't the only one following him. A black car with two moustachioed men inside followed the geneticist to his house, parked across the road and sat waiting.

"Sir, they look like plainclothes," Shashi reported to Tubelight, who ordered him to stay put and provide him with regular updates.

After assigning Zia to the first watch, Puri's chief operative then lay down on a rank-smelling mattress to try to get some sleep.

At five o'clock, he was rudely awoken. The gora director, Justus Bergstrom, was leaving in a car, Zia told him.

The two operatives set off after him.

Half an hour later, they found themselves at Agra airport.

Bergstrom left the car carrying a briefcase and hurried into the VVIP terminal.

Ten minutes later, a jet took off.

Tubelight watched it circle in the sky and then turn east in the direction of Lucknow.

Twenty-three

Ram awoke on the backseat of a moving car with his wrists handcuffed. He attempted to sit up, but the pain in the back of his head was too much to bear.

Grimacing, he lay back down again.

It was early morning—by the light in the sky he guessed it was around six A.M. How he'd come to be there was not immediately clear to him. He had to concentrate hard to remember the events of the night before.

There had been a car chase. In Agra. A black SUV had tried to force the car he'd been traveling in off the road. But it had crashed into a lamppost. At some point, they'd stopped at a dhaba. That had been later—on the side of a highway. A man who smoked a cigar had stood in the parking area talking on his mobile phone. There had been a couple of others working with him. One of them had arrived in another vehicle. Ram had recognized him. He'd been one of the men who'd chased him.

The events in the garden came rushing back to him.

"Tulsi!" he cried out.

A face appeared between the headrests of the front seats. It was the man who smoked cigars.

"Aaah, sleeping beauty is awake at last," said Hari with a smile. "How are you feeling, young man?"

Ram felt nauseous—the effect of the cigar smoke as much as the concussion he'd sustained.

"A little worse for wear?" asked Hari. "My apologies for the knock on the head. Rishi got a bit carried away. He's young and somewhat inexperienced."

"Where is she?" asked Ram, his voice hoarse.

"Tulsi is with your friend Vish Puri, I would imagine."

It took the young man a moment to place the name. "The fat jasoos? He's not my friend," said Ram.

Hari chuckled. "Well, I can hardly blame you. Such a pompous, irritating little man. I'm sure he told you that he's the best detective in all of India. He didn't? Well, he's absolutely convinced of it. And of his damn dharma. One of those self-righteous crusaders. And don't get me started on his fashion sense. Who wears safari suits and flat caps these days? He looks like he should be out walking a whippet."

Ram managed to sit up despite the pain. Through his window he could see high walls that demarcated large private properties. Farmhouses lay beyond. It looked like one of the wealthy suburbs of Lucknow.

"Where are you taking me?" he asked.

"To meet my client."

"Who's that?"

"You'll find out soon enough—ten minutes, give or take."

Hari handed Ram a bottle of water. Despite the handcuffs, he managed to gulp down a quarter of the contents and then wiped his mouth with the back of his hand.

"Why are you doing this?" Ram asked.

"I was hired to locate you and that's what I've done."

"Do you care what happens to me after that?"

"I'm taking you to the one person who can offer you the

protection you need. By lunchtime you will be reunited with Tulsi and the two of you can ride off into the sunset and live happily ever after."

Ram held up his hands and rattled his cuffs. "Then why these?"

"We can't have you running off again. I wouldn't give you a very high chance of survival. Half of Uttar Pradesh is looking for you."

An inquisitive smile crept across Hari's face. "By the way, I'm curious about something," he said. "How did you get away from the Gurkhas—the ones working for ICMB? They're former soldiers. It can't have been easy."

"Did they kill my mother?" asked Ram, his eyes as hard as flint.

Hari turned back in his seat. "No, it wasn't them," he said.

"Then it was Dr. Bal Pandey," said Ram.

Hari gave no indication of whether he believed this to be true. He simply stared ahead impassively. But Ram said to himself, "It was him. He murdered her," and buried his face in his hands.

The sedan pulled through a set of gates guarded by a dozen jawans armed with Lee-Enfield bolt-action rifles and the odd submachine gun. A driveway lined with pots of marigold flowers led to a modern bungalow clad in white marble. Hari's sedan stopped behind three white Ambassadors with Uttar Pradesh state government plates, their roofs replete with antennas and blue emergency beacons.

Ram was helped out of the sedan, his handcuffs were removed and he was led to the front door of the bungalow. It was answered by a male peon in a gray, half-sleeve safari jacket. With swift efficiency, he led them across a hall and down the corridor beyond. They passed a collection of multi-colored glass Buddha statues arranged on antique French side tables with delicate, bowed legs. On the wall hung a series of oil paintings featuring giant fluorescent roosters.

The peon stopped in front of the last door, knocked, waited for a second and then pushed it open. Ram stepped into the room beyond to find two men looking over a collection of architectural drawings spread out on a table. The man nearest to him appeared to be south Indian, the bright white of his kurta pyjama in striking contrast to his dark skin, wavy jet-black hair and big, bushy moustache.

More dazzling still was the sight of the second individual. Standing at just five feet and six inches tall and dressed in a dhoti with unshorn tufts of hair protruding from his ears, it was none other than the chief minister of Uttar Pradesh, the self-proclaimed "messiah of the Dalits," Baba Dhobi.

"At last you're here safe and sound!" he exclaimed as he stepped away from the table and greeted the young man with a large, generous smile.

Ram stooped down and touched his feet, but Baba Dhobi raised him up by the shoulders in an avuncular gesture.

"It is *I* who should be doing you such an honor, young man," he said, now speaking in Awadhi, his and Ram's mother tongue. "You have shown great courage and determination in the face of oppression and danger, and I for one am proud to call you brother!"

Baba Dhobi placed a hand on one of Ram's shoulders as the young man, who was speechless, raised his hands and pressed them together in another gesture of respect.

"We have been looking for you everywhere all these days," the chief minister continued. "When I heard about your poor mother, I called Hari Kumar personally and instructed him to find you right away. He has worked for us in the past once or twice and always proven reliable and proficient, and I had every confidence that he was the right man for the job. Fortunately, I was right. Thus you are standing before us alive and well. We are in his debt. Now come, I will introduce you. This is Viswanathan Narayanaswamy, the Vaastu practitioner who is overseeing the design of my new house."

By "house" Baba Dhobi meant "palace." And by "Vaastu," he was referring to the Indian science of construction in which invisible elements and natural forces were taken into account in order to ensure the well-being of the occupants.

"It is being conceived in a traditional way, mirroring a mandala," continued the chief minister. "See, the prayer hall will be in the northeast and the bedroom to the south. There will be a cow shed, of course. That will be positioned here, to the northwest of the building."

"The dwelling itself is a shrine," said the Vaastu practitioner in heavily accented Hindi. "It is not merely a shelter for human beings to rest and eat. Like a temple, it is sacred. Therefore the occupier should enjoy spiritual well-being and material wealth and prosperity."

"Very impressive, sir," said Hari.

"Truly beautiful, sir," agreed Ram.

"You really think so? I'm so glad!" declared Baba Dhobi, who was beaming with pride. "Construction is to start within the month," he added. "When it is finished you will all be my guests at the opening ceremony. Now come. We will eat together. We have much to discuss."

They sat in the dining room at a long table laid with china and silver and starched napkins folded to look like hens. Liveried servants came and went through a door to the adjacent kitchen bearing platters of food and pots of steaming tea.

With quiet deportment, they served each of the guests in turn and then stood with their backs to the wall, ramrod straight with impassive expressions.

Baba Dhobi looked out of place amidst these trappings. His cutlery went untouched and he slouched over the table eating halwa poori with one hand. Every now and again, he would raise his head from his food like an ancient hunchback, motion to his guests to eat more, and then continue demolishing his food, his lips smacking together with the sound of the sea lapping against a dock.

Ram, Hari and Viswanathan Narayanaswamy ate in an awkward silence, watching the chief minister out of the corner of their eyes. It was only after Baba Dhobi had cleared his plate, wiped his hands, signed a few documents brought by a hovering peon and dismissed all his staff from the room (the Vaastu practitioner included) that he addressed Ram again.

"You're aware your mother and I used to work together at Lucknow General Hospital," he said as he emptied a small packet of gutka into the palm of his left hand and began to run his finger over it to smooth out the lumps.

"Yes, sir, she told me many times."

"In those days things were different. I was a humble administrator. The job had come to me because of the reservation system. There were few of us in positions of power. The doctors were all from the upper castes. They ran the hospital like their own private Raj. We were powerless. Thus when your mother was badly treated . . . naturally, I conducted an investigation. But ultimately it was her word against his and she lost her job. I did everything in my power to help her. I did not strike her name from the employment roll, thus ensuring that she continued to receive her salary."

"Sir, she was your greatest admirer," said Ram. "She often

told me about your kindness. Even after all these years her salary came to her every month. You were like a father to her."

Baba Dhobi made a gesture with his hands, the kind that was intended to communicate humility but somehow betrayed self-satisfaction. He emptied the gutka onto his tongue and moved the tobacco mixture around his mouth.

"Now, there is an important matter that has been brought to my attention," he said, his mouth filling with saliva. "I understand that a medical research entity—this ICMB—has been operating illegally. Without a proper license, it has taken blood samples from yourself and your brothers and sisters in Govind village."

"That's right, sir. They told us that it was part of a medical study and paid everyone a hundred rupees each for their participation."

Baba Dhobi leaned over the side of his chair, spat saliva tinged red from the gutka into a spittoon on the floor, and then said, "Tell me what happened next."

"Sir, when they came to the village, I met Dr. Anju Basu of ICMB. I told her I was studying in Agra and she took my contact info. Some days later, she called me up. She said they wanted to conduct some drug trials and needed someone with my specific DNA. So I cooperated and went to their laboratories, where they took more blood."

"In return they gave you money?"

"Yes, sir—fifty thousand. But Dr. Basu also provided me with a lakh from her own pocket."

"So much?" Baba Dhobi spat again.

"Sir, she was very kind. She said I deserved the money—that it would help with my future. She knew about the difficulties I was facing with Tulsi's family." Ram hesitated. "Sir, I believe she felt guilty about what ICMB was doing and wanted to make amends."

The chief minister nodded thoughtfully. "Go on," he said.

"Sir, two weeks ago Dr. Basu asked to meet with me. She explained that she was leaving her job. She was facing personal problems with one of her coworkers who was harassing her. She had become scared. Also, ma'am said the organization was dishonest. She told me that they had analyzed my DNA and found a genetic trait that could potentially be used in the fight against cancer. She said it was worth a fortune to ICMB, but neither I nor anyone else in the village would get a share of the profits, that we were being exploited." Ram paused. "Sir, there was something else, also. She said that my DNA was different from that of my father's."

"Different?"

"Sir, she told me that my father was not my real father."

Baba Dhobi chewed thoughtfully on his gutka. "Your mother hid the truth from you all these years?"

"Yes, sir. I knew only that she had lost her job at the hospital a few months before I was born. But she had never told me why—never told me what really happened."

"Did Dr. Basu identify your real father?"

"Yes, sir. She said that the database had found an exact match. ICMB had taken samples from dozens of Brahmins as part of their research. She said that by coincidence they had my real father's records on file. He had participated in the program in order to prove that his blood was 'superior.'"

"And she provided you with this research?"

"Yes, sir. She gave me a computer data key with copies of ICMB's research as well as my father's DNA profile."

"Did you speak with your mother about this?"

"Yes, sir, I returned to the village. She confirmed everything. How he raped her and she fell pregnant"—there was a pause—"with me."

"And you told her you had proof."

"Yes, sir."

"Finally she could prove her case."

Ram gave a nod.

"So you gave her the data key."

"I told her to keep it hidden, sir."

"That was the only copy?"

"No, sir, I made another."

"You have it?"

Ram hesitated. "Yes, sir," he said.

"Good. Now, it is my responsibility as chief minister to ensure that the interests of our Dalit brothers and sisters are protected. An organization like this cannot simply be allowed to exploit our people without sharing the profit."

"Yes, sir, thank you, sir. And, sir—Dr. Basu was actually assisting me in this regard. We went to Delhi to consult with a lawyer. He advised me that a group-action suit can be filed against ICMB."

"No need, no need," said Baba Dhobi with a wave of his hand. "I have already given orders for the government of Uttar Pradesh to bring a case against this corrupt organization. But for this to proceed we will require a copy of their research. Do you have it with you?"

Ram shifted uneasily in his chair.

"Something is wrong?" asked the chief minister.

"Sir, Dr. Basu told me never to show it to anyone, not even the lawyer, until the case was ready to go to trial," said Ram.

"You are not talking to just anyone, my brother."

"No, sir."

Ram looked across the table at Hari, who'd been listening to their conversation in silence. He received a nod of encouragement in return. Then he reached down into his sock and took out a small data key.

He stretched across the table and placed it in Baba Dhobi's open palm.

The chief minister's stubby fingers curled around it slowly like the legs of a spider.

"There are other copies?"

"No, sir. That's the last."

Baba Dhobi dropped the data key into his shirt pocket. "Dr. Basu gave you good advice—you should have listened to her," he said.

In an instant, the mask of parental empathy fell away, revealing a hard expression beneath. Baba Dhobi's eyes now betrayed only cold triumph.

It took Ram a moment to understand.

"My mother came to you," he said in little more than a whisper.

"Your mother was weak and naïve."

"She came to you for help and you betrayed her."

"Sacrifices have to be made or they will trample us. I have fought all my life against them, fought for our rights. Your mother threatened to ruin all that."

"How?"

As if by answer the door opened behind them and two men entered the room. The first was a goon. He stood just over six feet tall and had the hooked nose and watery green eyes of an Afridi.

The second man, bald and bespectacled, was the Brahmin political leader Dr. Bal Pandey.

"He knows," said Baba Dhobi.

Dr. Pandey nodded solemnly and said, "I was listening."

"I'm getting tired of cleaning up your mess," added the chief minister.

"I told you I would take care of it," said the Brahmin.

Ram shot up from his chair, his eyes ablaze with hatred. "How can you conspire with *him*?" he bawled at Baba Dhobi. "You claim to fight for our rights!" Spotting a knife on the table, he lunged for it. But the goon grabbed Ram by the collar and shoved him back into his chair.

"You should really show your father more respect," said Baba Dhobi as the Afridi drew a revolver.

At the sight of the weapon, Hari balked. "What the hell is going on here?" he demanded.

"It's called politics, Hari," said Baba Dhobi.

"Politics? You and him?"

"We're going to form an alliance at the next election."

"Dalit and Brahmin?"

"Why not? Our communities share many of the same threats these days."

"You mean you'll lose power to the Yadavs if you don't."

"Like I said, Hari, it's politics."

"And when you were administrator of the hospital—that was politics as well?" demanded Ram.

"Let's just say Dr. Pandey and I have had a long-standing understanding," said Baba Dhobi.

"He paid you off, in other words—and now you're worried it will all come out, that the voters will learn about your betrayal," said Ram. "A coalition you can sell them on, but not if it came out that you'd helped cover up the rape of a Dalit woman by a Brahmin."

He tried to struggle free, but the goon dealt him a blow on the back of his head with the butt of the revolver and he slumped forward.

"Get him out of here," said Baba Dhobi. "And make sure I never see him again."

"Now, hold on," said Hari with alarm as Ram was dragged from the room. "What are you planning to do with him?

There are witnesses who saw me take him. How am I going to explain it if he turns up dead?"

"You'll tell them he escaped—he's done it before," said Baba Dhobi.

"You expect Vish Puri to believe that?"

"He won't be a problem."

"Don't tell me you're planning to eliminate him, too?"

"He's on his way here now."

"Now?" exclaimed Hari. He stood suddenly from his chair.

"Puri called on Inspector Gujar not one hour ago, saying that he had proof that Dr. Pandey and I conspired to get the woman killed and that he believes we now have her son."

"I'll take my money and be on my way," said Hari.

But Baba Dhobi told him to sit down. "You work for me now," he said, and then invited Dr. Pandey to join them for a cup of chai.

Although Puri woke Inspector Gujar well before his usual hour, he agreed to hear the detective's accusations against the chief minister, who, Puri claimed, had conspired to cover up the rape and pregnancy of Kamlesh Sunder by Dr. Bal Pandey while the two men had worked at Lucknow General Hospital.

He listened also to Tulsi Mishra describe how Ram Sunder had been abducted by Hari Kumar outside the Moonlight Garden in Agra.

When Puri provided him with photographic evidence taken by one of his undercover operatives of Hari's car entering the chief minister's private residence and threatened to go to the news channels if nothing was done, the police wallah picked up the phone and called his senior.

A decision was quickly taken to act and six jawans were assembled in front of the station.

Gujar even invited Puri along and they immediately set off together in the police wallah's jeep.

When they arrived at Baba Dhobi's private residence, the gates swung open and they were escorted inside by one of the chief minister's peons.

It all proved a little too easy, in fact. And when they entered the dining room and Baba Dhobi greeted them with the words "Aaah, there you are," Puri knew that he'd been betrayed.

"Inspector Gujar here is a fast learner, no?" he said as he felt the nozzle of the inspector's revolver press into the small of his back.

"He understands the value of loyalty," said Baba Dhobi.

"You ordered him to arrest Vishnu Mishra and frame him with the murder of Kamlesh Sunder," said Puri.

"It was too good an opportunity."

"And Hari? He's willing to take orders?"

"He's no Gandhi."

"On that point we are agreed."

The two private detectives eyed each other with disdain. "Tell me: how much you are paying him, exactly?" asked Puri.

"What's it to you?" said Hari with a snarl.

The detective shrugged. "For the longest time I've suspected there was a price tag somewhere on that fancy Italian suit of yours. Previously I would not have believed that murder would feature on your résumé."

"I told you before I had nothing to do with her killing."

"But now you are very much aiding and abetting. Kamlesh's killer is here very much in our presence, no?" he said, gesturing to Dr. Pandey, who was seated at the table listening to the conversation with smug placidity.

Puri added: "Unless I am very much mistaken the plan is to do away with Ram and my good self, also. If caught, you will hang with them, Hari."

"That's enough!"

"I wonder how your silk tie will look with a noose around it?"

Hari suddenly exploded: "*Shut up!*"

Puri didn't flinch. "Seems you have a hidden temper after all," he said.

"Give me a gun and I'll take care of him myself," Hari told Baba Dhobi.

"Not here," said the chief minister with a look that conveyed deep satisfaction. "You can accompany Dr. Pandey's man."

"Fine. Let's get it over with."

Inspector Gujar took Puri by the arm and, with his pistol still pressed into his back, led him out of the dining room, through the kitchen and out a side entrance to a waiting car.

Puri was cuffed and shoved onto the backseat, where he found Ram now conscious and sitting up.

The goon tossed Hari the keys. "You drive," he said before climbing into the front passenger seat, revolver in hand.

Hari got behind the wheel, started the engine and reversed down the driveway. He narrowly missed another car pulling in through the gates. Puri caught a glimpse of Justus Bergstrom seated in the back.

"Where are we going to do this thing?" Hari asked the goon once they'd pulled into the road.

"Same place I did the mother. It's a twenty-minute drive from here. Very secluded. Go straight."

After a quarter of a mile, they came to a red light. A blind beggar woman led by a young boy approached the goon's window.

"Saab, paisa dedo!" she called. "Mister, give me money."

He signaled for her to move on, but she persisted. "Bookhi hoon!"

"Hutt," shouted the goon.

Undeterred, she continued to rap her knuckles on the window. "We have nothing to eat," pleaded the boy.

"Oh, for God's sake, give her this," said Hari, and handed the Afridi a ten-rupee note.

With a curse, he placed his revolver on his knee and grabbed the money. Then he wound down the window and tossed the crumpled note at the blind beggar woman.

She in turn raised a can of pepper spray and said, "Hands where I can see them."

An especially insulting expletive left the goon's mouth and as he reached down for his revolver, she didn't hesitate to press down on the nozzle.

A full spume hit him in the face. There was a moment's silence like the one that comes between a child falling and starting to cry. And then from the back of the Afridi's throat came an agonized scream, and he smothered his face with his hands.

Hari managed to grab his pistol and, coughing and sputtering, opened the door and stumbled out onto the road.

"That wasn't part of the plan!" he complained, his eyes streaming with tears as he helped Puri and Ram out of the car and unlocked their handcuffs. "You could have warned me that she was going to do that!"

"Don't talk to me about plans, yaar!" bawled Puri, his eyes also watering from the pepper spray. "You were supposed to disarm him *before* I arrived!"

"You two are working together?" said Ram.

"I was prepared to make an exception just this once," said Hari.

"An exception, is it?" retorted Puri. "It is thanks to me

you are off the hook and this young man is not lying with a bullet in the head."

"Do you really think I would have walked into such a situation unprepared? I had a Plan B. And a Plan C. Ram was never in danger."

Flush arrived on the scene and started to unbutton Hari's shirt to retrieve the pinhole camera and transmitter he'd fitted on him earlier that morning on the edge of Lucknow.

"Boss, we got all of them—Baba, Dr. Pandey, Gujar. Every frame," Puri's operative reported.

"Tip-top, very good," said Puri. "I will join you momentarily. Make two copies. One I want taken directly to the *Action News!* bureau. Then we two—Hari and I—will go directly to the CBI as per the plan."

The beggar woman, the boy and two other young men pulled the Afridi from the car and tied his wrists.

"Her I know," said Hari, who'd recognized Facecream through her disguise. "But who is the boy?"

"A new addition," said Puri.

"And the other two helping her—yours?"

"Some extra pairs of hands were required. They're volunteers—Love Commandos, in fact."

"*Love Commandos?*"

"My clients, so to speak."

Hari tilted his head back and glanced up at the sky. "*Now* I understand," he said with a slow, deliberate nod. "I've been racking my brains trying to figure out how you came to be involved in the case."

A look of sheer delight came over Puri's face. "Glad to hear it," he said. "But one question is there."

"Your pistol?"

"I want it back, Hari."

"Not to worry, Mr. Vish Puri, saar, it's safe and sound."

They watched as the Afridi was bustled into a car and driven away.

"What's going to happen to him?" asked Ram.

"He will be delivered to the CBI and charged with murder," said Puri.

"You trust the CBI?"

"No. But that is why we are releasing the video to the TV news outlets first. Public outrage will force them to act."

"And me? I'll be able to testify?" said Ram.

"You will get your day in court, young man. Many days in fact, if you so choose."

Ram gave a nod. "I'm sorry, Mr. Puri, I misjudged you. I can't thank you enough for everything you've done for me."

"Please, I beg of you, young man, don't give him a bigger head than he already has!" said Hari.

"I do have one question for you, sir," said Ram. "Dr. Basu—did Baba Dhobi and Dr. Pandey conspire to have her killed?"

"Not at all. It was one of her work colleagues, in fact."

"Because they discovered the leak?"

"That I cannot say exactly—but most probably, yes."

"But as we were pulling out of the gates, I saw in that other car—"

"Justus Bergstrom, the ICMB director."

"Yes, sir. He interrogated me before I escaped—wanted to know where I'd put the data key."

"And no doubt that is why he has come calling on Baba Dhobi this morning—to retrieve his property."

"For a price," said Hari.

Puri gave a nod. "Knowing Baba Dhobi, he will extract the quantum amount. That is all he is after, no? Wealth at any cost."

• • •

Two hours later, Puri sought out Justus Bergstrom in the VVIP terminal lounge at Lucknow airport, where he was waiting for his executive jet to refuel. He was sitting back in a comfortable leather lounger with his legs crossed, toying with a USB data key like an expert gambler with a casino chip.

"I see you got what you came here for, sir," observed the detective.

Bergstrom surveyed him with patient eyes. "I did indeed, Mr. Puri. And you?"

"One piece of the puzzle is missing, in fact."

"You're referring to the Dr. Basu affair?"

"Affair, sir? It was murder, as you well know. Even here in India we have laws against it. Allow me to assure you that the guilty will be brought to book."

Bergstrom played hurt. "You believe I'd stand in the way of justice, Mr. Puri?"

"Sir, I have seen what you are capable of—kidnapping, intimidation, exploitation. In the past few days you have done all within your power to recover that data key you hold in your hand. Profit is your number one goal. Would you cover up a murder to avoid scandal and bad publicity? Of that I am in no doubt at all."

Bergstrom slipped Ram's data key into his trouser pocket, sat up and adjusted his cuffs. "I think you misjudge me, Mr. Puri," he said. "I can hardly run a successful operation if my employees start murdering one another, now, can I?"

He picked up his briefcase and popped open the two locks. From inside he retrieved a file. He held it out for Puri to take.

"After Dr. Basu's death last week, I ordered an investigation into the circumstances," said Bergstrom. "My security team—I believe you have crossed paths with them once or twice—quickly came to the conclusion that she'd been murdered. It also became clear from her phone and computer records that Dr. Basu had been in regular contact with a certain Ram Sunder, who was participating in one of our drug trials. After reviewing footage taken by our security cameras as well as our computer records, we came to know that she'd taken a copy of some of our research from the building—illegally."

"At which point you tracked down Ram Sunder and abducted him. You got his mobile number from Dr. Basu's phone records. His device was switched on, thus making the task child's play."

"I wouldn't know anything about that, Mr. Puri. Kidnapping is not something we indulge in at ICMB."

"No, sir. You've others to do your dirty work—two former British army Gurkhas no less."

"The point is, Mr. Puri, that we came to the conclusion that Ram Sunder had played no part in Dr. Basu's murder. Our focus then turned to another individual."

"Dr. Sengupta, your head of research."

"Unfortunately, yes. Dr. Sengupta has always been passionate about his work. But the passionate can also be obsessive. And it seems he became obsessed—totally infatuated, in fact—with Dr. Basu. In that file you will find copies of pages from his private diary in which he describes having erotic fantasies about her in the laboratory where they worked side by side. He talks about 'owning her body and soul.' On a number of occasions she went on dates and he spied on her. The men she met are described in disturbing terms and he considers using violence to scare them off."

"Must be Dr. Basu had some idea of his feelings, no?" said Puri. "Any complaints were made against him on her behalf?"

"Several, Mr. Puri. I have included copies of her e-mails in that file. Dr. Sengupta visited her at her apartment on no less than three occasions late at night. Naturally she felt uncomfortable about this and brought his improper behavior to my attention."

"You acted on her complaints?"

"Yes, I spoke with Dr. Sengupta. He told me he'd gone to see Dr. Basu to discuss work—the project they'd been working on. I warned him that this was highly unprofessional and he assured me that it wouldn't happen again."

"No further action was taken?"

"I received no further complaints."

"But then Dr. Basu announced her engagement and her departure from ICMB, also."

"She submitted her resignation the day she was killed."

"And you believe Dr. Sengupta confronted her that very night?"

"Perhaps he stopped her on the road, there was an argument, he strangled her and then arranged the scene to look like an accident."

"Some further proof is there?"

"He answered a call from his mother soon after midnight in the vicinity of the bridge."

Puri searched through the file and found a copy of Dr. Sengupta's phone records with the incriminating call highlighted.

"Who is to say that you are not framing him?" said Puri.

"And why would I do that?"

"You were worried she would spill the beans, so to speak, on your work—and as for Dr. Sengupta, he was unstable."

"I think you've been watching a little too much Bollywood, Mr. Puri. This is the real world."

"Aaah, the real world, is it? My apologies, sir. For a moment I thought I was dreaming about genetics research companies exploiting Dalits for their DNA and innocent midwives getting raped and murdered."

The Swede looked mildly irritated. "Please, Mr. Puri, spare me the sarcasm. I played no part in this tragic affair and have taken it upon myself to get to the bottom of what happened. Last night, I submitted a copy of the same file to the Agra police and they arrested Dr. Sengupta this morning."

"From his residence at seven thirty in fact," said Puri.

"You knew?" For the first time, Bergstrom showed surprise.

"It is my business to know," said Puri with triumph. "This is for me to keep, no?" he asked as he held up the file.

"By all means. And now I believe that concludes our business together." Bergstrom stood and picked up his briefcase. "I trust that there will be no further contact between us."

"Sir, one thing is there, actually," said Puri.

"And that is?"

"Contrary to what you have been told, he is alive and well."

"He?"

"Ram Sunder."

"Alive?" Bergstrom's eyes narrowed.

"Yes, sir."

"Well, I'm very glad to hear it, Mr. Puri."

"He is now under the special protection of the CBI, in fact, and no doubt his lawyer will be contacting you in the coming days."

"Regarding?"

"The rights of he and his fellow villagers."

"Rights? I believe that is something of a gray area here in India, is it not?" said Bergstrom, his lips drawn in a tight smirk.

"That is what the Britishers believed, sir, before they faced a certain Mohandas K. Gandhi," answered Puri.

And then he watched as the Swede strode purposefully out of the terminal and crossed the tarmac toward his waiting jet.

Twenty-four

Mummy and Rumpi didn't reach Jammu until dawn, by which time the robbery of the Vaishno Devi shrine had become national news. Bundles of thousand-rupee notes with a value of one million dollars had been stolen, it emerged, and the police were hunting for a young woman going by the name of Gauri Nanda. An artist's impression of the suspect was being circulated. Extra security had also been put in place at the airport and railway station. There were checks being carried out on all major roads leading in and out of the city.

Jagdish Uncle hadn't been heard from since midnight, when he'd reached home. Mummy and Rumpi soon discovered that there was a simple explanation for this: he was tucked up in bed sleeping soundly.

"But, Uncle-ji, you said you would not rest until you tracked them down—that no one could pass through Jammu unnoticed," said Rumpi after they woke him.

"Everyone in the city is known to me," he replied with a lordly flourish as he stood in the kitchen in his undershirt, sarong and black socks.

"So where is Pranap Dughal?" asked Mummy.

"Kindly allow me to explain," he replied. "See, after my poor Sweetie met her fate, I called ahead to Ranvir at the toll. Thus he saw that same Toyota entering the city boundary on Palace Road. From there, Manvir who sells guavas spotted their vehicle racing past Government Dental College. Five minutes later, they reached Purani Mandi, where Raju, who sits playing cards with Amit and Gurshan, did not fail to notice the vehicle, also."

Jagdish Uncle helped himself to some cold rajma from the fridge, eating it straight from a Tupperware container.

"You were saying, Uncle-ji?" prompted Rumpi.

"Right, so, after that they passed through Lakhdatta Bazaar."

"Aur?" asked Mummy, who was fast losing patience.

"Then they crossed New Tawi Bridge. Arjan, the Kwality ice cream vendor sitting on the far side, is well known to me. From him I was able to trace the vehicle to Gandhinagar, where Puneet Sahib's driver was sitting idle doing timepass."

"Any person in Jammu did not see them, Uncle-ji?" asked Rumpi.

"At that point, in fact, madam, the trail went stale. Had Mr. Julhar been feeding the pigeons in his usual place, their direction thereafter would have been duly noted, but alas, he went to attend his sister's wedding in Jalandhar three days back and while there got admitted to hospital with an abdominal infection."

Rumpi took a deep breath to calm herself, exhaled slowly and said, "Uncle-ji, were you able to trace them or not?"

"I was not."

This disclosure drew a joint sigh of disappointment from the two women.

Jagdish Uncle, however, made light of it. "Ladies, not to worry, be happy," he said.

"How you can say that?" asked Rumpi.

"Situation is under control."

"Uncle-ji, you just told us you weren't able to locate the Dughals."

"That is true, *I* was not. But Surender, who works at Anand Auto Parts—*he* saw them entering Paradise Guesthouse."

Rumpi screeched, "Uncle-ji!" and picked an apple up off the kitchen table as if to throw it at him. "How can you joke at a time like this?"

"It is easy when you know how, madam," he said with magisterial dignity.

Mummy looked less than amused. "Did they do check in?" she asked.

"They are in room number four. And," Jagdish Uncle added, "I came to know they have tickets for the Jet Airways flight at eleven. Now we can inform Inspector Malhotra and he can do the needful."

But Mummy was already heading for the front door.

"Where are you going?" he called after her.

"Just I must reach," she called over her shoulder.

Rumpi hurried after her. "Wait, I'm coming with you," she said.

Jagdish Uncle was left in the kitchen holding the Tupperware container of rajma. "What's the hurry?" he called out. And then after a moment's hesitation, "Wait for me!"

It was still too early to find an auto plying Jammu's streets, but they came across one parked at the end of the galli that ran in front of Jagdish Uncle's home. The auto wallah, who was asleep in the backseat with his feet sticking out the side of his vehicle, was perhaps the one person in all of Jammu with whom Jagdish Uncle was not acquainted, and it took the latter a few minutes to persuade him to forgo his wash and breakfast and transport them the couple of miles to the Paradise Guesthouse.

"You are providing an important public service," Jagdish Uncle kept assuring him.

These blandishments appeared to make no impression whatsoever on the auto wallah, who took his time slipping on his chappals, combing his beard and relieving himself on the nearest wall.

He then spent a couple of minutes communing with the collection of deities on his dashboard before hand-cranking the engine. Soon, the auto was putt-putting through Jammu's narrow lanes.

They were about halfway to Paradise Guesthouse when Jagdish Uncle remembered to turn on his phone and found a couple of missed calls from the clerk. The Dughals, he learned, had checked out and were headed for the train station and *not* the airport.

The Delhi-bound Shatabdi was due to depart in twenty-five minutes. The auto wallah was duly informed of the change in destination—at which point he rebelled.

"Sahib, nahin," he said, and pulled to a stop.

No amount of pleading or indeed name-calling—"stupid duffer!"—would persuade him to budge and only an offer of double the usual fare assured his continued co-operation.

This princely sum didn't guarantee that the vehicle moved any faster. But thanks to its compactness and maneuverability and the driver's knowledge of a number of shortcuts, they were able to make up for lost time.

With ten minutes to spare before the departure of the Delhi-bound train, the trio pulled up in front of the station and hurried to the entrance.

They found a crowd of passengers waiting to pass through the extra police security check, where an X-ray machine was in operation.

Mummy spotted the Dughals at the front of the queue, but there was no way to reach them.

"The stationmaster is known to me," said Jagdish Uncle.

"Go find him, na. We two will stay here meanwhile," said Mummy.

She and Rumpi watched Mrs. Dughal being wheeled around the metal detector arch before being searched by a female jawan. Her husband then passed through the arch without triggering the alarm and the police waved him on toward the waiting train.

An announcement came over the tannoy system saying that the train would be leaving in five minutes.

"Requesting all passengers to kindly board," said a female voice.

With just two minutes to spare, Jagdish Uncle returned with the stationmaster. He led them through the cargo-storage area, where railway officials and porters were sorting parcels of all shapes and sizes wrapped in muslin cloth. A barrow of crates blocked their exit for a crucial thirty seconds. They heard a whistle followed by the slamming of doors.

By the time they reached the platform, they were too late. The train had pulled out of the station.

"Had it not been for that duffer we would have reached here in time," said Mummy, who was referring to the auto wallah.

"I still don't know what you expected to do once we caught them," said Rumpi as she watched the rear carriage disappear from sight.

"What with so many police around we could get them delayed, na."

"Well, Mummy-ji, we tried our best and that's the most anyone can ever do. Uncle-ji, you also deserve a medal. Where would we be without—"

Rumpi looked dumbstruck. She had spotted something at the end of the platform and was staring hard. "That looks like Inspector Malhotra and—"

"*Them!*" exclaimed Mummy.

The trio walked toward the Dughals in a kind of astonished daze.

Inspector Malhotra greeted them warmly.

"Mrs. Puri, I owe you an apology. You were right all along," he said. "One of the Vaishno Devi priests has confessed to drugging the security guard and planning the robbery with this man, Pranap Dughal, or rather Dhiru Bhatia, a charge-sheeter, believed to have been involved with the Bhutan Bank robbery last year."

Mummy was all grins. "Most probably he started life as a pickpocket," she said. "Thus he could not resist taking Chubby's wallet. Old habits and all."

"I'm sure you're right, Mrs. Puri," said Malhotra. "But to be honest we are still a little stumped." He took her to one side and whispered, "We are unable to locate the loot. I'm concerned that they might have hidden it somewhere or it is being transported by another accomplice."

"No, no, Inspector. Just you are looking but not seeing," said Mummy.

"I don't understand, madam."

"See here." She rummaged through her purse and retrieved a safety pin. Thus armed, she approached Mrs. Dughal.

The woman shot dagger eyes at her. But Mummy didn't hesitate to jab the pin into her side several times.

There came a slow hissing sound.

Mrs. Dughal began, imperceptibly at first, to reduce in size.

"See," said Mummy.

Malhotra lifted up the woman's kurta. Beneath lay a deflating fat suit and, beneath this, wads of thousand-rupee notes strapped around her stomach, thighs and legs.

"Her chin is fake also—and she is wearing so much of makeup," said Mummy. "But underneath you will find the young lady you are doing searching for high and low. Gauri Nanda no less."

Once the money had been recovered and the Dughals led away, Inspector Malhotra escorted Mummy to the police station, where she was required to make a statement.

It was the sand in the Vaishno Devi guesthouse that gave the game away, she explained, adding, "Just they were doing disposal of it down the shower."

"Are you saying she—Mrs. Dughal, aka Gauri Nanda—carried the sand beneath her fat suit all the way up Vaishno Devi?"

"Correct. Everything was deception, na—her weight, candy bars, ordering of large meals from room service, shouting abuse at her partner in crime. Thus she and he were setting the stage like magicians. Aim was to make all and sundry believe she was obese. No one should be in doubt. Porters included. It was she who returned Chubby's wallet in the wee hours on the train. Just she slipped it unseen under the curtain. That is after taking off all her getup and thus going unrecognized."

"So once they reached the top of the mountain she changed out of her fat suit and got rid of all the sand she'd been carrying about her as well," said Malhotra. "But I don't understand how she checked into the guesthouse as Gauri Nanda."

"I believe I know the answer to that one," said Rumpi,

who was sitting in on the debriefing. "Once the two of them were in their room in the Vaishno Devi guesthouse, she waited until the foyer was crowded and then slipped outside unnoticed. The priest had her backpack waiting. She put it on, returned to the guesthouse and checked in under her assumed name. Then in the middle of the night she left again—fooling even Mummy. She broke into the vault, made off with the loot, and returned to her room. In the morning, she taped all the wads of notes to herself and donned her disguise again, although the fat suit probably didn't have to be inflated quite as much as before, I would imagine."

"That is how we came to recover her backpack and climbing rope from her room," said Malhotra. "Had the couple's chartered helicopter been allowed to land they'd have got clean away."

"Scot-free," agreed Mummy.

"But thanks to you, Mrs. Puri, these two were brought to my attention—thus when the priest confessed I knew who to look for."

"So kind of you," said Mummy.

Malhotra escorted them out of the station to an auto.

"Naturally I will mention your invaluable assistance in my report and, furthermore, recommend you receive the five lakh reward, madam," he said.

Rumpi smiled. "Seems you were right after all, Mummy-ji," she said as she gave her mother-in-law a fond hug. "Old really *is* gold."

Twenty-five

Puri had lost count of the number of weddings he'd attended in his time. During the height of the season, he was often left with no choice but to make an appearance at four or five "functions" every week, the vast majority for business associates, neighbors and distant cousins.

Invariably the venues were "marriage halls" or "lawns" with spaces large enough to accommodate hundreds, sometimes thousands, of guests. Vast cathedrals of frippery and bling, they were generally so garish and ostentatious—not to mention bright—that the detective often wondered if they could be spotted with the naked eye from space.

The last wedding he'd attended (or was it the one before?) had been held at Seven Star Banquet Hall in Moti Nagar. The daughter of a childhood friend who'd made a fortune in kitchen and bathroom tiles (and, like most people with cash and half a brain during the past decade, a second fortune in "realty") had married the son of a Delhi marble dealer.

"No expense has been spared!" the bride's proud father had boasted.

As was so often the case, this proved no exaggeration. His daughter and her betrothed posed for photographs while sitting on Louis XIV–style thrones atop a stage straight out of a Miss World contest. Fountains spewed multicolored water, laser beams pierced the sky and a Bollywood starlet in a plunging sari blouse gyrated atop a podium.

Puri was spoiled for choice when it came to food, with a buffet as long as a football pitch offering Continental, Indo-Chinese, Punjabi, south Indian and numerous varieties of street food. The gol gappa was especially good. But along with a severe case of indigestion, he left feeling somewhat subdued by the crassness of it all. In a country with so much want and need, the Great Indian Wedding was truly out of control.

It was, therefore, with marked relief that Puri arrived outside the venue for Ram and Tulsi's wedding.

The Arya Samaj temple at the "Ashram red-light turnoff" on Delhi's Inner Ring Road was a simple building, barely recognizable from the outside as a Hindu place of worship. Maintained by a reform movement that emphasized the importance of meditative prayer over idol worship, the entrance was markedly peaceful, with no loudspeakers blaring mantras. Puri joined a small group of guests made up of the bride and groom's most trusted friends, as well as Facecream, two of her fellow Love Commandos and three plainclothes CBI officers charged with protecting Ram.

In the absence of a brass band and white steed, the baraat was an improvised affair. When the groom arrived on the back of a motorbike dressed in a simple sherwani and pagdi, he was showered with ten-rupee notes and everyone jigged to the female guests' rendition of "Le jayenge, le jayenge dil wale dulhania le jayenge!"

Tulsi had arrived ten minutes ahead of Ram and was waiting inside the temple. She looked stunning in a gold and red lehnga, the delicate henna patterns on her hands and feet and strings of jasmine tied in her hair more than making up for the absence of extravagant bridal jewelry.

The room where the ceremony was to be conducted was simply decorated with strings of fresh flowers hanging from the walls and Kashmiri carpets laid on the floor. The priest, or arya, wore none of the usual regalia of traditional pandits; in a plain shirt and trousers, he could have been mistaken for an office worker. Ram handed him the items required for the ceremony—two marigold garlands, half a kilo of ghee and a box of ladoos—and the couple sat cross-legged on the floor before a shallow hearth.

Once all the guests had arranged themselves in a semi-circle behind them, the ceremony began with Tulsi draping a garland around Ram's neck. The groom then washed his feet, hands and face before eating from a concoction of curd, honey and ghee.

"It's good of you to come, sir," Facecream whispered to Puri as they sat side by side, watching the sacred fire being lit.

"I would not have missed it for all the world, actually," he replied. "So much courage Ram showed, I tell you."

Even when his mother's killer had led him away with the intention of putting a bullet in his head, the young man hadn't begged for his life. He hadn't even cried.

And now, when the CBI was preparing to charge Baba Dhobi and Dr. Pandey with murder and Ram faced the ordeal of years in protective custody as the star witness in what would hopefully be a political trial the likes of which India had never seen, he was holding firm.

"I want justice for my mother" had been his words to the CBI director yesterday after being warned of the possible dangers of testifying.

It had been wrong of him to prejudge Ram, Puri acknowledged privately. And he'd been wrong to condemn Ram's union with Tulsi. Family was the bedrock of society—on that the detective held firm—but like anything else, families could "malfunction." Vishnu Mishra's rejection of an upstanding young man like Ram on the basis of caste was at best misguided.

Puri felt the urge to write a letter to the honorable editor of the *Times of India* on the subject and penned a few lines in his head.

Tradition and customs have their place and provide us with key reference points and a certain continuity. However, rigidity in thinking is the enemy of progress. Likewise, babies should not be thrown out with the bathwater. It is for young people also to act responsibly during times of change. A successful marriage is built on mutual understanding and compatibility. Love should also be there.

As Puri watched the bride's and groom's hands being joined together, he was suddenly struck by an intense longing for his wife. It felt like an age since they'd spent any proper time together and he was glad that she would finally be home from Jammu in a few hours. Tomorrow he would take her to that restaurant she liked—the Chinese one in that godforsaken mall in Vasant Kunj. Then this weekend there was his birthday bash to look forward to. Their three daughters were all coming home and the house would be filled with grandchildren and laughter.

Ram and Tulsi recited their wedding vows and began to circle the flames. When they had completed four turns, Tulsi placed her foot on a stone while the groom repeated a mantra expressing his wish that their marriage should be built on firm foundations. The arya then filled Tulsi's hands with puffed rice.

"You have grown in your parents' home but, like a seed,

must be replanted in another home in order to blossom and mature," he said.

Ram and Tulsi were now husband and wife. Only the paperwork remained. Two witnesses were required to sign the marriage certificate, and the happy couple asked Facecream and Puri to oblige.

"Nothing would give me more pleasure, young man," said the detective as he pinched Ram's cheek hard in a show of pure Punjabi affection.

On the way back to his office, Puri watched the sky through the window of his Ambassador. A dark cloud was moving over the city like a menacing alien mother ship, casting Delhi in a gloomy half-light. Everyone out on the pavements or standing in the doorways of shops and businesses had their eyes cast upwards. But their expressions spoke only of joy and expectation. The monsoon proper had finally arrived. Relief was only minutes away.

When he reached Khan Market, Puri didn't linger outside, however. He went straight up to his office and started dictating his notes on the Case of the Love Commandos to Elizabeth Rani. His executive secretary, who had finally enjoyed a couple of days off, typed his words on a laptop computer, stopping him occasionally to confirm a date, a time or the spelling of an unfamiliar name, like Justus Bergstrom.

"As for the killer himself, he was indeed an Afridi, as Tubelight had guessed—a descendant of Muslim Afghans who settled in Uttar Pradesh," said Puri. "Vishnu Mishra has since been released and all charges dropped. He has offered a substantial reward for anyone who leads him to his daughter."

The detective ended with the words "Madam Rani, it is without doubt one of the most challenging cases I have solved in my long and illustrious career 'til date."

Usually this would have been Elizabeth Rani's cue to marvel at his acumen. But fearing the evil eye as much as her employer, she restricted her congratulations to "Well done, sir, I don't know how you do it."

She then followed this up with a few questions about the case.

"Sir, Ram's mother, Kamlesh, was violated by Dr. Bal Pandey at Lucknow General Hospital and Baba Dhobi, who in those days was an administrator, failed to file a case against him," she said.

"Quite correct, Madam Rani," said Puri as he sat back in his executive swivel chair with his fingers knitted together and hands resting on his belly.

"But then she—"

"You are wondering what benefit Baba Dhobi gained from turning a blind eye and not pressing charges against Pandey?" he asked with a hint of magnanimity in his voice.

"Actually, sir, that I understand. Being a man with no scruples, he turned the circumstances to his advantage. What I was wondering was—"

"Why Kamlesh Sunder continued to place trust in him?"

She gave a nod. "Yes, sir."

"Madam Rani, a female such as she, coming from the village and all, never thought for one second that Baba Dhobi was playing a double role," said Puri. "He presented the situation as *us* versus *them*—that being his forte so to speak. He was a fellow Dalit in a position of authority and yet he could appear to be powerless against the Brahmin oppressor."

He paused. "Anything else is there?" he asked, knowing full well that more questions were to follow.

"Yes, sir. I don't understand how Hari came to know that Ram escaped his captors."

"That is an easy one, actually, Madam Rani. He was

working for Baba Dhobi, who in turn was in touch with Bergstrom, who was desperate to get back his data key with the research."

"They had links beforehand—Baba Dhobi and Bergstrom?"

"ICMB could not build such a facility in Uttar Pradesh without the express permission of the chief minister, Madam Rani. So many kickbacks and all are required."

"So it was Baba Dhobi's goondas who went to the village and thrashed Ram's father and the chowkidar in the village?"

"Not at all. That was the work of the two Gurkha gentlemen in the employ of Bergstrom. After coming to know that Dr. Basu leaked the research, they were charged with searching high and low for Ram."

"I still don't understand how Ram escaped, sir."

"He revealed the details yesterday, only. After getting abducted, he was interviewed by Bergstrom at some undisclosed location in Agra. Some violence was used—beatings and all. Afterward, Ram was confined to a room and one ankle was chained to the wall. Later that night he pulled a few threads from his shirt and used them to tie three links in the chain together, thus shortening it and making it so tight that it dug into his skin. He then called to the guard and demanded to use the toilet. This was allowed and so the chain was removed. After Ram returned from the toilet, the chain was placed once again around his ankle. The guard, not noticing the threads with the links still tied together, made it a little loose. Once he had departed from the room, Ram snapped the threads, thus rendering the chain loose enough to slip it off his ankle. He then made his getaway out a window and went to ground once more in Agra while searching for Tulsi."

"A remarkable young man," said Elizabeth Rani. "I do hope he's being properly protected."

"What with all the publicity in the case, the CBI would not want to be found wanting," said Puri. "Priority will be given to his safety, that is for sure. But he and his lovely bride will be forced to live with separate identities 'til the end of their days. For everything in this life there is a price to be paid, Madam Rani, is there not?"

"Yes, I suppose, sir," said Elizabeth Rani, who didn't sound altogether convinced.

She stood up from her chair and lingered in front of the desk with a puzzled look. Puri could see that there was still something on her mind.

"Tell me, Madam Rani?" he said with as much patience as he could muster given the hunger pains that were developing deep in his belly.

"Facecream, sir. You don't think she would ever leave us, do you—go and work for the Love Commandos full-time?" she asked.

Puri's mouth curled into a smile. "To be totally and perfectly honest, I have had my concerns, also," he said. "What all she was doing mixed up with such an underground organization? I wondered. Where were her loyalties lying these days? But now all concerns are gone. I salute her commitment, actually. She identifies with the cause. It is heartfelt, that is for sure. Why . . . ? I cannot tell you. Could be when she was younger, she was forced to marry. Or she was forbidden from marrying some boy. Frankly speaking, it is not for us to ask. She is a privately minded person. And I am proud to say, one of the most remarkable people I have had the honor to work with 'til date."

The pitter-patter of rain drew the detective's attention to the window. Streaks were starting to appear on the grimy panes.

"Aaah, at last Madam Rani—baarish!" he said as he stood up and went to get a closer look. "Better late than never, haan?"

"Yes, sir, the city certainly needs it."

They stood by the window watching as the deluge grew in intensity and the surfaces of the road and pavement below began to effervesce as if the water gathering upon them was boiling.

Puri pushed open the window. The stale, fetid air that had been hanging over the city for weeks was dissipating. He found that he could breathe easily again.

"Madam Rani, we should celebrate," he said. "Send the boy for some nice hot pakoras."

"But, sir, the weather?"

He looked out the window again. The other side of the street was no longer visible. It sounded like they were standing at the bottom of a waterfall.

"Come now, Madam Rani," said the detective, "it is only a little rain, no?"

At a few minutes to eight in the evening, Puri fixed himself a drink, sat down on the sofa in his sitting room and switched on the TV.

"News is coming!" he shouted to Rumpi, who was in the kitchen.

The detective could barely contain his excitement as he switched to *Action News!*

Often when he solved a big case, he didn't get the recognition he deserved. Either because some cop stole the limelight or, more often than not, out of a need to remain anonymous for fear of retaliation.

Occasionally, he also stayed away from the cameras for

fear of prejudicing the outcome of the trial. He and Hari had agreed to adopt such a policy with regard to the Case of the Love Commandos.

If the special court acted properly and Baba Dhobi and Dr. Pandey and all those associated with the murder of Kamlesh Sunder were convicted, then the two rivals would break their silence.

The Jain Jewelry Heist, however, was different.

Puri had finally solved the case that very afternoon after he'd found himself thinking about Baba Dhobi's south Indian Vaastu practitioner.

Vaastu was becoming increasingly popular amongst India's "creamy layer." The wealthier they got, the more paranoid they became about losing everything, it seemed. Thus the thought had occurred to him that the Jains might have consulted with a Vaastu practitioner.

He soon discovered that they had.

His name was Gopal Jaipuria and he'd advised Jay Jain in the design, positioning and construction of the house.

Jaipuria, a specialist in astro-numerology and gem therapy, had also been given access to all of the Jain family's birth dates, anniversaries and favorite numbers. With these, he'd been able to crack the combination to the safe.

"What part did the other thieves play—the ones you caught with the earrings and cash?" asked Rumpi as she settled onto the sofa next to him.

"The Vaastu practitioner set them up—gave them the job, so to speak."

"So they arrived after he'd emptied the safe?"

"By a good hour at least. Must be he opened the safe with some ease, left them a token amount and made off with the mother lode. After, the gang came bungling in, blowing up the safe with dynamite. A bunch of jokers they were."

At five this afternoon, Jaipuria had been arrested and the jewels recovered. Puri had thus concluded that his bad fortune was gone. The evil eye's gaze was focused elsewhere. When *Action News!* arrived at the scene and asked him to comment, he hadn't been able to resist taking credit for single-handedly solving the case.

Now, fifty million people were about to share his moment of triumph.

"Here it comes," said Rumpi when the graphics rolled and the sensational music pumped from the speakers.

"Tonight—an *Action News!* exclusive!" announced the anchor.

Rumpi took Puri's hand in hers. "I'm so proud of you, Chubby," she said, and gave it a squeeze.

"Our reporter is live in Punjabi Bagh, Delhi, and we cross to her now. Vineeta, I understand the real hero of the Vaishno Devi heist has been revealed?"

Puri exclaimed, "What the bloody hell!" as a young woman appeared on the screen, standing in front of an apartment block.

"That's Mummy's house!" cried Rumpi.

"Yes, my dear," mumbled Puri, who looked like he'd lost the will to live.

"It's emerged tonight that an aunty in her seventies cracked the case single-handedly," the reporter was saying. "Thanks to this heroic senior, the thieves together with the loot were apprehended by the police as they were making their getaway. Koomi Puri, known to one and all as Mummy-ji, is here with me now. Mummy-ji, the Jammu police have called you a national hero. How does that make you feel?"

Mummy glanced apprehensively at the camera. Staring down at the handheld microphone, she spoke into it. "Just I was doing my duty as a concerned citizen of India, na."

"I understand the thieves masqueraded as yatris on the

pilgrimage, but you realized there was something fishy going on?"

"Pranap Dughal—sorry, Dhiru Bhatia—was a bad sort. So crafty he was. A daku through and through."

"And you saw through the lady thief's disguise?"

"At first, no. She was doing so much of abuse and all and eating everything in sight."

"And I understand you identified the priest involved, also."

"He was on the train from Delhi doing planning of the robbery with Pranap Dughal."

"Now, I've come to know that sleuthing runs in the family, Mummy-ji. Is it true your son is a private investigator in Delhi?"

"My late husband Om Chander Puri was a police inspector, also."

"And it was because you were trying to help your son that the thieves came to your notice on the train?"

Puri could hardly watch. He'd managed to contain news of the embarrassing pickpocket incident, and his professional reputation remained intact.

"Please, Mummy, don't . . . I'm begging you," he muttered.

But he was wasting his breath. She came straight out with it.

"See," she said, "it all started when Chubby—that is my second eldest, the private investigator one—he got his wallet stolen on the train by that Pranap Dughal."

Puri covered his face with his hands.

"By God," he groaned.

Epilogue

The city was loud—car horns blasting, people shouting. Billboard advertisements showed half-naked, fair-skinned girls. Everyone seemed to be in a big hurry.

The cost of everything was equally bewildering. The bus ticket alone had been more than each of the three women spent on lentils in a week. The price of a plate of subzi and three rotis quoted at a roadside stand had persuaded them to go without food until they returned home to the village in the evening.

An auto wallah quoted them a fortune to take them to the address written on the business card.

They would have to walk, they decided. Poonam knew better than to ask the police for directions. Instead, she approached another Dalit woman and asked her son, but he only pretended to be able to read the address and sent them in the wrong direction.

Finally, as they stood at a busy junction looking this way and that and wondering if perhaps their journey had been in vain, a young woman wearing glasses stopped to cross the road. In her appearance, she was like the village teacher who'd helped them. Poonam summoned the courage to ask her to point the way.

The young woman didn't speak Awadhi but looked at the piece of paper and nodded. The place was very close, she seemed to say—a five-minute walk at the most.

Soon, the three women found themselves entering a building and then being shown into a strange metal box with a mirror on one wall and some buttons next to the door. A man wearing a uniform asked them where they were going and Poonam showed him the card. He then pressed one of the buttons. Two metal doors slid together. Finding themselves trapped inside, they panicked and screamed. Then they felt a strange sensation as the box moved upward and, a moment later, the doors opened again.

They staggered out and were greeted by a plump, middle-aged woman in a sari, glasses and maroon lipstick. Her name was Kukreja.

She led the three women into a small, cramped room full of papers and books and gave them chairs to sit on.

Kukreja Madam said she was pleased that they had come to see her and said she knew all about their situation. She even had a file on her desk, containing official documents about their village, Govind. They detailed how much rice and lentils the Dalits had been allotted under the government ration scheme over the past year. But when Kukreja Madam read out the figures the women said that they had received less than a quarter of the official count.

"How many days' work have you completed under the rural employment-guarantee scheme?" she asked.

"None!" they chorused.

Kukreja Madam pursed her lips and then riffled through another file. She found their names listed on another piece of paper and explained that, according to the official record, they had worked for one hundred days each and been paid accordingly.

A young man appeared carrying three cups of tea and a plate of biscuits.

When he was gone, the village women began to giggle, telling Kukreja Madam that no man had ever served them anything before.

She smiled. "I can help you," she said. "But it's not going to be easy and will take time. First, I need to understand how things work in your village and the name of the pradhan in charge of distributing the rations."

His name is Rakesh Yadav, they said, but he'd been arrested a few days ago for processing and smuggling heroin. His eldest son was now in charge.

Would his family come to know about their visit to Lucknow? Poonam wanted to know.

Yes, they would find out eventually. But as Kukreja Madam explained, she ran a charity that would take up their case and place two volunteers in the village. They would monitor the situation and report to the police.

"The police do exactly what the Yadavs tell them to do," Poonam pointed out.

Kukreja Madam repeated that she was not promising change overnight. But if they were strong, it would come.

The three women talked amongst themselves and agreed that they were prepared to stand for what was rightfully theirs. They believed others in their village would join them.

"Good," said Kukreja Madam. "Then we will fight them together."

Mouthwatering Dishes from the Vish Puri Family Kitchen

Lucknow Mutton Biryani

The city of Lucknow is synonymous with Biryani. The dish is traditionally cooked using the *dum pukht* method (in Persian, *dum* means "to breathe" and *pukht* "to cook"). The idea is to use a low heat and to seal the rice and meat in a pot using dough around the lid, allowing the juices and flavors to slowly infuse the dish. Do this in an earthenware pot with a lid on the stove or in an earthenware dish in the oven.

Serves 4

Meat

2 pounds lamb, mutton, beef, or chicken, cubed

1 cup stock

Marinade

4 tablespoons garlic paste (or mashed garlic)

4 tablespoons ginger paste (or chopped in a food processor with a little water)

1 cup yogurt

Pinch of saffron (optional)

½ teaspoon lime juice

½ teaspoon salt

2 teaspoons ground coriander

2 teaspoons ground cumin

Red chilli powder to taste

1 tablespoon garam masala*

Rice

2 cups basmati rice

Hot water

Available in Asian grocery stores. Contains dry roasted green cardamom, black pepper, coriander, cloves, bay leaf, cinnamon, nutmeg, star anise and fennel seeds.

Garnish

- ½ cup ghee/vegetable oil/ butter
- 1 cup onion, thinly sliced and fried in ghee until brown
- ½ cup slivered almonds, fried (optional)
- ½ cup slivered cashews, fried (optional)
- 2 tablespoons finely chopped coriander leaves
- 2 tablespoons finely chopped mint leaves

Dum Pukht Seal

- 1 cup chapati or whole wheat flour
- ½ cup water
- 1 to 2 tablespoons oil (optional)

Mix the marinade ingredients with the meat and let it sit at room temperature for 2 hours.

Meanwhile, using half the ghee/oil/butter, fry the onions and then the nuts separately in batches until the onions are crispy and the nuts are several shades darker. Drain on paper towels.

Wash the rice in cold water and cook till half done: test by mashing a grain between your thumb and forefinger; it should squish but still have a firm inner core. Drain and set aside.

Heat the remaining ghee/oil/butter in a heavy-bottomed pot (if you're not using the dum pukht seal method, use a pressure cooker) and fry the meat until sealed. Add the stock, cover, and cook until the meat is tender.

If using the oven for the next step, preheat it to 350°F/180°C.

Mix the dum pukht seal ingredients to form a dough.

Layer the rice and meat in your pot or baking vessel. Cover with dough if using the dum pukht seal method, or cover with two layers of baking foil, shiny side down, and secure with cooking string.

On the stove, cook on medium heat for 10 minutes. Reduce the heat to low and let simmer for 30 minutes.

In the oven, bake for 20 minutes.

Serve hot, opening the dough seal at the table. Garnish with the onions, nuts, coriander, and mint. Serve with yogurt.

Chubby's Peckish Pakoras

Pakoras are to Indians what potato chips or crisps are to Westerners. They can be made with any vegetable, chicken, fish or even bread and can be served with any lip-smacking dip, including the fiery coriander chutney below!

Makes 10 servings

- 2 cups chickpea flour (also called gram flour or garbanzo bean flour)
- 1 tablespoon lemon or lime juice
- Water

- If you like them spicy, add a chopped green chilli or ½ teaspoon red chilli powder
- Salt to taste

You can also optionally add

- 1½ teaspoon garam masala
- 1 teaspoon ground cumin

- ½ teaspoon turmeric
- Sunflower oil for deep frying*

Choose your pakora: cauliflower, onion, spinach, potato, whole chillies . . . the sky's the limit, really. Just make sure whatever you choose is bite-size and will cook quickly. You can, of course, mix things like cauliflower florets, peas, and corn kernels.

Sift the chickpea flour. Add the lemon juice, dry spices, and enough water to make a thick batter that sticks to the back of a spoon. Add your meat or vegetables.

*A healthy though less crisp alternative is to bake your pakoras. Preheat the oven to 500°F/260°C. Grease a baking sheet with olive oil. Follow directions above but instead of deep frying, bake pakoras for 8 to 9 minutes. Flip and bake again until golden brown. Rumpi would approve!

Heat the oil in a deep frying pan or wok until a drop of batter sizzles on contact. (Careful, hot oil is dangerous. Never leave it unattended.)

Carefully fry tablespoons of the pakora mixture in batches until cooked and a deep golden color, 5 to 6 minutes. Serve hot with chutney or dip.

Coriander Chutney

A big handful of fresh coriander, large stems removed

4 to 5 sprigs of mint, rough stems removed

2 to 3 green chillies, or to taste

4 cloves garlic

Juice from half a lemon

Salt to taste

Put all the ingredients except the salt in a blender or food processor and chop until smooth. Add the salt and more lemon juice to taste.

Hungry Hungry Halva

Serves 4

¾ cup ghee or butter (no oil)　　1¼ cup sugar

1 cup semolina　　　　　　　　2 cardamom pods

4 cups water　　　　　　　　　½ cup nuts—almonds,
　　　　　　　　　　　　　　　　　cashews, and raisins

Put the ghee or butter in a wok or frying pan on the lowest flame possible.

Once the pan is slightly warm, put the semolina in and stir gently. Keep stirring until the two are thoroughly mixed and the semolina takes on a darker, golden color. Be careful, semolina burns easily!

Meanwhile, separately boil the water and add the sugar and the cardamom pods, cooking it until the sugar dissolves.

Keeping the heat low, pour the sugar water mixture into the semolina mixture, stirring continuously to avoid lumps. Once the mixture is less watery, add the nuts, cover and cook until the water is absorbed.

Serve hot. Good for auspicious occasions like love marriages!

Glossary

Note: The rupee exchange rate at the time of this writing is
$1 = 54 rupees.

AAILA	Nepali homemade liquor.
AARTI	Hindu fire ritual, often performed daily, in which a plate holding a flame and offerings is circled in front of a deity or guru while devotional songs are sung.
"ACHCHA"	Hindi for "OK," "good" or "got it." Can also be used to indicate surprise and as a form of reproof.
AFRIDI	Pashtun tribe of Pakistan and Afghanistan.
ALMIRAH	cupboard, most commonly made of steel.
ALOO	potato.
"ARREY!"	Hindi expression of surprise, like "hey!"
ATTA	flour, mostly milled from wheat.
AUR	Hindi for "and"; also used to ask "what's new?" or "what else?"
AWADHI	a dialect of the Hindi dialect continuum, spoken chiefly in the Awadh region of Uttar Pradesh and Nepal.

BAARISH	rain.
BALTI	bucket.
BANYAN	*Ficus benghalensis*, the national tree of India. Older banyans are characterized by their aerial prop roots.
BARAAT	wedding procession that leads the groom to his marriage venue.
BARFI	sweetmeat made from condensed milk and sugar.
BATCHMATE	former student who attended the same school, college or military or administrative academy.
BAUL	minstrels from Bengal, eastern India. Bauls constitute both a syncretic religious sect and a musical tradition.
BETA	"son" or "child" used in endearment.
BHAI	brother.
BIDI	Indian cigarette made of strong tobacco hand-rolled in a leaf from the ebony tree.
BIHARI	a person from the state of Bihar in eastern India.
BIRYANI	a rice-based dish made with spices, rice and a choice of either chicken, mutton, fish, eggs or vegetables. The name is derived from the Persian *bery*. Biryani is believed to have been invented during the Mughal period.
BOGIE	Indian English for a train carriage.

BONG   slang for a Bengali.

CASTE   English word that derives from the Spanish and Portuguese *casta*, meaning "race, lineage or breed." The Indian word is Varna.

CHAI   tea.

CHALLO   Hindi for "Let's go."

CHAPPALS   sandals usually made of leather or rubber.

CHARGE SHEETER   a person with a criminal record.

CHARPAI   literally "four feet." A charpai is a woven string bed used throughout northern India and Pakistan.

CHART   a train passenger manifest.

CHHATRI   an elevated, dome-shaped pavilion. Common in Rajasthani and Mughal architecture.

CHICKAN   traditional embroidery style from Lucknow, Uttar Pradesh.

CHICKEN FRANKIES   India's answer to a burrito, a parantha stuffed with spicy chicken.

CHOWKIDAR   guard.

CHUDDIES   Punjabi for underpants.

CHUNNI   Punjabi word for a long scarf worn by South Asian women. "Dupatta" in Hindi.

CHUP   Hindi for "shut up."

CREAMY LAYER   the elite.

Glossary

CRIB — Indian English for "complain," "moan."

CRORE — a unit in the Indian numbering system, equal to 10 million.

DAAL MAKHANI — rich Punjabi dish of spiced black lentils, red kidney beans and cream.

DACOIT/DAKU — a member of an armed band.

DALIT — a designation for a group of people traditionally regarded as untouchable. Dalits are a mixed population, consisting of numerous social groups from all over South Asia.

DARSHAN — generally used to mean worship before an idol or guru.

DESI SHARAB — Indian-made liquor, usually cheaper and of lower quality than imported or foreign liquor.

DHABA — roadside restaurant, popular in northern India.

DHARMA — Sanskrit term used to refer to a person's righteous duty or any virtuous path.

DHOTI — traditional men's garment, a rectangular piece of unstitched cloth, usually around seven yards long, wrapped around the waist and legs and knotted at the waist.

DICKIE — a car trunk or boot.

DIPPERS — headlights.

DISHOOM — sound effect when someone lands a punch in a Bollywood movie, like "pow" or "bam."

300

Glossary

DIYA   a lamp usually made of clay with a cotton wick dipped in vegetable oil.

DOUBLE ROTI   Indian English for sliced white bread.

DURGA PUJA   an annual two-week festival in South Asia that celebrates the goddess Durga.

FARMHOUSE   a large house with grounds, more often than not built on agricultural land illegally. Owners often list their occupation as "farmer" despite deriving their income from other means.

FIR   a First Information Report is a written document prepared by the police when a complaint is lodged with them by the victim of a cognizable offense or by someone on his or her behalf.

GALAUTI or GILAWAT   flat spicy mutton kebab.

GALLI   Indian English for a narrow street.

GHAZAL   a poetic form consisting of rhyming couplets and a refrain, with each line sharing the same meter.

GHEE   clarified butter.

GOLGUPPA   a thin fried shell used to hold spicy tamarind water; very popular north Indian street snack.

GOONDA   thug or miscreant.

GORA   a light-skinned person; the term is often used in reference to Westerners.

Glossary

GOTRA — a term that broadly refers to people who are descendants in an unbroken male line from a common male ancestor.

GULAB JAMUNS — a dessert made of dough consisting mainly of milk solids in a sugar syrup. It is usually flavored with cardamom seeds and rosewater or saffron.

GURKHA — Nepali hill tribesmen who serve as soldiers, mostly in British and Indian army Gurkha regiments.

GUTKA — a preparation of mostly crushed betel nut, tobacco, slaked lime and sweet or savory flavorings. A mild stimulant, it is sold across India in small, individual-size packets. It's consumed much like chewing tobacco.

HAAN — Hindi for "yes."

HALVA — a sweet dessert (see recipes).

HAVELI — private mansion, sometimes with architectural or historical significance, much like a Moroccan riad.

HOLI — spring Hindu festival.

HOWZAT! — the cry of a fielding cricket team when appealing to the umpire for a ruling following the delivery of a ball on whether a batsman is out.

IDLI — a South Indian savory cake popular throughout India. The cakes are usually two to three inches in diameter and are made by steaming a batter consisting of fermented black lentils and rice. Most often eaten at breakfast or as a snack.

JAI! — Hindi for "hail!"

JALEBI — a sweet made from batter fried in swirls and then soaked in sugar syrup.

JALLAD — a designation in Uttar Pradesh for the men who do the work of cutting open dead bodies and removing organs so they can be inspected by doctors or surgeons to analyze the means of death.

JASOOS — spy or private detective.

JAT — originally a pastoral or agricultural caste in the Punjab region. Jats can be Hindu, Sikh or Muslim. Today, the term Jat has become synonymous with "peasant."

JAWAN — a male constable or soldier.

JHARU — a broom made of reeds.

JI — honorific suffix.

JUGAAD — an improvised arrangement or work-around that has to be used because of a lack of resources. Jugaad tractors are essentially wooden carts powered by agricultural water pump engines or customized motorbikes.

KABARI WALLAH — an individual who collects recyclable refuse from households; most are Dalits.

KACHALOO CHAAT — a spicy, sour snack made with the taro root.

KATHAK	one of the eight forms of Indian classical dance. Traces its origins to the nomadic bards of northern India known as Katha-kars or storytellers.
KATHI ROLL	a type of street food similar to a wrap, usually stuffed with chicken tikka or lamb, onion and green chutney.
KHANA	Hindi for food.
KHEER	milky pudding often made with rice ver-micelli and raisins.
KHUKURI	a Nepalese knife with an inwardly curved edge.
KOHL	a type of eyeliner smeared around the rim of the eyes.
KSHATRIYA	the military and ruling order of the tra-ditional Vedic-Hindu social system as outlined by the Vedas; the warrior caste.
KURTA PYJAMA	long shirt with fitted pajamas.
KYA?	Hindi for "what?"
LADOO	a sweet often prepared to celebrate fes-tivals or household events such as wed-dings. Essentially, ladoos are sugar and flour balls.
LAKH	a unit in the Indian numbering system, equal to a hundred thousand.
"MAADERCHOD"	motherfucker in Punjabi.
MANDALA	a spiritual and ritual symbol in Hindu-ism and Buddhism, representing the uni-

verse. The basic form of most mandalas is a square with four gates containing a circle with a center point.

MANDIR — a place of worship for followers of Hinduism.

MASALA — a mixture of spices.

METRO — a city or big town.

MOTU — slang for fatty.

NA — meaning "no?" or "isn't it?"

NAMASTE — traditional Hindu greeting said with hands pressed together.

NAMAZ — Muslim prayer.

NAUTANKI — drama queen, fool.

NAWAB — an honorific title ratified and bestowed by the reigning Mughal emperor to semi-autonomous Muslim rulers of princely states.

NAZAR LAG GAYI — The evil eye in northern India is known as Buri Nazar, or often just Nazar.

NETA — politician.

NIMBOO PANI — lemonade, salty or sweet or both.

ODISHA — Indian state formerly known as Orissa.

"OM NIMAH SHIVAYAH" — a popular mantra in Hinduism.

PAAN — betel leaf, stuffed with betel nut, lime and other condiments and used as a stimulant.

PAGAL	literally crazy, but generally understood as "idiot."
PAISA	one hundredth of a rupee.
PAKORA	fried snack, one of Vish Puri's favorites (see recipes).
PALLU	the loose end of a sari.
PANDIT	Hindu priest.
PAPAD	a thin, disc-shaped crunchy snack or appetizer usually made of ground lentils or chickpeas and cooked with dry heat.
PAPRI CHAAT	a popular snack found in northern Pakistan. Papris are crisp dough wafers cooked in oil. They're filled with potato, chickpeas, chillies, yogurt, and tamarind chutney and topped with chaat masala and crunchy noodles.
PARANTHAS	flat Indian wheat bread pan-fried and served with yogurt and pickle. Often stuffed with spiced potatoes, cauliflower or cottage cheese and eaten for breakfast.
PATIALA PEG	measure of liquor equivalent to 90 milliliters—that is to say, about 50 percent larger than a shot glass. Originated in the Punjabi city of Patiala.
PHAT-A-PHAT	"hurry."
POORI	puffy wheat bread deep fried in oil.
PRASAD	offerings of fruit or sweetmeats sanctified in front of deities during prayer and then passed to devotees to consume as blessings.

Glossary

PUJA	prayer.
PUKKA	Hindi word meaning solid, well made. Also means definitely.
PURSE	Indian English for handbag.
RAAT KI RAANI	night-blooming jasmine.
RAJMA CHAWAL	red kidney beans cooked with onion, garlic, ginger, tomatoes and spices. A much-loved Punjabi dish eaten with chawal, rice. See recipes in *The Case of the Deadly Butter Chicken*.
"RAM! RAM!"	a form of greeting in Hinduism, Ram being an avatar of the god Vishnu and considered by many as a deity in his own right.
ROTIS	an unleavened bread made from stone-ground wholemeal flour known as atta.
RUDRAKSHA BEADS	a large broadleaf evergreen tree whose seed is traditionally used for prayer beads in Hinduism.
SAAB	"sahib" meaning "sir."
SAFARI SUIT	a square-cut short-sleeved jacket with a broad collar unbuttoned at the top, epaulettes and four pockets, worn with long pants; usually khaki or sky blue and popular in India until the late 1990s.
SAHIB	an Urdu honorific now used across South Asia as a term of respect, equivalent to the English "sir."
SALLA	derogatory term, expression of disgust.

SALWAR KAMEEZ	baggy cotton trousers and long shirt.
SANYASSI	a Hindu who has renounced all his material possessions and adopted the life of begging for survival.
SCOOTIE	a scooter or motorbike.
SHAADI	Hindi for "wedding."
SHATABDI	Shatabdi trains are known in India as being "superfast," but that's a relative term. They do, however, offer the fastest service between the country's major cities.
SHIKHARA	this term, which in Sanskrit means "mountain peak," refers to the rising tower in the Hindu temple architecture of north India.
SHIVA	a Hindu god.
SHLOKA	a verse from the Hindu holy scriptures.
SHUDRA	fourth in the pecking order of castes, traditionally ordained to serve the Vaishyas (agriculturalists), Kshatriyas (warriors) and Brahmins (priests) above.
SHU SHU	peepee, go to the toilet.
SIGRI	rudimentary stove often fueled with cow dung.
SINDOOR	a red powder used by married Hindu women and some Sikh women. During the marriage ceremony, the groom applies some to the parting of the bride's hair to show that she is now a married woman. Subsequently, sindoor is ap-

plied by the wife as part of her dressing routine.

SONF   fennel.

SUBZI   vegetables.

TAMASHA   a form of theater in western India, but in colloquial Hindi it means a public spectacle.

TARKARI   a spicy vegetable curry.

TEEN PATTI   "three cards," also called flash, a gambling card game popular in South Asia.

THANDA   cold.

THARRA   cheap country-made booze.

TIFFIN   a lunch box, invariably made of stainless steel and consisting of a number of round containers that stack on top of one another.

TIMEPASS   Indian English for lazing about, doing something trivial to pass the time of day.

TRIBALS   term used to describe indigenous tribal people of India.

TULLI   drunk.

UTTAR PRADESH   the most populous state in India, with a population of more than 200 million people, it is also the most populous country subdivision in the world.

VISHNU   in almost all Hindu denominations, Vishnu is either worshipped directly or in the form of one of his ten avatars.

Glossary

The most famous of these are Ram and Krishna.

WALLAH   generic terms in Hindi meaning "the one." Hence "auto wallah," "phool (flower) wallah," "chai wallah," etc.

YAAR   equivalent to "pal," "mate" or "dude."

ZEBU   a type of cattle that originated in South Asia; characterized by a fatty hump on the shoulders.

About the Author

Tarquin Hall, a British writer and journalist, has spent almost a decade living in South Asia. He is the author of the Vish Puri mystery series—*The Case of the Missing Servant, The Case of the Man Who Died Laughing,* and *The Case of the Deadly Butter Chicken*—in addition to dozens of articles and three works of nonfiction, including the highly acclaimed *Salaam Brick Lane,* an account of a year spent above a Bangladeshi sweatshop in London's notorious East End. He and his wife, Indian-born journalist Anu Anand, live in Delhi with their two young children. Tarquin can be reached through his website and blog www.tarquinhall.com. Puri sahib also maintains his own site www.vishpuri.com and is active on Twitter @vishpuridelhi.